MOVING ON

H.J. HOLT

Dreamspinner Press

Published by
Dreamspinner Press
382 NE 191st Street #88329
Miami, FL 33179-3899, USA
http://www.dreamspinnerpress.com/

Moving On

Cover Art by Anne Cain   annecain.art@gmail.com
Cover Design by Mara McKennen

ISBN: 978-1-61372-592-4

Printed in the United States of America
First Edition
July 2012

eBook edition available
eBook ISBN: 978-1-61372-593-1

CHAPTER ONE

"AND yes, I do want fries and cola with that."

The teenager in front of Luke turned back to his friends and grinned as if he had just quoted Shakespeare. Luke forced his features into a humoring smile instead of squeezing the contents of the ketchup dispenser over his head and turned to get the order. *"Tonight I am going to get laid. Everything else is just so much bullshit,"* he repeated in his head for the twentieth time that evening. He couldn't look at his watch again yet—he'd challenged himself not to check the time until he served ten more customers and he was only up to six. These little games got him through the shift. And the shift would get him the money to hit a club and get laid. Luke turned his empty smile back on and greeted the next customer.

At 11:00 p.m., finally, it was over. He grabbed his stuff from his locker and ran to the bus stop. If he got out right on time and the bus was running just a little late, he could catch it. Otherwise, it would be another twenty minutes before he'd be heading home to wash the fast-food smell away, change, and hit a club. Tonight, he was lucky. As Luke sat looking out the window of the bus, he again went through the arguments for and against getting a car. Against: he could only afford something that would probably end up spending more time with a mechanic than with him, and parking in the city was a bitch. For: he would *have a car,* dammit!

He'd been in England long enough now to get his head around the whole "driving on the wrong side of the road" thing, and he even thought he had roundabouts figured out (which was more than could be said for many English drivers). Bristol had a pretty good public transport system, but it still meant planning his time around someone else's timetable. His car back home in Chicago had meant everything to him, even though it was a wreck. It was the most expensive thing he had ever bought, and it felt almost as if he had gained some entry into the whole "just like everyone else" life that he'd longed for.

Finally, it was his stop. It was a short two blocks to the apartment building where he lived, then three flights up. He started undressing as he walked to the bathroom, then turned the shower on to heat up while he cleaned his teeth (he had learned the sly tricks of his building's plumbing the hard way), and was back out the door again within thirty minutes. His hair was still damp, but what the hell? He wasn't in the mood to hang around.

Luke headed for Crush. It wasn't the best club in town, but it was within walking distance (even when intoxicated) and attracted a clientele that was there for a good time with good music. As soon as he walked through the doors, he got the same buzz he always did. Sometimes he wished he could be more like the bored, disinterested type than a schoolboy in his first gay club, but Luke always got that rush—the lights, the music, the bodies, the dancing. He truly believed the world was a better place when he was in a club, and even a stint working the bar at one back home hadn't convinced him otherwise.

Forty-five minutes later, Luke was on his second drink and starting to look around with more purpose. He'd managed to avoid someone he didn't want to talk to (no one should have that much to say during sex) and speak to several other people he knew to varying degrees, as well as enjoy the dance floor. He'd been approached by a couple of guys while dancing but hadn't been interested enough to take it further.

He had started to wonder if he should be a little more open to what was on offer when he spotted someone leaning against one of the walls. Luke caught something in the eyes and the shape of the face that he liked and maneuvered closer so he could get a better look. The man was quite a bit older than Luke, probably midthirties, and, it had to be said, looked a bit out of place. He had thick, short, dark hair and a pair of eyes that seemed to be able to look right through whatever they focused on. His face was serious, perhaps even sad. Then Luke got it— he looked as lost and lonely as Luke felt, although somehow he wore it with dignity.

Luke watched the man look down at his drink and then tip back the remaining contents of the glass. He was getting ready to leave, and Luke knew he didn't want to let him go. He hated approaching men— he always felt stupid and ugly when they looked at him, but there was something about this guy that made it worth the risk.

"Hi." As an opener, it was a classic, although perhaps more than a little unoriginal. Luke followed it with a smile and the realization that he didn't know what to say next. He just managed to stop himself before he blurted out something about not having seen the guy at Crush before. It was true, but corny enough to kill his chances stone dead.

"Hi." A slow smile back. "I'm Paul."

"I'm Luke," he replied, delighted that he had thought of something to say, before realizing that this still wasn't enough to get them back to his place. *This is why I always wait for the other guy to make the move*, he thought.

Fortunately, Paul was able to pick up the slack. Still smiling, he asked "So why did you come over to say hello?"

"I...."

Paul tipped his head to one side as if he was curious to hear what Luke would come up with.

"I saw you and... I thought... I wanted to talk to you...."

"That's nice. But I'm not looking for conversation." The smile didn't change, and Paul's eyes stayed fixed on Luke's.

"What *are* you looking for?" Luke asked.

Paul reached up and lightly drew his knuckles down Luke's cheek. "I'm looking for someone to fuck," he said quietly, never taking his eyes from Luke's.

"That's a relief, because I'm a lot better at fucking than I am at talking." Luke's smile grew into a grin.

Paul placed his hand on Luke's hip and pulled him closer for a kiss. Soft, confident lips on lips. No grabbing or thrusting. Paul was roughly the same height as him, just a couple of inches taller. Luke silently congratulated himself on his choice. This was going to be good.

WHEN they arrived at Luke's apartment, he held the door open for Paul and then followed him inside. As soon as it was closed, Paul pulled Luke close to him and started kissing him again, running his tongue over Luke's lips and sucking them softly between his. Luke tried to lead him toward the bed without breaking off the kiss, tugging at Paul's shirt and moving backward. Luckily, Luke's flat was small, and it wasn't long before he felt the bed behind his legs. Paul pushed him down so he was sitting on the edge of the mattress and then pulled off his own T-shirt. When Luke looked up at him with a smile, Paul smiled back and began unbuckling his belt.

"Let me help you with that," Luke suggested, and he took over while his mouth started to cover Paul's stomach with kisses.

So this is why I always do an extra ten sit-ups, Paul thought as Luke's tongue flicked lightly over his abs. When Luke's hands pushed down his jeans and briefs, Paul's cock was ready for him.

Luke had been in this situation enough times to know that not every cock fulfilled the promise its owner's physique made, but there were no disappointments here. Paul's cock was hard and straight, and a good size for jacking, sucking, and (most importantly) fucking. Yeah, it would stretch him, but his ass could use the workout.

Luke reached out to stroke the cock and heard a soft sound in Paul's throat. There was always something about the first touch. His hand slid up and down the shaft as he looked back up at Paul.

Paul wanted to fall into those eyes, that mouth, and he couldn't move or look away as Luke licked his lips and bent his head down to take the tip of Paul's cock into his mouth. Luke kept one hand firmly around the base so he could keep control and rolled his tongue round the head, slowly sucking Paul in as his mouth moved down before swirling his mouth back up again.

Paul could have stood there all night feeling that tongue and lips going up and down, up and down, but he wanted to touch Luke too much, to see what his clothes were hiding. He slowly pulled back and pushed his fingers into Luke's dirty-blond hair, smoothing it back from his eyes.

"You're wearing far too many clothes," Paul told him. Luke smiled and quickly undressed while Paul pushed off his own shoes and removed his jeans and briefs. He lay down on top of the bed with Luke lying next to him and began to let his hands run over Luke's slim body, slighter than his own. He had the easy tone of a fit young twentysomething, and a hard, good-sized cock to go with it. Paul looked back at Luke's handsome face and stroked his cheek.

"I bet you've been told this a thousand times, but, fuck, you are beautiful." A look came over Luke's face that Paul didn't understand— not the arrogant certainty he'd been expecting, more like confusion and doubt. He took Luke's face in his hands and began kissing his full mouth again, moving his hands over his bare skin, taking ownership of his body. As he moved his hands lower, he felt Luke moving his hips, pushing his cock up to meet Paul's touch. Paul's grip was firm and sure as it worked Luke's cock, as though he'd read Luke's mind and knew exactly how he liked it. His thumb knew just how much pressure to place under the ridge to drag a moan from Luke's lips, to make those eyes grow drowsy and unfocused.

He moved on top of Luke and dipped his head down to his tight nipples. Not all guys liked to be sucked and licked here, but the gasp from Luke's throat told Paul that he was in luck. He made his mouth soft around the nipple and surrounding skin, sucking in long gentle pulses that fell into rhythm with his hand on Luke's cock. Luke's nipple became swollen and increasingly sensitized, ready for Paul's firm tongue to flick and circle until Luke's breathing was coming quick and shallow. He moved his mouth to Luke's other nipple and repeated the motions. Precome had started to ooze from Luke's cock, lubricating the shaft as Paul's right hand continued working it and his left played with the swollen nipple that had escaped his mouth.

"If you're going to fuck me, you're going to have to do it soon." Luke smiled but his eyes were dark. It had been a long time since anyone had given him this much attention, and done it so well, but he really wanted this guy inside him.

"Where do you keep the lube?" Paul asked, his voice low, and Luke reached over and opened a bedside drawer. Paul caught a glimpse of condoms and a few other items that were certainly interesting, but grabbed the lube and pumped some out onto his fingers, working it between them and ensuring they were completely covered. He pumped more onto the tips of his first two fingers and moved down between Luke's legs. Paul felt Luke flinch a little as the cold lube came in contact with his skin, but soon he was pushing insistently against Paul's fingers as they worked the cold lube around his hot little hole. Paul wanted every nerve awake and begging for more.

"Inside me. Please," Luke murmured, and Paul pushed past the tight muscle with first one, then two fingers, and began easing deeper, pressing against the soft walls until he found the prostate and heard the sounds from Luke's throat grow more intense. Once he could feel Luke was okay with the stretch, he withdrew his fingers, quickly replacing the two with three, twisting and pushing as he ground them in, watching the intensity on Luke's face as he gripped the pillow under his head and bit down on his lip. He seemed to want to hold Paul's gaze, but the sensations kept forcing him to close his eyes.

Paul slipped his fingers out and grabbed a condom from the drawer. He wanted this guy so much, was so aware of the strength of his desire to be fucking that tight ass that he had to keep reminding himself to take it slow; he didn't know how fast Luke could take it. Luke had rolled over onto his stomach, waiting for him. For a second Paul thought about turning him over—he really wanted to watch Luke's face while he was fucking him—but then he decided anything that would use up valuable seconds before he could get his cock into that ass wasn't worth it.

Kneeling between Luke's open legs, he pressed the head of his cock against the lubricated hole and felt Luke give under his weight. The tightness hugged him so snugly he had to push harder, leaning forward over Luke's back and supporting himself with his arms on either side of Luke.

Luke felt the pressure and fullness moving deeper and forced his hips back against Paul. Sweat started to prickle on his forehead as he took more and more, until he finally felt Paul's balls against his ass.

Paul took a moment to just enjoy the squeeze all around him, leaning down closer to move his lips over Luke's nape. Slowly, Paul started rocking inside Luke, drawing sighs that grew into moans with each stroke. He used his weight to drive the thrusts by pushing down on his hips and then shifting back to his arms.

Luke felt Paul in him, on top of him, whispering to him, and knew he had needed this so badly. A tension in him that he had hardly known was there opened and relaxed as Paul fucked into him.

Paul felt Luke's body taking each thrust and gripping him, and he pressed himself down over Luke's back, skin against skin, his mouth against Luke's neck, his ear. "Ahhhh, it's so good, so good," he whispered between thrusts.

The pitch of Luke's moans changed as Paul focused his attention. Luke's hand reached for his cock, with its throbbing pulse. It only took a few strokes before Luke felt the overpowering force pushing his senses higher and harder until there was nowhere left to go and it exploded through him, and he splattered come over the sheet beneath him. As Luke regained awareness, he felt and heard Paul moaning his climax against his throat as he took his last thrusts into Luke's now-aching ass.

Paul got rid of the condom and curled around Luke on the bed. Luke was surprised, but not in a bad way. He was so tired of being alone and of feeling like an outsider. He would have liked to blame it on living in a new country, but he'd felt this way his whole life. Lying here with this guy—Paul—for a few minutes let him put down that weight and feel close to someone. Paul's breath was warm and calm on his neck, and he closed his eyes and relaxed into him. In moments, he was asleep.

PAUL lay next to Luke's sleeping body and gave himself five more minutes. After that, he would definitely—*definitely*—get up and go home. He was very aware of all the points where his body and Luke's came into contact, and he liked lying there imagining the things that he could do to make Luke moan again. It had been a while since he had felt like this, as if he had found a door that led from the real world into a room where he could just "be." He would love to fall asleep next to this man and love fucking him all over again in the morning, but he'd never get to work in time. Could he call in sick? That wasn't really him. He was Mr. Responsible, Mr. Reliable, never Mr. Impulsive.

So then what was last night? Paul had always told himself that he would never set foot in a club after he was thirty. He didn't want to be an annoying old queen like the ones he and his friends had laughed at when they were heady with being young, gay, and out. When you believe you're invincible, it's easy to laugh at other people's frailties. Paul had been so sure that he was going to be one of the lucky ones, and for a while he had managed to have the dream—a "life partner," his one and only—it was just that the dream had been cut short. Was this all that was left for him? Hanging around clubs and going home with random young men who wanted a quick novelty fuck with an old guy? Thirty-odd more years of this was too depressing a thought, until he looked back at Luke. Okay, it was hard to feel sorry for yourself when you had just fucked something that delicious. Had he really told him he was beautiful? Thirty-six years old, and he still didn't understand how to play it cool. At least he wouldn't have the embarrassment of seeing him again.

Very slowly he peeled himself away from Luke and slipped out of the bed. He considered waking him, but Luke seemed deeply asleep and maybe it would just be awkward, anyway. That meant that he had to feel around in the dark for his clothes and try to dress without making a sound. The absolute worst thing would be for Luke to wake up and see him half dressed, sneaking out like a letch. He found his clothing one piece at a time, trying to make sure it wasn't Luke's before putting it on.

Luke slowly eased out of his dream and back to reality. Someone was moving around in his bedroom in the dark. His brain caught up with his senses, and he remembered the man he'd brought home last night. A quick check of the bedside clock told him it was 4:37 a.m. He had a choice to make—let him know he was awake and risk awkward exchanges as he delayed him mid-escape, or let him slip out without a word and never see him again. He tried to remind himself of all the times he'd wished a guy would hurry up and go, and be grateful that he didn't have to work out how to lose this one. But he thought he'd had a connection with this one that Paul clearly hadn't felt with him. A tiredness came over Luke that had nothing to do with it being the early hours of the morning. He was so tired of it always being so hard, so complicated. It almost made him wish he was still in Chicago with Kit. Almost, but nothing would ever be quite that bad. He lay still with his eyes closed and let Paul go on his way.

Paul caught the change in Luke's breathing and his stomach plummeted. *Why didn't I wake him when I had the chance? Now he'll think I'm a total asshole.* But it seemed that Luke had just been disturbed in his sleep and was now fully embroiled in his dreams again. Thanking whatever higher powers might exist, Paul quietly edged out of the bedroom door and closed it as softly as he could behind him.

They had left the light on in the living area in their hurry to reach the bedroom, and Paul looked briefly around at the sparse room. Luke's fresh American accent had curled around his words, and the apartment had the feel of a place where someone stayed rather than a home. He had to admire Luke's tidiness. It looked as though Luke was one of the few people who really could live in one of those minimalist apartments that always looked so good but was ruined as soon as someone left a sweater over a chair or a pen on a table. Paul smiled. It was probably just as well they hadn't gone to his place.

Then he realized why he was hanging around. He didn't want to go. Once he left, it was unlikely he would see Luke again, and if he did it would be an uncomfortable acknowledgement that Luke would probably ignore. He briefly considered undressing again and returning to bed, but had to admit that was not an option. His eyes fixed on Luke's phone. Next to it was a small pencil pot and notepad. Without giving himself time to overanalyze or doubt what he was doing, he scribbled down a quick note, remembered to add his phone number at the bottom, and left before he could change his mind.

Once Luke heard the door to his apartment shut, he got up to use the bathroom and get a glass of water. On the kitchen counter, he saw a piece of paper left out, and when he picked it up he saw it was a note from Paul.

> *Luke*
>
> *I'm sorry I have to leave without speaking to you. I start work early and I have to get home first. I really enjoyed being with you last night. If you ever want to meet up again, call me. I hope you do.*
>
> *Paul Blackwell*

His mobile number was jotted at the bottom of the note.

Luke read the note several times, and each time made him smile just a little bit more. He took it back into the bedroom with him and was soon fast asleep.

CHAPTER TWO

LUKE woke up late, but soon had a smile back on his face. As he showered, he remembered Paul's touch on his skin, on his cock, the way Paul had fingered him until he'd ached for more, and he knew he'd have to jerk off before a day at work. He began rolling his semi-erect cock between his two hands as good feelings flowed through him, and then he gripped the base firmly with his left hand and lightly rubbed his right palm over the head. Luke closed his eyes and imagined Paul was standing there watching him. It wasn't long before precome was covering his palm. He rubbed it over the shaft before encircling it with his thumb and forefinger and worked them up and down. In his mind, he saw Paul lasciviously licking his lips, and then Luke was moaning as strings of come shot out of his cock. Luke leaned back against the cold tiles. His erection was gone, but his thoughts of Paul weren't. *I hope you do.* Why did those words keep coming back to him? Maybe because they sounded so uncomplicated and honest. If only life were really like that.

When Luke arrived at work, the smell of stale grease turned his stomach and he felt a familiar tension tighten his muscles. He'd been grateful when he'd first gotten this job. Although Bristol was the biggest city in the south of England, it hadn't been easy to find work when he arrived. There were plenty of low-skilled jobs available in London, but he soon found out why. There was no way you could live in the city on the wages they paid. Bristol had seemed like a good alternative and he hadn't regretted the move. His job was boring, but he'd worked at places like this before and usually you could have a laugh during the quiet times. Plus it was something he knew he could do easily, and that had given him the confidence to go for the job.

Things had seemed all right at first, until one of the girls who worked there had gotten the wrong idea and hit on him. She was only seventeen, and Luke remembered how that felt, so he'd tried to explain that he wasn't interested as gently as possible, which included telling her he was gay. It wasn't something he flaunted or hid, and he tended to assume that anyone who wanted to know could work it out pretty quickly. Unfortunately it turned out that she had been bragging to the other staff and telling them she was going to nail Luke. They wanted to know what had happened, and she had given them a full account.

As in every other place like this that Luke had worked, there was a manager who kept his distance from the staff wherever possible, and only came out of his office periodically to complain. The real "bosses" were always the most dominant personalities, often people who had been working there the longest. They set the schedules and told everyone else what to do, and most people were happy enough go along with it.

Here, those people were Brian, Ross, and Kelly, and it turned out they were suffering from a severe case of homophobia. They were full of not-so-hilarious ideas for jokes at Luke's expense, such as squirting lube all over the inside of his locker, sticking gay chat line ads on his locker door, or shouting warnings whenever any of the male staff had to get past him.

At other times, they would pretend to be consumed by curiosity about his sex life and ask question after question, which was clearly intended to humiliate and embarrass Luke. Instead, anger at their bigotry simmered. He supposed he should be grateful that he didn't get a lot of the references as he still wasn't completely up on English slang. You didn't have to be Sherlock Holmes to work out the underlying meaning, though.

"Hey, Kelly, is it just me, or is gay-boy walking funny today? Do you think he's had a cock stuck up him all night again?" Brian called out loudly when he saw Luke. Kelly laughed like this was the funniest thing she had ever heard. Although this was the type of greeting Brian offered on a regular basis, today Luke could feel a hot blush on his cheeks. Shit! If they thought they had hit a nerve, he'd be in for one hell of a shift. He quickly made himself very busy replenishing the napkin dispensers, until he was back in control. Then he put his hand on the pocket containing Paul's note and smiled to himself.

PAUL sat down at his desk with a cup of coffee and quickly glanced over his plans for the afternoon. Three children drifted into the classroom, wanting him to sort out a dispute over a game they were playing, but it was quick to solve and they were soon on their way again. He couldn't resist any longer. He dug out his phone and checked messages and voice mail. Nothing. Of course not, he told himself, trying to cover his disappointment. It was only lunchtime; even if Luke were going to call, he would probably leave it for several days at least.

Paul hated this. Hated not knowing if the other person felt an interest or if he was out on his own. As far as he knew, Luke had forgotten his name by now and the note he had left was rotting in Luke's garbage can. When he thought back, he remembered there had been many fantastic things about being with his long-term partner, Craig, but he had quickly taken for granted the feeling of always knowing there was someone there for you. Someone who understood, someone who could argue with you and yet stay with you, someone you didn't have to guess with—you just knew, and if you didn't, you just asked. There was no way round it—"dating" totally sucked. He knew he had to move on—people kindly reminded him of this most days, and his loneliness was finally pushing him to take the risk of reaching out again. Unfortunately, that didn't make Mr. Perfect suddenly appear.

Nicki put her head round the door. "Hi. I need to pick your brain! Do you have any idea how I can get my lower group to understand equivalent fractions?" Nicki was a new teacher and Paul was her mentor. He'd resented being given the additional responsibility at first, but it turned out that her enthusiasm and freshness were just what he'd needed to give his teaching a lift, while his experience helped hers along.

"Sure. Have you tried folding up a piece of paper into different parts?" And Luke slipped to the back of his mind again.

LUKE closed the door to his apartment behind him, checked the bolts were in place, and relaxed. He knew the tiny flat wouldn't seem like much to most people, but it was the most important thing in his life. A place that was just for him, with a secure lock on the door. When he first came to England, he'd had to make do with youth hostels, and although some of them were surprisingly good, he had usually shared a room with at least one other guy. That always reminded him of his time in foster care, and made him paranoid about his things going missing, or worse. One of the main reasons he had taken his current shitty job was so he would have a regular income and could look for his own place.

His flat was made up of a tiny "bathroom," which was actually too small for a bath and only had a shower, a bedroom that could just hold a double bed and a single wardrobe, and a slightly larger room which had a basic kitchen unit at one end and a saggy couch in the middle. To Luke, it was heaven. He had scrubbed the place with every cleaner he could find before unpacking his small collection of possessions and calling it home. He was still waiting for it to really feel like that.

After showering away the smell of the burger bar, he pulled on a baggy T-shirt and sweatpants, tipped some cereal into a bowl, and booted up his netbook. When the machine had finally finished whirling and humming, he logged into his e-mail account and checked his messages. Along with all the usual crap, there were two from guys he was kind of friends with from Chicago, and the one he'd been hoping for: a message from Brooke.

He'd met Brooke when he had been working as a washer at a Mexican restaurant and she had been a waitress. She was older than him, with two kids (neither of whom seemed to have a father), and she smoked and drank more than was good for anyone. Luke had very little in common with her except the fact that they were both limping through life with a few more hurts than they could handle. It hadn't taken long before they were the closest thing to family in each other's lives.

Brooke wasn't much of a writer, but she was the one thing he really missed from home. He opened her mail and started to read.

hey babe hope u r ok and still fuckin yor way thru englend!!!! life here is shit but u no that!!! bennie got a prise in scool 4 riting but im pretty sure hes my kid (just jokin) and tina is singin a bit on her own in the show on friday wish u were gonna be there cause I no I'll just blub the hole time gonna vid it 4 u (her singin not me blubin!) that peece of shit we dont talk abowt came round work and was askin afta you no 1 nos shit so no 1 said shit I didnt no to tell u or not but I have and I hope ur ok I met a guy!!!!! hes probly no good but ur not here to tell me so im going out with him on sataday I'll give you all the detayls!!!! babe I miss u but im savin som mony evry week so I can com c u 1 day take care of u caus I cant from here but send u lov anyway xxxxxxxxxxxxxxx

Luke read back over the message several times, first to make sure he had decoded Brooke's spelling correctly, and then just to imagine she was there, talking to him. He hoped this new guy would be an improvement on her usual choices but wouldn't bet on it. That was one thing they shared—lousy taste in men. It sounded as though Kit had come around to the restaurant, but Brooke was right when she said no one knew anything; no one but her, anyway. Luke had finally managed to crawl away from Kit, and it was Brooke he had crawled to, Brooke who had looked after him until his bruises had faded enough for him to go and sort out his passport and visa and get on a plane. It didn't matter what Kit found out now, but Luke couldn't have faced seeing him before he left. Even now, just thinking about him made Luke's stomach cramp.

When Luke had first met Kit, he had just turned twenty. Kit was only a few years older, but he appeared to be everything Luke longed to be himself. Kit was supremely confident, seemed to know everything, and was sexy as hell. Luke had been grateful that Kit had chosen him, and he hadn't had the sense to hide it. At first Kit had shown Luke warmth and even tenderness, getting Luke truly hooked before things had started to change. Kit began to criticize him more frequently, and Luke blamed himself for getting so much wrong. Then Kit explained to Luke that he just wasn't enough to satisfy him sexually, so he needed to fuck other people. Finally, he convinced Luke that it was his fault when Kit's anger overwhelmed him and he left Luke bruised and shaking. At that time, two things were clear to Luke: all the faults in the relationship were down to him, and he couldn't face life without Kit. Now, whenever he thought of Kit, he felt one thing—shame. Shame at letting Kit beat him, shame at all the things Kit had said to him, shame at the things he had done to try to please him. Ultimately, Kit had taught him that there were worse things than being alone, and it was a lesson he wouldn't forget.

Luke took Paul's note from his wallet and read it again, although he could have recited it by heart. Would he call him? The safest thing would be to throw it away, find someone new to fuck, keep moving and keep to himself. It seemed a waste, though, when Paul had fucked him so well he still got hard thinking about it. He decided to leave it for a few more days, and if he still had an ache for Paul's cock, then one more time couldn't do any harm.

PAUL somehow found space to dump his bags of books in his hallway and pulled the door shut behind him. He couldn't avoid it. He was royally pissed off. He'd been friends with Steve since his last year of school, and Steve had been one of the first people he'd told he was gay. Of course, this had been made easier by the fact that Steve was already out, and one of the few gay people Paul knew at the time. Since then they'd gone through a lot together (including sleeping with each other twice—both times they agreed they had made a mistake), changing from teenagers to twenties to thirties. He had found Craig, Steve had found Rich, and before they knew it they were inviting each other over for dinner like old married couples. Only now there was just Paul, and the shock of a partner's death was something Paul hoped Steve would never have to understand.

Like a lot of his friends, Steve had given Paul a huge amount of support and love to help him get through that time. People talked a lot about the friendships women had, but Paul had learned that friendships between men (gay or straight) could be just as powerful. Somehow it seemed that people could tell what he needed then, but now it was different. Now he found his friends grating on him, not understanding where he was.

Steve had called him and asked if he wanted to meet up for a drink after work to catch up, which had sounded great and was, at first. Before long, it had slid toward the usual "you need to get back out there" lecture, and Paul had felt sparks of irritation massing inside him. These conversations tied him in knots. He knew he had to move on, dammit, he even wanted to, but it wasn't as easy as people in cozy couples imagined. When he tried to talk about the difficulties, it was taken as evidence that he was still mourning Craig, and while there were times when losing Craig was still painful enough to make him forget to breathe, that wasn't the biggest problem anymore. It felt almost like a game of musical chairs. The music had stopped but Paul didn't have a place, and everyone else had moved on to a new game. There had been a time when pretty much everyone he knew had been single; now it was the reverse.

Paul had even told Steve about going to the club, but that was interpreted as another bad move on his part. *"Is that what you want to go back to, one-night fucks? Jesus, Paul. You're not twenty-five anymore. What happened? Did you end up with someone?"* Paul wished he'd never mentioned it. He could tell already that going on to describe Luke (young, hot, and hadn't called him since) would only give Steve more fuel. What was the point in saying he'd felt something between them, that Luke had reminded him that he was still alive, that Luke had given him that ache of wanting to know more about someone that he hadn't been sure he would feel again?

And so he'd ended up agreeing with Steve, acting as if he bought into all his lecturing bullshit, knowing that Steve would go home happy and repeat the conversation back to Rich, oozing self-satisfaction (probably after great couple sex, as well). He, on the other hand, still had a load of tests to mark, a silent phone, and an empty bed. He stabbed his frustration out on the plastic lid of a microwave meal and watched the clock count down the seconds. When his phone rang, his first thought was that it would be Steve, continuing his great advice, but he didn't recognize the number. "It's not him, so don't even think it," he told himself before taking the call.

"Hi. It's… um… Luke. Luke Kearsey. From the other night…."

It was him.

"Hi!" Okay, way too excited. *Keep it calm, keep it casual*, Paul told himself. "How are you?"

"Fine… um… I saw your note. I don't know, maybe if you still wanted to get together sometime…?"

"Yeah, yeah, that would be great."

"I work evenings sometimes, but tomorrow I'm off. You're probably busy already."

He could play games and pretend he was busy, or…. "No, tomorrow would be good. How about something to eat? Do you like Italian?"

A few minutes later their plans were set and Luke was gone.

Paul stood in his kitchen, grinning like an idiot. Luke had called. Paul remembered the taste of his mouth, the blueness of his eyes, the squeeze of his ass. Paul wanted him now. Tomorrow was too long to wait. He looked over at the stack of papers he had to mark and sighed. Well, whatever rubbish his class had come up with, they were all getting good grades tonight!

CHAPTER THREE

LUKE stopped at the corner and took a couple of deep breaths. He could count how many "dates" he had been on using one hand, not including Kit (and he definitely didn't include him). You met someone, they let you know they were interested, you had sex with them, the end. He didn't like follow-ups. People had all kinds of expectations and hopes when they met you for the second time, and Luke knew what disappointment looked like. He wasn't interested in watching it spread over the face of the person he was trying to impress. His brain had told him again and again that this was a mistake, but he ached with loneliness, and it was that ache that had brought him here.

He appreciated it was cheating, but he had made sure he was ten minutes late because there was no way he was going to wait around on his own. Even then, if Paul wasn't already there, he would go. He didn't need any more humiliation in his life. However, as he approached the restaurant and glanced in through the window, he could see someone who he thought might be Paul at the bar. He smiled and realized how much he wanted Paul to be there. He took another breath and walked in.

Paul hadn't been surprised to arrive before Luke, as he always tended to be early in an attempt to make sure he wasn't late. He ordered a drink at the bar and decided to sit facing away from the door so he wouldn't be grinning aimlessly at everyone who came in. Instead, he enjoyed his drink and indulged in some "people watching" while trying not to be too obvious. He homed in on a couple who were clearly together, but seemed to be desperately trying to appear as if they weren't. They didn't speak and rarely made eye contact. Was it the awkwardness of a blind date or a longer relationship in its death throes?

"Hi." Paul turned around and saw Luke standing behind him, smiling a little hesitantly. He was just as gorgeous as Paul remembered, with those too blue eyes and hair that couldn't decide whether to be blond or brown. He felt all the blood rush to his groin as he smiled back and tried to push away the flashback of being inside Luke's ass.

"Hi. It's good to see you." He saw Luke's face relax and the smile reach his eyes. He caught the eye of a waiter, who escorted them to a table and presented them with menus before leaving them to make their choices.

Luke glanced around and saw that the restaurant was about half full, mainly with couples but one or two bigger groups as well. Most of the couples were male/female, and he wondered how straight this place was. He was glad to see that it wasn't uncomfortably upmarket and that he had gotten the dress code right—no jeans and T-shirts, but no need for ties either. He flicked his eyes to Paul, who was checking out the menu, so he quickly did the same. The prices weren't too bad, but this was definitely going to put a dent in his weekly budget. He looked back at Paul—it was worth it.

They ordered their food, and Paul suggested a bottle of wine, which Luke had absolutely no idea about but agreed to in a way that he hoped seemed knowledgeable. As the waiter left, Paul leaned forward and softly said, "I'm really glad you came. I was hoping I would see you again." How could Paul do that—just say what he thought like he knew it was always going to be okay? Luke tried to triple-check everything before he opened his mouth, but with Paul there was no self-doubt. Where did that kind of easy confidence come from? Luke wasn't sure whether it was admirable or foolish, and he sure as hell wasn't going to drop *his* guard.

He shrugged in a way he hoped appeared casual. "I don't really know that many people in town yet." When he heard it out loud, he sounded a lot colder than he had been aiming for.

Paul sat back, but moved the conversation on smoothly. "How long have you been in England?"

"About four months now. I was in London for a bit, then came here to Bristol."

"And what brought you to the UK?"

Shit, was this whole evening going to be about him? *Well, I realized that my boyfriend was only going to keep getting more violent and I had nothing and nobody, so I ran as far as I could afford to go. Now I have nothing and nobody, but a lot less bruises.* "I'm a student at the university. I thought it would be interesting to study abroad."

"Really? What are you studying?" Luke looked quickly at Paul, but he wasn't questioning the truthfulness of what he was saying, just being interested.

"Law." It sounded impressive, and it was the first thing Luke thought of.

"Wow, you're not making life easy on yourself, are you?" Paul laughed. He took a breath, and Luke guessed Paul was going to ask another question, so he got in first. "What about you? What do you do?" Luke had to change the focus of this conversation quickly.

Either Paul really liked talking about himself, or he'd sensed Luke's discomfort. He began to tell Luke about being a teacher and how much he loved his job despite the workload and strain, because of the kids he taught. Luke watched Paul talk. He spoke about his work with such warmth and commitment it was contagious. Luke found himself asking questions about the kids, laughing at some of Paul's stories, wanting to hear more and more. He watched the way Paul's eyes changed when he moved from discussing a joker in the class to a child who concerned him, from describing teaching math (which he loved) to teaching art (which he hated). It seemed as if the more Luke learned about him, the more he wanted to know.

As they ate their main course, Paul told himself to shut up. He had heard from some of his blunter friends that he could be a total bore when he got started on his job, and he knew he was getting into full flow. However, in his defense, Luke was definitely more relaxed now and seemed to be having a good time. His blue eyes crinkled when he smiled, and he had even offered some stories of his own about school, although these had been about his days as the pupil rather than the teacher, and always focused on other children who had been in his classes. Paul could feel the current between them, flowing from one to the other, relaxed, easy, and undeniably sexy. Right now there was no hurry, but it was there.

"So, do you miss home?" Paul tried to bring Luke back into the conversation to stop it from becoming a monologue.

Luke's stomach tightened a little, but he answered quickly enough. "Sometimes, but not too much. Lots of things seemed different to start with, like the money and the accents and the cars on the wrong side of the road." They both laughed. "But I'm pretty used to all that now."

"What about your family? I think the phone bills would make it impossible for me to live in another country!"

Perhaps it was the wine, or perhaps it was that Luke didn't want to just be with Paul, he wanted to be like Paul.

"Oh, God, yeah! My mom and dad are always calling me up, so luckily they get stuck with most of the bills. I call my brother a lot, though. We've always talked a lot, and I really miss him." What the hell was he talking about? He'd heard once that his "father" had two other sons with another woman, but he had only met his dad twice and certainly never been introduced to any brothers. But he wanted it so much—to be the kind of person who should be with someone like Paul.

Paul went on to tell him about his own older brother and younger sister, and Luke nodded with shared understanding when Paul talked about loving his brother but feeling competitive with him as well. Luke noticed that he was focusing more and more on Paul's lips as he spoke, and the way he moved his hands, his fingers. The desire that had been quietly simmering in him all evening was becoming increasingly demanding. There was one thing that kept coming back into his head, though, something he had said at the beginning of the evening.

"What I said before? About not knowing anybody? Well, it's true, but… I came tonight because I really wanted to see you." Luke bit his lip to try to stave off the embarrassed flush on his cheeks. He didn't usually talk like this. He also had no idea how incredibly sexy he looked to Paul right then.

"Let's go."

Luke heard the lust in Paul's voice and found himself back on surer ground. He licked his lips slowly. "What if I want dessert?"

"Oh, I'll make sure you get dessert." Paul caught the waiter and asked for the bill. Luke reached for his wallet, but Paul stopped him. "I'm paying. I asked you, remember? That means I pay."

"I can pay my half," Luke replied a little sharply. Hadn't he phoned Paul? But Paul chose the restaurant... shit, he didn't have a clue how this dating thing worked.

"Do you want to argue, or get out of here?" Paul held his hand over Luke's and let his index finger lightly stroke the skin beneath it. Luke caught his breath.

"I'll pay next time."

"Good. Let's go."

Paul pulled Luke down into the alley next to the restaurant and pushed him against the wall before pressing his broader body against Luke's slighter frame and kissing him hard. Luke's hands were under Paul's jacket, holding him tightly as the tips of their tongues lightly stroked against each other. All the need that had built up quietly over the evening wasn't going to wait much longer. Luke felt like he could melt into Paul and leave behind all the shit he hated about his life. Paul's mouth dropped to his neck, his tongue flickering over Luke's skin under his jaw, making Luke tilt his head to expose his throat to him as his nerves sparked and crackled.

Paul's hand rubbed against Luke's groin, drawing a sound from his throat that told Paul all he needed to know. "I'm going to take you home and watch you come with my cock in your ass," he whispered slowly in Luke's ear, enunciating every word. He remembered the feel of Luke around his cock and felt his balls ache.

"You better live nearby," Luke replied breathlessly.

Paul laughed and grabbed his hand, leading him back out of the alley and along the street. Luke slipped his arm around his waist and felt Paul's around his. He looked over into Paul's sharp gray eyes and returned his smile. This felt so good he was almost starting to hope Paul didn't live too close. They walked to the end of the street and turned right, then left onto a road lined with narrow terraced houses. Paul unhooked the gate of number 16 and walked up to the door.

"You have your own house?" Luke asked before he heard how childish that sounded. But Paul didn't seem to notice when Luke said something dumb.

"Yeah. I'm lucky, I know," Paul replied as he turned the key in the lock and pushed against the door. "I came into some money and I've always wanted my own place. You'll have to excuse the mess, though!" he added as he remembered Luke's pristine apartment.

Luke was thinking about his flat as well, and what a dump it was next to Paul's home. He asked himself again what Paul could be seeing in him (other than his lies) and how long it would take him to see Luke for what he really was. Then he saw the desire in Paul's eyes and decided to have fun until that happened.

Once Luke was inside the door, Paul took his face in his hands and started kissing him again, slowly moving his tongue deeper and feeling the heat pass between them. He didn't know why this gorgeous man was back in his arms, but he sure as hell was going to enjoy it.

Luke remembered how Paul had cut him short when he had been blowing him last night, and tonight he wanted the whole deal. "I think you need to sit down," Luke told him, nodding to the stairs behind them. It didn't take long before Paul was leaning back against the stairs with Luke kneeling between his legs two steps below. Luke covered Paul's lower stomach and thighs with short, hard sucks before turning his attention to the very alert penis in front of him. He teased Paul by covering the shaft in quick flicks of his tongue until Paul groaned with frustration. Then he began moving his tongue more slowly and firmly over the shaft, raking his tongue up the length and over the ridge. Luke let the head slip into his mouth for one long suck before he moved his mouth and ducked his head down to Paul's balls, which he enveloped with soft, wet kisses. He could feel the tension in Paul's thighs and knew he was longing for more so Luke gave him what he needed and started taking his cock deeper into his mouth.

Paul let out a low moan as Luke sucked a quick low pulse over the head of his cock. "You are going to have to stop that. I promised to come in your ass, remember?" Paul groaned.

Luke lifted his head long enough to shoot back, "Oh, my ass will make you come all over again, don't worry about that." All evening he'd been feeling like he was trying to keep up with Paul; now he was calling the shots and controlling how Paul felt, and he had no intention of stopping.

Luke had moved his mouth further down the shaft, intending to take Paul right back into his throat, when an icy chill shot through him and it was all he could do not to pull his mouth away. Shit. Snatches of the bad times with Kit had an unfortunate habit of flashing into his brain when he least expected it. He remembered Kit's cock thrusting into his throat, his hands tied, Kit's hands in his hair holding his head in place. He remembered the panic of not being able to breathe, and the pain in his throat. When Paul's hand lightly stroked his hair, he felt himself flinch.

"Hey, you okay?" Paul whispered softly.

Fuck. The evening had shattered. His muscles were tight with tension, and he could feel his erection fading. Paul was so far out of his league. He should never have called him and now, of course, it had ended in humiliation. Paul would see how useless he was. He couldn't meet Paul's eyes.

Paul forced himself to stop thinking about his cock and focus on Luke. Something was definitely wrong. He thought he'd been careful not to push into Luke's throat, but maybe he had. Or maybe his precome was tasting really bad. He did a quick check back over what he had eaten that day—nope, definitely no asparagus.

"I'm sorry. I… I'm okay," Luke muttered, still not looking at Paul. Maybe he could save this situation if he could just get a grip. He bent his head down and started to go to town on Paul's now semierect cock, using every trick he knew.

It took more willpower than Paul thought he had, but he pulled away from Luke.

"Hey. Stop, stop. You don't have to 'perform' for me, y'know. I only want to take what you want to give." Luke was still looking away from him, his face a mixture of embarrassment and sadness that caught at Paul's heart. He reached down to touch his shoulder. "Look, come up to bed… if you want to."

Luke finally met his gaze for a second and nodded. The only thing worse than staying here with Paul would be leaving. Was this what they meant when they talked about being caught between a rock and a hard place? He got up from the stairs and followed Paul up to the bedroom with no idea how this scene was going to play out.

Paul stood very close to Luke and let his fingers stroke his cheek, rub over his lips, and then slide down his throat and slip under the collar of his shirt. Leaning forward, he began to kiss Luke's mouth as he moved his hand to the back of Luke's neck and stroked the skin there. With his other hand, he started unbuttoning Luke's shirt and pulling it free from his trousers. Something in Luke gave up and he let Paul take the lead, stopped trying to impress him. Paul's hands were inside his shirt now, stroking his back in the way Luke loved as his mouth kept finding new ways to make contact with Luke's. His hands found Luke's belt, and once it was loosened and his jeans undone, Paul slipped his hand under the band of Luke's briefs. Paul moved back slightly from Luke so he could watch his expression, waiting to see Luke's eyes grow heavy and dreamy with arousal. He worked the shaft of his cock until he could feel it hard and full in his hand and Luke had begun to bite on his full lower lip. *Now I've got you*, Paul thought, *and I am not letting you go*. He moved in to take that lower lip between his own and sucked gently as he worked his hand up and down a few more times. Luke tilted his head back slightly and sighed.

Paul stepped back. "Take off the rest of your clothes," he told Luke firmly, and he waited to see how Luke would respond. The corners of Luke's mouth turned up slightly, and there was a different light in his eyes when they met Paul's. Without speaking, Luke held Paul's gaze and undressed until he was standing naked in front of him. Paul let his eyes drink in everything Luke had to offer—his firm, slim body, the toned but not muscular arms, narrow hips, strong legs, and of course his hot, hard cock, radiating heat for Paul. "Lay down on the bed. Show me how you like to touch yourself. Do *not* come."

Luke's smile widened, but he did as he was instructed, lying on his back with his legs apart. His mind flipped back to his fantasy in the shower, and he gripped the base of his cock with his left hand. With his right, he cupped his palm over the head and rubbed in a circular motion, and pleasure washed through him.

Paul watched him while he undressed, leaving his clothes where they dropped. He opened a drawer and took out some lube and condoms, and chucked them onto the bed next to Luke. He walked around the bed, watching Luke from different angles and noting the tightening of his muscles, the way he kept slowing down his hand or changing the pressure slightly in an effort to maintain control. Finally, he climbed onto the bed and knelt at Luke's side. Luke stopped, but Paul corrected him. "I didn't tell you to stop."

Luke took in a deep breath to steady himself and resumed moving his hand while Paul stroked the inside of Luke's thigh. The closeness of Paul and the feel of touch were too much for Luke. "I can't," he begged. "Please."

Paul was impressed that he still didn't stop without permission. Luke had definitely played this game before. "Stop," he whispered very softly, and Luke let his right hand drop with only a little reluctance. He licked his lips and tried to steady his breathing, waiting to see what Paul would do next.

Paul moved between Luke's legs. "Bend your knees. Bring them up. That's right." Luke curled his knees into the sides of his body, exposing himself completely to Paul. Paul felt his power over Luke and remembered what he had said to him on the stairs. *"I only want to take what you want to give."* Luke was watching him closely, but offering his trust. Paul was going to make sure it was rewarded. "Grab a pillow. Put it under your hips," he murmured to Luke, who quickly obeyed.

Luke wondered fleetingly if he was repeating a past mistake, but when he looked at Paul, he felt that Paul would always keep him safe, even if he took him to the edge. Had he ever felt that way with Kit? But he didn't want to think about Kit now, not when Paul's hands were pressing up from his buttocks and along his exposed thighs, pressing him down and opening him up. Paul squeezed lube onto the palms of his hands and rubbed them together to warm the gel. Then he applied his warm, slippery hands to Luke's balls, caressing and rolling them in his grip. Luke realized he was holding his breath and forced himself to suck in air and push it out again as his balls rolled in Paul's big hands. Paul kept holding his balls in his left hand while he slipped his right hand underneath, stroking very lightly on the place where Luke's balls joined his body. Slowly and lightly, he began to move his index finger in small circles over the most tender skin, working over Luke's perineum. Luke arched his back and moaned from the sensation.

If he had been able to open his eyes, he would have seen Paul smiling down at him, high on the pleasure he was giving Luke.

Paul felt torn. He almost wanted to give up his original plan of fucking Luke and instead take that cock into his mouth while his fingers continued to drive Luke mad, but he knew that would be just plain cruel if he didn't intend to let Luke come. He continued moving his finger up and down, always lightly circling the flesh beneath, only stopping to add more lube. In this way, he pulled more and more sounds from Luke, whose brow was furrowed with intensity.

When he had worked his way around Luke's asshole several times, he knew he couldn't wait any longer and had to start getting him ready. Making sure his finger was coated with lube, he placed it against the tight entrance. "Push against me," he whispered to Luke, who responded immediately by rocking his hips up and taking the tip of Paul's finger through the ridged muscle. "Look at me," he commanded, and Luke forced himself to meet Paul's gaze and hold it as his finger touched him so intimately. Paul slipped further in and pressed lightly against the soft, tender wall until he found Luke's prostate, and Luke tipped his head back as waves of pleasure rippled from Paul's finger. Paul knew he couldn't wait much longer, had to get inside him. "Give me your hand," he instructed Luke, and when he did, Paul smeared lube over Luke's first two fingers. "Now put them inside yourself. Find that spot—that's it. Hold it there." Luke's breath was ragged and precome oozed from his cock. Paul watched him finger himself while he slipped on the condom and wondered how the hell he was going to stop himself from coming as soon as he was inside Luke.

He placed his hand over Luke's, and Luke withdrew his fingers, pulling his knees up higher and watching Paul's face. As soon as his ass was free, Paul thrust forward and began stretching Luke open with his cock. Luke moved his legs over Paul's shoulders, raising his hips further onto Paul's dick, and with another hard thrust, Paul was all the way inside him. Luke bit down on his lip but held Paul's gaze. Paul leaned further forward, making Luke gasp as the pressure changed inside him. He pushed Luke's hair back and then stroked Luke's face, curving down to his mouth. When his thumb rubbed against Luke's full lower lip, he began to make short, hard thrusts, and Luke opened his mouth to suck on Paul's thumb for release.

Liquid pleasure pumped through Paul's veins as Luke's ass held him in a vice. The smallest movements created friction all along his cock, which ignited in his balls. Once he could feel Luke had relaxed a little, he began hammering into him with more force, driving them both toward their climax. Luke's hand reached for his own cock and worked it with strong, hard movements in time with Paul. Paul gripped his hips and thrust in harder, knowing he was lost now and just riding it out wherever it took him. He heard his own grunts of bliss mixed with Luke's higher moans. He saw Luke's body arch, his head thrust back as strings of come shot from his cock and he shook with the force of his orgasm. Luke's ass muscles spasmed around Paul's cock as he came, taking Paul with him as everything turned to light.

Luke sank back into the bed, his eyes closed. He felt totally drained. Worrying, analyzing, doubting himself were all too exhausting to bother with. He felt every sensation as Paul withdrew from his ass, and he slowly lowered his knees, stretching out his legs. Paul disposed of the condom and even grabbed a tissue to wipe the come from Luke's stomach before grabbing the corner of the duvet.

"Come on, get up," he said, nudging Luke.

"Yeah, I've got to go," Luke murmured hoarsely. Somewhere at the back of his mind he remembered telling himself that this was just going to be one more fuck. He had definitely lost track of that tonight.

"What do you mean?" Paul asked, slipping under the duvet as Luke moved to the edge of the bed. "Have you got to be at work early tomorrow?" Tomorrow (or later today) was a Saturday, and Luke had the late shift as usual, thanks to Brian's schedule.

"No, but…."

"Then get under here with me and stop talking," Paul suggested. Luke briefly considered that and then let his smile match Paul's. He moved next to him slightly awkwardly, but Paul pulled him close. Luke found himself resting his head on Paul's chest, with Paul's arms around him. Paul seemed totally relaxed, and slowly Luke felt that sense of peace flowing from Paul's skin into his. The duvet was soft and warm, and Paul's heartbeat pulsed steadily against his ear. Luke felt so good it made his heart ache. *This must be what it feels like to be loved*, he thought, *to feel like this all the time*. He knew it wouldn't last, but he wanted it for as long as he could get it. He closed his eyes and relaxed into Paul.

Paul felt Luke's breathing gradually become slower and deeper. It had been a long time since he had wanted to fall asleep with someone and know they would be there when he woke up. Luke seemed so nervous sometimes, so unsure, yet he was sexy as hell, had traveled on his own from the USA to study in another country, was smart… something wasn't quite right. On the other hand, when he saw Luke smile as if the sun had come out from behind a cloud, or watched his eyes narrow and darken with desire, Paul knew he wanted more. But did Luke want to give it?

CHAPTER FOUR

LUKE slowly became aware of his surroundings and realized he wasn't at home. Although the curtains were dark, light was pushing in around the edges, and he could feel someone in the bed next to him. Then he remembered where he was and let go of the breath he'd been holding. He lay still and tried to work out if Paul was awake. His breath was slow and regular, so Luke guessed he was still asleep. Trying not to move too much, he looked around for a bedside clock. 8:32 a.m. He relaxed a bit more. He had plenty of time to get to work and he could afford to just lie there for a bit.

His mind drifted back over the previous night, remembering how Paul had taken charge of him and made it so much better than Luke had expected. He remembered the lies he had told at the restaurant, or he hoped he did, because the one thing a liar needs is a good memory. And he remembered how it had felt when he was sitting opposite Paul, listening to him, watching the way he moved, learning how he thought. *Just remember who you are*, he thought. *You can enjoy this, but don't get carried away.*

He felt Paul shift position a bit, then stretched his arm over Luke's hip.

"You awake?" he whispered.

Luke smiled. "Yeah, I'm awake." He rolled over to face Paul, and something caught inside him somewhere between his heart and his dick. Paul's face was still soft with sleep, and Luke put his hand to his cheek, kissed his mouth, and felt the slight scratch of stubble on his face. Paul's hand lay lazily across Luke's buttocks as he returned the kiss. Luke had already decided how this day was going to start, and he worked his mouth down to Paul's chest, pushing the duvet back with his hands and moving lower and lower.

Paul moved onto his back and fingered Luke's hair as Luke's tongue ran up and down the line of hair extending down to his groin. Luke could smell their sex from the night before and wanted to get Paul into his mouth so he could taste it again. He rubbed his moistened lips over the head and shaft, feeling the warm silky skin caressing him before parting his lips and taking the large head into his mouth. As it entered his mouth, he remembered the sensations from the head of Paul's cock penetrating his ass last night, and Paul's sigh of pleasure only heightened the connection in his mind. He wished he had Paul's fingers inside him right now, but there was no way he was going to stop and ask. He pulled back slightly, holding the shaft in one hand and flicking his tongue over the slit until he was lapping up the precome as it spilled out. Moving down the shaft, he let the head rub from the roof of his mouth to the softness at the back of his throat. He held it there for a few moments until he was sure he was okay, then tilted his head to a better angle and let Paul's cock nudge deeper.

Luke could hear Paul moaning his name as he slowly eased back, working his tongue against the underside of his cock. Paul's thighs were trembling around him, and his hands made fists in the sheets. After a couple of breaths, Luke moved forward again, this time swallowing to help him take Paul right in, creating a vacuum around his cock that was dragging come up from his balls.

The urge to thrust was becoming overwhelming. "Babe, I can't...," Paul managed to gasp.

Luke understood what he needed and slid his mouth back over the head, taking the shaft in his hand again. "I've got you, you can push into me. I won't let you go too far." As soon as Luke's lips were in contact with his cock again, Paul gave in to his body and drove forward against Luke's mouth and hand. Luke sucked firmly on the crown and upper shaft, working the lower part of Paul's cock with his hand and taking Paul's thrusts until he was crying out and coming into his mouth.

Paul sank into the mattress and tried to get his breath back. This was definitely the right way to start the weekend. Luke scooted up next to him, and he tried to coordinate his hand and arm enough to reach out and touch him. Luke laughed. "Is it okay if I have a shower?" Paul was pretty sure he managed to nod, and Luke climbed off the bed and wandered out of the bedroom.

Everywhere you turned in Paul's house, there was stuff. Books, magazines, CDs, items of clothing—Luke couldn't imagine how anyone could collect so many things. Two doors other than the door to Paul's bedroom led off from the landing. He didn't want to snoop, but he didn't know which was the bathroom. He pushed lightly against one door and looked hesitantly inside. It was a small office, piled high with yet more books, papers, and a computer. There was a photograph of a laughing Paul on the desk, and Luke thought again how handsome he was. He moved into the room for a better look and saw that Paul had his arm around another man, who was looking over at Paul with undisguised adoration.

A tightness spread over Luke. Was Paul still seeing him? If not, why did he still have the photograph? Maybe he was out of town and Luke was just Paul's distraction while he was gone. Obviously, he'd known Paul wasn't serious about him, he told himself. How could he be? Paul would definitely go for just the type of guy in that photo, and that most certainly wasn't Luke. It was just sex, good sex, and that was all Luke had ever expected. He tried to push anything else into a corner of his mind.

The second door turned out to be the bathroom, and Luke quickly showered, feeling like he needed to get out of there now. When he returned to the bedroom, Paul was gone and Luke could smell toast (burning?) and coffee from what he guessed was the kitchen. He pulled on his crumpled clothes from last night and went downstairs.

The ground floor of the house was really one big room, with a lounge area at the front of the house and a kitchen and dining area at the back. Paul turned to him as he walked up to the breakfast bar, and

Luke saw he was still in a bathrobe. "I thought the least I could do was make you breakfast," he said, smiling. "Tea, coffee?"

Now that Paul was right in front of him, Luke felt the need to leave dissipate a little. "Coffee would be great," he answered. As he looked around, Luke realized that Paul's kitchen was probably the tidiest place in the house. Through the back windows, he could see a garden, but somehow even that seemed chaotic. Luke sipped his black coffee and glanced around a bit more, trying not to be too obvious, but looking for any further sign of the mystery man in the photo.

In his head he kept telling himself to let it go, but then he heard himself say, "This is quite a big place for one person. There's another floor above your bedroom, right?"

"Yeah, it is a bit big. But the extra bedrooms are great when people are visiting."

"Has it always been just you living here, then?" His brain was telling him to shut up and leave, but Luke just couldn't let it go.

"Yep. I moved in about five months ago. I'm afraid there are still boxes lying around here and there," Paul added apologetically. *Really?* Luke thought. It was hard to see them underneath everything else.

"I know it's a bit silly, but to be honest I'd always wanted to live in one of these houses, and then I came into some money, so I thought 'why not?'," This was the second time Paul had mentioned "coming into money." Didn't that usually mean inheriting money or something? At any rate, Luke was no closer to working out who the guy was in the photo, and he hadn't spotted any other clues. Perhaps Paul was just telling him a pack of lies, anyway. A bolt of guilt shot through Luke; after all, he could hardly complain about that.

He declined Paul's offer of blackened toast and accepted an apple instead.

"So, have you got any plans for today?" Paul asked him. What did that mean? Luke wondered. Did he want him to go or to stay?

"I've got to work later," he replied honestly. He glanced at his watch and did some quick calculating. His shift started at midday, and he'd have to get home and change before travelling to work. It was nine thirty now, so he had a little time, but he didn't want to wear out his welcome. Paul seemed surprised. "You've got a job? That must be tricky on top of all that studying."

Shit. "Umm, it's only part-time and I need the extra cash," Luke said, maybe a little too quickly.

Paul, as always, either didn't notice his discomfort or lightly brushed it off. "What do you do? I remember working in a bar when I was at uni for a couple of semesters, but I couldn't really keep it up." Now it was Paul's turn to wish he hadn't spoken. Did that make it sound as if his university days were a million years ago? He wondered how old Luke thought he was, but absolutely wasn't going to ask.

"Oh, it's okay. It's just at that hamburger place on Victoria Street? If you're ever in the area, I wouldn't recommend it," he said, laughing. "Actually, I've got to get going."

Luke finished his coffee and dropped the apple core into the bin, then washed his cup, dried it, and asked where it should go.

Paul stopped himself from smiling. Luke really was a bit of a neat freak. What on earth did he make of Paul's organized chaos? "What time do you finish?" Paul wondered if he was pushing too hard, but Luke had chosen to hang around long enough to give him a mind-storming blow job, and looked for nothing in return. And it felt good when they were talking, just being together. Maybe Luke felt it too.

"I've got the late shift. We don't close up until twelve, and then we need to clean up for the Sunday morning guys. I won't be done until really late."

Paul didn't push any further, but he couldn't quite let go. He didn't want Luke to walk out the door without any idea of when he would see him.

"Well, if you feel like it, give me a call tomorrow. Or maybe later in the week."

Even Luke had to acknowledge it. Paul wanted to hear from him again. The corners of his lips curled with the knowledge, and he walked up to Paul and leaned in for a kiss. Paul wanted to reclaim that mouth, that body, but Luke was soon pulling back. "I really do have to go. But I will call you."

Once he was out of Paul's house Luke felt like dancing down the street. Paul liked him, he was sure of it, and he even wanted to see him again. And when he did, Paul would kiss him and fuck him and touch him…. He couldn't stop grinning, even though he knew he looked like an idiot. He had briefly considered asking Paul to drop him back at his apartment, but Luke wanted to walk, to breathe in the morning air and to enjoy all his thoughts of Paul before the drudgery of work. He knew this wasn't going to last, but he could still enjoy it while it did.

PAUL made himself another cup of tea and sat down on the sofa. Was it weird that the person he most wanted to talk to now was Craig? Probably. He had shared so much with him for so long he sometimes wondered if he had forgotten how to think for himself. He frequently found himself trying to decide between two types of cereal or what to watch on the television, and Craig would be there in his head. But now Craig was silent, and Paul either had to decide for himself or procrastinate forever. Maybe that was why he hadn't redecorated the house at all since moving in, or why he grabbed whatever microwave meals were on special each week. If he stopped asking himself what Craig would want, he would be letting go of him a bit more. Was he ready for Craig to just be a memory instead of a presence in his life? It felt like a betrayal.

Unexpectedly, being with Luke didn't make him feel that way. It wasn't like Luke was the first guy he'd slept with since Craig's death (that really had been a complete guilt trip), but he hadn't wanted to see anyone as much as he wanted to see Luke, hadn't felt the buzz. Then there was the question of if or when to tell him about Craig. "If" wasn't really an option; he couldn't pretend Craig hadn't been an important part of his life, and there was nothing to hide. It was difficult, though, to land the whole "dead partner" thing on someone. They tended to either feel awkward or start feeling sorry for him, and sympathy just wasn't sexy. He didn't want to be anyone's charity case. He'd almost been tempted to say something to Luke that morning when he was asking about the house, but he hadn't wanted to scare him off by dumping his problems on him.

Paul gave himself a mental shake and got up. This was no good. He had to get busy. First, he would shower, then plan out what work he needed to get done for school next week. If he completed his planning and any marking that was outstanding today, he would be free tomorrow, and if Luke happened to call.... He also decided he would certainly make time for the gym. He really needed to make sure he was going at least twice during the week. Suddenly, that seemed important again.

THE good thing about Saturdays was that they were always busy, and lots of customers made the time go much more quickly. It also meant that Brian and his little cohort had to keep their jibes to themselves, as even they weren't stupid enough to shoot their mouths off in front of customers. For once, Luke's smile came easily when he was serving, although he preferred working back in the kitchen where he could let his mind drift back to Paul.

The only thing spoiling his mood was an e-mail he'd received from Brooke. She was still excited about her new man, but she had mentioned Kit again. One of the guys who had worked with her and Luke had asked her for Luke's address, saying he wanted to get in touch as he was hoping to come over to England for a vacation. Brooke had given it to him without thinking there could be a problem, but later on she had seen the same guy talking to Kit outside the restaurant. She hadn't known that he knew Kit, although they might have met when Kit had been around the restaurant a while back asking if anyone knew where Luke was.

Anyway, she said, she thought Luke should know, but Luke didn't really know what to do with the information. Once Kit knew Luke was in England that would surely be the end of it. The worst that could happen would be him writing to Luke, which he really didn't want, but he could deal with that by tossing any letter without reading it. It had been months now, and Kit must have moved on to someone new. It pissed him off that Kit was still wriggling around in his brain after he'd put so much distance between them.

When he finally had a break, Luke went through the kitchen to the yard outside. It was where the smokers hung out, but it also caught the afternoon sun and he couldn't hear the constant repeating soundtrack of the restaurant. He was glad to see the only other person out there was Liam, who was leaning against the cement block wall enjoying a cigarette. Liam only worked at the restaurant part-time and was studying for his "A" levels at college. He kept to himself and had never given Luke any trouble.

Luke nodded to him in acknowledgement when he stepped outside.

"Hi. It's pretty busy in there today." Liam nodded back toward the kitchen.

"Yeah. Makes the time go faster, though. You on lates tonight?" Luke leaned against the wall and felt the warm sunshine sinking into his skin.

Liam shook his head. "Nah. I'm off at five. Actually, I've got a date with this girl tonight. Lucy. We're going to see *Finding the One* at the cinema. It's not really my kind of thing, but I thought she'd like it. It's one of those chick-flick films." Liam shrugged, but looked at Luke to see what he thought.

He thinks I know more about dating than he does because I'm older than him, Luke realized, *when the opposite is probably true.* Luke wanted to boost his confidence for his date, though. He was on the side of the romantics today. "That sounds like a really good idea. Movies are always a good choice because you don't have to keep thinking of things to say, and then afterwards you can talk about the film. Gives you some common ground." Maybe he should suggest a movie to Paul; he saved that idea for later.

Liam smiled, reassured. "So how did you meet her?" Luke asked, and Liam was soon telling Luke the whole story. Luke closed his eyes and relaxed against the wall as Liam talked, wondering if he should call Paul tomorrow or leave it for a couple of days. His brain told him to play it cool. Keeping Paul at a distance would make things easier when their "thing" had burned itself up. His heart/dick told him to grab as much of Paul as he could while he could.

The kitchen door banged as someone else came out into the yard. Luke's thoughts and Liam's ramblings were interrupted by Brian's arrogant voice.

"So, you been sucking any cock lately?" he sneered at Luke.

Liam turned away with a look of distaste. Brian's stupidity grated against him, but his instinct was to avoid drawing that attention to himself.

Luke briefly considered adopting his usual strategic ignoring approach, but today he just couldn't. He found himself turning to face Brian and smiling.

"Yeah, actually I have. A really good one. And when he fucks me, it's fantastic!" He walked back into the kitchen, leaving Brian lost for words and Liam half laughing, half choking on his cigarette.

CHAPTER
FIVE

LUKE woke up and checked the clock—9:17 a.m. He stretched out in his bed and rolled over, noticing the sunlight pushing round the curtains. It looked like it was another pretty good day out there. He had started to dislike Sundays, as they tended to be the day of the week that brought home to him how alone he was in England, but knowing there was someone he could call (someone who might actually be hoping he would call) gave it a different feel. Maybe things were going to work out for him over here after all.

He stayed in bed for another half hour, almost falling back to sleep and enjoying the sensation of not having to face going to work. He smiled as he remembered Brian's face after he had answered him back, but niggling inside him was the suspicion that it might not have been the smartest thing to do. Brian hadn't spoken to Luke again for the rest of the day, which was a positive result, but he'd definitely been shooting evil looks his way. There was nothing he could do about it now, though.

Luke stripped the bed and put the washing machine on before heading for the shower. He turned around under the shots of water to get the most from the sensation of them hitting his skin. He still hadn't made up his mind whether to call Paul today and kept playing with different scenarios in his mind. In Luke's experience, imagining something was usually a lot better than the reality. He wondered what Paul was doing right then, and he saw that photograph in his mind again—Paul relaxed, smiling at the camera, and another man next to him with his arm around Paul, looking directly at him. Maybe it was his brother, or a friend? Not unless they had a very unusual relationship. The look on "photo man's" face hadn't been platonic. Luke was sure there was a well-fucked contentment about it.

What did it matter? Sex with Paul was great and that's what this was about. He had to stop these fucking stupid daydreams and remember that, or he deserved to get his heart ripped out again. He knew that a lot of the things Kit had said were bullshit, but he also had to recognize he wasn't great relationship material. Several counselors had told him he had trust and attachment issues when he was a kid, and while he didn't have time for much of their bullshit, he couldn't really argue with that.

He'd always felt separate from other people, like the kid with his face pressed up against the glass window of toy shop. From an early age, he had known that there were things about his home life he had to hide, and being taken into foster care when he was five hadn't helped. It was easier for his mom to get by before he started school, but teachers soon started noticing all the little things she forgot or couldn't keep up with. He had been taken into care due to neglect that first time, and the social worker had told him that it was just for a short spell while his mom learned how to look after him a bit better. He could still remember the absolute terror of being alone and being taken from everything he knew. Despite his caregivers' best efforts, he had been sure that he had done or said something wrong and that his mother wouldn't want him back. Although he had frequently been hungry before, now he couldn't make himself eat, kept wetting himself, wouldn't speak, and refused to do anything in school. His loneliness had been a horror to him, and when he was returned to his mother, he would scream whenever he had to leave her.

But of course he'd had to leave her again and again; when she took up with Chris, who felt Luke needed more discipline and he was the one to give it, when she slipped back into taking drugs (twice), and the final time, when he was fourteen, when she had been arrested trying to bring a large quantity of cocaine over the border from Mexico. The hardest part for Luke had been the realization that she had planned to use him as a scapegoat. He had been so excited about their surprise vacation, but the real surprise had been when the border patrol searched his suitcase and found the drugs. She had denied all knowledge and claimed Luke was acting alone.

Fortunately, the police had been monitoring the operation for a while and had recorded phone conversations between Sylvia and the dealers. After a lot of interviews and wrangling, her lawyer had persuaded her to plead guilty to a lesser charge. Taking her previous convictions into account, she had been sentenced to twenty years with little chance of early release. Luke hadn't seen her since. At first he had waited for a letter or some kind of reaching out from her, but there had been nothing, so the conversation rolled on and on in his head—the one that always began with him asking why.

Even Luke had to admit that his rage had made him pretty difficult to reach at that time. He wore out a stream of foster parents with his sullenness and unpredictable explosions of anger. Everyone had been relieved when he had reached sixteen and insisted he didn't want to start another new school after a second expulsion. He had argued that he could get a job and look after himself, and set about proving it. His social worker had persistently visited him every month until his eighteenth birthday to make sure he was taking care of himself, and in hindsight, he wished he had been nicer to her. She had often brought him things and sorted stuff out for him that she didn't need to do, and he realized now she hadn't been the enemy he'd assumed. At least he had wised up enough to thank her during her final visit.

All this had given Luke a pretty clear idea of what he should expect from people. At first he had thought Kit was an exception, but he had learned the hard way that there were no exceptions. Well, maybe Brooke, but that was as far as he was willing to go. He had to admit he'd never come across someone like Paul before, but he would be a fool if he supposed it was going to end any differently. Luke knew he would only be able to keep up the "university student from happy background" act for so long, or alternatively, Paul would get bored with him, and it would be over. He had to be ready for that.

Outside the sun was shining and he had the whole day ahead of him. He could sit in the flat and remember the bad times, or he could call Paul and have some good times while they were on offer. Luke didn't think of himself as particularly smart, but even he had no trouble working that one out.

PAUL had decided he wasn't going to sit at home waiting for Luke's call and was getting ready to go and explore the monthly markets down by the quay when his mobile flashed up Luke's name. When he heard Luke's voice, hesitant and a little defensive, his first thought was that he wanted to drop his plans and fuck all that uncertainty out of him. However, even he could see that if he wanted his time with Luke to be about more than fucking, well, they would have to do more than fuck when they were together. So instead, he asked Luke to join him.

It wasn't long before he was outside Luke's building, buzzing for him in more ways than one. Luke answered the intercom and said he would be straight down. When Luke opened the door, Paul couldn't help but lean in for a kiss. He looked as gorgeously fuckable as ever in a tight blue T-shirt and jeans. Luke could look so guarded, but there were times when he smiled and his whole face opened up, and this was one of them.

Paul seriously considered changing his plans, but Luke laughed. "C'mon. I thought we were going out." Paul wondered if he was doomed to get hard every time he heard an American accent from now on, as he unlocked the car and walked round to the driver's side.

A dark blue Toyota Verso was a very "Paul" kind of car, Luke thought as he climbed in. After clipping on his seat belt he couldn't help but notice the school books stacked up on the backseat. A messy dark blue Toyota Verso, Luke corrected himself, trying to hide his grin.

"What?" Paul asked, catching Luke's expression.

"Nothing. It's a nice car," he added, still smiling. Paul looked at the car with fresh eyes. It was a nice car, but it certainly wasn't the kind of car he'd have wanted when he was in his early twenties. Shit, it was a reliable, boring car. Luke probably felt as though he was going out with his dad. Paul made a mental note to start looking at new cars on the Internet tonight.

"Have you been down to the markets before?" Paul asked, trying to shift the conversation.

"No, but I've been meaning to." If he were honest, wandering around market stalls had felt more like something you would do with somebody else, not alone, so he hadn't bothered going. Paul started telling him about the different kinds of things for sale while Luke glanced around to see if he could spot any CDs to indicate Paul's taste in music, but it was the one thing missing from the usual clutter. He had a pretty hot looking stereo though, not the type to come as standard, so maybe he was an MP3 guy. Luke loved his iPod but rummaging through someone's CDs had always been a good way to get a handle on them.

The market was full of people making the most of the early summer sunshine, but they got lucky with a parking space and soon joined the crowd. The stalls were placed along the quayside so visitors could enjoy the proximity of the water and sailboats, and of course the nearby bars did a roaring trade. There were stalls selling everything. Books, jewelry, food, clothes, and antiques, and in among them, street performers and buskers entertained the crowd. It wasn't long before Luke and Paul were pulling each other from one thing to another, comparing prices, asking what the other thought and laughing at each other's bad taste. Luke hadn't felt so comfortable with another person since he had hugged Brooke goodbye four months ago. Every so often his eyes caught Paul's, and something less relaxed passed between them, something that made him have to touch Paul, even if it was just for a second.

"Hey, Paul!" a voice called from behind them. They both turned and saw two men about Paul's age walking over to them.

"Jack, Matthew, hey, how are you?" Paul gave both men a quick hug in greeting. Luke quickly checked their faces but neither was the mysterious "photo man." He was aware they were equally unsure about him, and the critical voice in his head started guessing what they must see when they looked at him.

Paul turned to Luke and introduced him, just saying, "This is Luke." Luke tried to smile at them as his stomach churned. They both said hello and shook hands with him before starting to chat with Paul about the market. Luke arranged his face as if he was listening but he found it hard to hear what they were saying. He kept being drawn back to their expensive clothes, their easy manner, and their occasional but purposeful glances at him. He wondered if Paul was embarrassed to be seen with him; if he was, it didn't show.

"So, how do you two know each other?" the one called Matthew finally couldn't resist asking. Luke looked at Paul, not knowing what he would want to say.

Paul caught Luke's eye and saw the flash of vulnerability before it was covered with defensiveness again. He liked Matthew, but the man was a gossip and a bastard for putting him on the spot. Paul understood why the question was so difficult. Right now, Luke was a fuck buddy with potential, but Paul had been keeping himself a bit vague when it came to how much potential. There was the age thing, the fact that he was pretty sure Luke wasn't being honest with him about a whole raft of stuff, and Luke's habit of becoming distant and defensive. Strange how none of that really mattered when Luke looked into his eyes and smiled like Paul was the one good thing in his life.

Paul took a slight breath and gave Matthew a smile that said "this far and no further." "Luke's a friend," he told him in almost the same casual tone. Luke watched him closely. For all his gentle easiness, there was a seam of iron in Paul that Luke had glimpsed in the bedroom but now understood could be called upon in other circumstances. He turned to Matthew and saw him get the message and move on to another subject. A friend. Yeah, that sounded pretty good.

The conversation continued for a few more minutes, mainly about other people the three of them knew, and Luke focused on sending them telepathic "go away" messages, but his powers obviously needed some work because they seemed in no rush. Finally he picked up on the signs that they were leaving and managed to join in with the "nice to meet you" exchanges as they went.

Paul slipped his arm around Luke's waist and pulled him closer. "You okay?" he said casually, as though there were no reason why he wouldn't be.

He took a deep breath and let it go, leaning slightly into Paul's side. "Yeah," he replied, not adding, "I am now."

"I'm hungry. You want to get something to eat?"

"Yeah, that sounds good."

Once they were armed with bottles of Coke and piping hot samosas, they found a spot further along the quay where there were fewer people and they could sit and enjoy their food. The sun sparkled across the water and the spicy food was delicious. They could still hear music from one of the bands playing near the market. When Paul looked over at Luke drinking Coke from his bottle, he felt happier than he had for a very long time.

Luke finished his samosa and made a production of licking and sucking each finger clean while Paul watched and yearned to put his own fingers (and other things) into that mouth.

"Want me to do yours?" Luke asked with a wicked glint in his eyes.

"Maybe not here," Paul had to concede. "But I'm going to take you up on that later."

Luke's grin spread across his whole face, and he tipped his head back to feel the force of the sun on his face, his eyes closing. Paul watched him and thought about how he would cover him with kisses once he got Luke home and had him naked on his bed.

Luke sensed Paul looking at him and it felt as good as the warm sun. "Let's go back to your place," he said without looking at him; then he turned and met Paul's eyes.

"Yeah. Let's go," Paul replied hoarsely.

Luke led the way back to the car, and Paul was sure Luke was putting an extra jiggle in his step as he walked, looking back over his shoulder at Paul with his lips slightly parted. Paul looked around the car park and saw there was no one else around. His cock was screaming at him to fuck Luke right there, but luckily his head hadn't given up all control just yet. Luke leaned against the car door, smiling at Paul, and Paul couldn't resist taking that face into his hands and sinking into a long kiss.

Luke's hands wrapped around Paul's hips and pressed his groin against his, feeling how hard Paul was for him.

Paul didn't want his mouth to be away from Luke's, but he had to get him home so he moved back and walked round to the driver's side. By the time he got into the car, Luke was already inside waiting for him, reaching forward for his mouth again, and Paul had to stop and feel Luke's tongue dipping between his lips before he could think about driving.

Luke had a different plan. His hands were busy with Paul's belt, then unbuttoning his jeans and sliding the zipper down so he could get his hand inside, tight against the fabric of Paul's briefs. Luke's tongue flicked lightly against Paul's as his hand rubbed against Paul's cock, gradually feeling the dampness of precome through the material.

The voice in Paul's brain was becoming increasingly drowned out by the messages coming from his dick.

"Stop... let's get home...."

"I don't wanna wait. There's no one around. I'm still hungry," Luke breathed against his cheek.

Using both hands, he pulled at Paul's jeans and briefs, lowering them further, and Paul found himself lifting his hips to help. Luke was right, there wasn't anyone to see, but still... and then Luke's mouth was on his cock and there was only one way this was going to end. Paul sank back into the seat and gave in to his dick.

It wasn't exactly comfortable for Luke, and it was hard to get the right angles or offer much variety, but he got the feeling that Paul wasn't going to be critiquing his style.

Paul looked down and watched Luke's head moving up and down in his lap, heard the wet sounds of his mouth, felt the irresistible suck pulling his come up from his balls, and his thighs trembled under Luke's hands.

"Fuck... Luke... babe...." His words dissolved into a soft cry of pleasure as he jerked his come into Luke's mouth.

They both leaned back in their seats for a moment, catching their breath.

"When we get home, you are so fucked," Paul murmured.

"I know." Luke grinned at Paul, but his eyes were hard with lust.

CHAPTER
SIX

IT HAD taken all of Paul's concentration to drive safely back to his house. Luke had rolled down the window, and the wind blew through the hair he wanted to be touching. The sunlight made Luke's eyes shine a brighter blue than he had thought possible, and that mouth…. *Just don't think about his mouth*, he told himself.

Once they were home it didn't take them long to get upstairs and undressed. Paul rolled on top of Luke and propped himself up on his elbows, dipping down to kiss him again and again. Luke stroked Paul's sides and back and rolled his hips so their cocks nudged against each other. Looking down at Luke, Paul saw anticipation and desire in his face.

"You want to play?" he asked, his voice low and clear. He could have sworn he saw Luke's eyes darken with arousal.

"Yeah," Luke breathed back.

"Roll over," Paul instructed, and Luke didn't hesitate. He felt the smooth sheets under his skin and burned for Paul's touch. His cock pressed into the mattress, giving him just the right kind of hurt. Paul straddled his back and placed his right hand over Luke's, their fingers interlocking. He lifted their hands and placed them on the rail of the metal bedstead above Luke's head. "You're going to keep this hand here," he told him. "And this hand—" He did the same with Luke's left hand. "Here. Do not move them." He pushed his own hand into Luke's blond-brown hair, firmly pressing his head into the pillow before letting it go.

Luke's cock was on fire but he let Paul take charge. He wanted to give in to Paul, knew that he would get something he needed from it, without even knowing what that was.

Paul moved down Luke's body, sometimes stroking, sometimes pinching the flesh under his hands. "Bend your knees underneath you. Keep them apart—I want your cock exposed." Luke obeyed, finding it just a little bit harder to keep breathing as he spread, his ass and balls open and vulnerable for Paul to play with.

Paul began moving his hands over Luke's thighs and buttocks so lightly the touch was hardly there, but Luke tightened his grip on the rail and resisted pushing up into the caress. He was rewarded by Paul's lips rubbing the inside of his thighs, then opening his mouth and pressing with tongue and teeth. The sensation of Paul's teeth against the tender skin made Luke's heart catch, and when he sucked breath into his mouth and gritted his teeth, Luke forgot to breathe until Paul let go again. All of Luke's consciousness was focused on the area of his body under Paul's mouth. It felt like hours passed as Paul covered every inch of Luke's thighs and buttocks slowly, methodically, as if he either didn't realize or didn't care that Luke was being pushed further with every touch. It started to occur to Luke that he had made a mistake when he blew Paul in the car; he had eased Paul's urgency and need for release while only heightening his own.

Using his hands, Paul spread Luke's ass further, exposing the nerves packed into his crack and the tight, wrinkled hole. When Paul's tongue first made contact with the skin there, Luke made a sound that seemed to vibrate right through Paul's dick. He let his wet tongue drag over the trembling surface again and again as each time Luke made a soft, high sound in his throat. Once Paul had worked down over his balls and back up to the hole again, he placed the tip of his tongue against the entrance and held it there.

Luke's senses exploded. "Oh, fuck, please," he cried as the frustration of not pushing back almost drove him to tears. When Paul finally forced his tongue through the unyielding opening, Luke raised his head from the pillow, his lips parted, tension freezing his body. All he could think about was that tongue.

Paul worked his tongue inside Luke's ass, loving the sounds Luke made as sensation flooded him. He eased his tongue out to lick over the hole again and again before pushing back inside, this time roughly hooking two fingers into his anus to stretch the opening further. Luke's muscles were still tight and needed to be stretched, but Paul could tell from Luke's groans that any discomfort was balanced by pleasure. Now Paul was free to push his tongue in deeper, press against the sides, and work around the nerve-packed sphincter.

When Paul finally lifted his mouth from Luke's ass, he squeezed some lube onto his thumb and eased it up into the still wet hole. He found Luke's prostate and lightly rubbed it with the ball of his thumb, circling the sensitive spot and flexing his thumb so the knuckle stretched against Luke's tightness. "Need more… please," Luke begged.

Paul took his tongue from the tip of Luke's crack right up to his throat, to whisper in his ear. "I know. But you don't get to decide when you get it."

Luke groaned with frustration but kept his hands on the bedstead, although they were damp and slipping with sweat. Another minute. He would just make himself think about lasting one more minute. He would make himself wait for Paul if it killed him. His breathing was labored now, his knuckles white as he gripped harder and harder to keep himself from reaching for his cock. When Paul slowly withdrew his thumb and Luke could hear the tear of the condom wrapper, his body strained with anticipation.

Paul hadn't just taken Luke to the edge; he found he was burning up with the need to ram into that tightness and take everything he wanted and needed from it. He pushed the head of his cock through Luke's sphincter, heard the sigh of pleasure from Luke's lips, and gave in to the urge to fuck into Luke and take the breath right out of him. He drove in, digging his fingers into Luke's hips as he braced him for the next lunge. He felt Luke completely surrender to him, pushing back into his thrusts so Paul could fuck all the way in. He wanted more and more of Luke, and he leaned down over his back, skin against skin, forcing his cock to press down hard against the front wall of Luke's ass.

Luke didn't need a hand on his cock now. Every thrust was so intense it was all he could take. He felt himself falling and falling, with Paul's weight pressing him down. Paul was murmuring, "So good, so good," into his ear. His body turned to liquid and his climax smashed through him, leaving him broken.

Paul tore the last thrusts he needed from Luke's ass and hot waves rushed up through his body from his balls. As it subsided, he became aware of Luke trying to get his breath back underneath him, their bodies slick with sweat, but he still didn't want to let Luke go.

After Paul eased out of him, Luke somehow managed to straighten his legs and roll onto his back, but after that, he didn't think he would ever move again. When Paul had gotten rid of the condom, he dragged the duvet up onto the bed from the floor where they had pushed it earlier and covered Luke and himself. He lay beside him, lazily pushing Luke's damp hair back from his face. The corners of Luke's lips curled upward, but he was too exhausted to do anything else. He adjusted his position slightly, and in a minute he was asleep.

It was only just dark outside, and Paul knew it was still early, although he didn't care enough to look at the clock. There was nowhere else he wanted to be than right here next to Luke.

HOURS later, Paul roused and stretched out, seeking contact with Luke. Nothing. He woke up a bit more and realized Luke wasn't there. He turned on the bedside light and sat up. Luke's clothes were still on the floor, so he couldn't have gone far. After waiting a couple of minutes, he climbed out of bed, pulled on the bathrobe hanging on the back of the bedroom door, and went searching for him.

He found Luke sitting in the dark on the sofa in the living room, wrapped in an old blanket Paul used as a throw. He couldn't help but compare this Luke with the one who had been lying in his bed a few hours earlier. Then, Luke had given himself over to Paul without reservation, surrendering both his body and his mind. Now, his face was closed and tense, consumed by thoughts he would probably never share.

"Are you okay?"

Luke was quiet for a few moments, weighing his answer. When he did speak, his voice was soft, as if there were someone in the next room he didn't want to wake up. "You told them I was your friend. Is that how you see me?"

Although he was still half asleep, Paul understood what Luke was talking about. He sat down on the rug in front of Luke and looked up at him. He could just make out Luke's face in the dark of the room.

"In a way."

"I guess you have lots of friends."

"Not like you. I don't have anybody like you." Paul reached up and took Luke's hand. "Come back to bed."

"I need to know…. Who's the guy in the picture?" he said in one quick breath.

"Okay." Paul tried to refocus his sleepy thoughts. "Which picture?" he asked, but he already had a pretty good idea who Luke was talking about.

Luke bit his lip, but he wasn't going to back down. "The one in the office. I was looking for the bathroom," he added defensively, but Paul just nodded.

"Yeah. The guy in the picture." So it was time for that talk, Paul thought. He wondered how long ago Luke had seen the photograph and how long he'd been thinking about this. To buy himself some time, he got up from the carpet and settled at the opposite end of the sofa from Luke. How to start? He took a breath. "You want the short or the long version?"

"Long." If he was going to hear this, Luke wanted the whole story, with nothing left out.

"Okay. His name is Craig, was Craig. Craig Mitchell." God, he still couldn't use the past tense without getting a hit in his stomach. "I met him six years ago. He was a friend of a friend, and we met at someone's thirtieth birthday party. We hit it off and started seeing each other." Paul shrugged in the dark. "He was the person I had been looking for, the one I'd been hoping to meet. We understood each other, excited each other, and we wanted the same things from life. I moved in with him after about four months, and it worked. We both knew we were serious about our relationship and we decided to buy a house together, which taught us both how to compromise." Paul laughed a little at the memory. "We planned our holidays together, argued together, and celebrated together. We even talked about a civil partnership, but everything seemed so perfect the way it was, we didn't need anything else. We thought we would grow old together. I thought we would grow old together."

Luke heard Paul sigh deeply. He was glad it was dark and he didn't need to think about his reactions. He couldn't help but remember how he had felt about Kit when they first got together, and how excited he had been when he moved into Kit's apartment. He had thought he was going to belong somewhere. He understood the hope Paul felt at the start of the relationship, but not the fulfillment of that hope.

"It was coming up to our five-year anniversary, five years since we first met. We were going to have a party with all our friends, and the guest of honor, of course, would have been Jordan—that was the guy whose party we met at. Then Craig didn't come home one night. I called and called his mobile, but it was switched off. I left messages, but he didn't call back. I called our friends, but they hadn't heard from him either. I knew something was wrong. I went on the Internet and searched his route home. There had been a road accident involving an articulated lorry and a Peugeot. Craig drove a Peugeot. I could see which hospital the drivers had been taken to, so I called them, but they wouldn't tell me anything. I was going to drive there, when I got a call from Craig." Paul was quiet for a minute, but Luke didn't jump into the silence. He knew there was more.

"Only it wasn't from Craig. It was from Craig's phone. The police were trying to trace his relatives, and they had accessed the messages I had left. They asked me who I was, what my relationship was to Craig, his parents' names, phone number, and address. I remember the woman I spoke to was very calm, almost cold, like she was working through a checklist she had to complete. She wouldn't answer any questions. I could hear her radio in the background, heard the name of our street. Then she told me that a police car had just turned into the street we lived at and that they would be able to answer all my questions. I knew then, I could hear it in her voice. She'd been stalling me until they got there. Later, I appreciated that; that they had sent someone round to tell me to my face. At the time I just wanted answers.

"He had died at the hospital. He never regained consciousness after the collision. He suffered massive internal injuries." Paul closed his eyes. It had been a while since he'd gone through all this, and he realized again how much he hated the words, hated that they were describing someone he loved, not some anonymous stranger on the news.

"That was fourteen months ago. Now I live in a new house and I have some of his things, but they're packed away with all the photos and other stuff. I have one photograph out because I miss him too much to not have any, and too much to have any more."

"You still love him."

"Yes. I guess I've realized I don't have to stop loving him to let him go. I just have to stop waiting for him to walk back through the door."

Even in the dark, Luke couldn't ask his last question, *"Have you stopped waiting?"* He knew he didn't have the right, not yet, maybe not ever.

They sat in silence on the couch, both lost in their own thoughts. Paul was glad Luke was able to let him be, wasn't fussing at him to make him feel better. Nor was he making his excuses to get the hell out of there. He knew Luke probably had more questions, but he wasn't sure he had any more answers. As time passed, he heard the faint sounds of traffic and birdsong start up from outside. It was still early, but beginning to get light—perhaps five thirty or six o'clock. There was no point in going back to bed now, since he had to leave for school in a couple of hours, and he doubted he would sleep, anyway.

"I'm going to make some coffee. You want some?"

"Yeah. Yeah, that would be good."

Luke watched Paul walk through to the kitchen and turn the light on, then heard him filling the coffeepot with water from the tap and getting out the mugs. His head was spinning, but he was too tired to get a grip on his thoughts and too awake to go back to sleep. He did know that when the shit had hit the fan in his own life, the last thing he had wanted was platitudes, and if he ever shared those times with anyone, he wouldn't want their pity or fake understanding.

Still wrapped in the blanket, with his thick hair messed up from too much sex and too little sleep, Luke wandered into the kitchen and sat down at the table.

Paul gave him a tired smile. "I don't know how, but you can carry off the whole 'nothing but a blanket' look." Luke smiled back, looking even more adorable. But Paul could sense Luke's brain processing everything he had heard and knew something was still unresolved between them. Maybe he needed something from Luke now, after he had laid out his hurts in front of him, some confidence or sign that the trust and openness were reciprocated. He brought the coffee over to the table and sat down facing Luke.

"What are you up to today?"

"I've got work at twelve," Luke answered without thinking.

"At the burger bar? Don't you have lectures or anything?"

Luke's brain sharpened into focus. "No, not on Mondays. I work Saturdays and Mondays, sometimes some evening shifts. The rest of the time it's studying."

Paul couldn't help but feel disappointed. He was sure Luke wasn't being honest with him, and sharing his experiences with Craig hadn't made a difference. Although that wasn't why he had told him, he had to acknowledge now that he had been hoping it would bring them closer together and further from being just "fuck buddies." Perhaps that was his answer. Luke didn't want to move any closer; fuck buddies was just fine with him.

Suddenly Paul wanted his house back to himself. He wanted to stop thinking about Luke, and Craig, and relationships, and the whole damn thing. He got up from the table. "I know it's still early, but if you want me to run you back to your place, we better go now. I have to leave for work at seven, and I've got some stuff I need to do."

"Sure. I'll just get dressed." Luke knew when someone wanted him gone, even if he wasn't quite sure what he had done wrong. Should he have said he was sorry about Craig? Did Paul want all that sympathy and understanding stuff from him? He couldn't tell him it was all going to be all right because what the fuck did he know? The chances were that it wouldn't be all right. In Luke's experience life was consistently pretty shitty. Maybe talking about Craig had reminded Paul how low-rent Luke was in comparison. Luke had let Paul do whatever he wanted with his dick and now it was time to move on.

He pulled on his clothes and quickly searched his memory for the nearest bus stop. He was pretty sure there was one a few streets from Paul's, and that seemed a better option than an awkward car trip. His mind flipped back to the day before, when he had felt so good sucking Paul off in his car. Then it had seemed hot, but now it felt cheap and tacky. He would bet good money it wasn't the kind of thing Craig would have done.

Luke went and found his jacket.

"I'll just throw something on," Paul said when he saw him, but Luke shook his head.

"There's no need. I can catch the bus around the corner. It's not a problem." Before Paul could say anything else, Luke was gone.

After the door closed, Paul felt a pang of guilt. He knew he'd been a bit shitty, but fuck it, sometimes he needed something. Didn't he ever get to put that first? He walked back upstairs and opened the bedroom windows to clear the lingering smell of sex and hot bodies before going to take a shower. He tried to turn his thinking toward the coming day at school. That was one good thing about his job, he could lose himself in it and leave all this confusion and shit behind.

CHAPTER SEVEN

LUKE had showered away the smell of Paul and sex, and gone to bed when he got back home from Paul's house, mainly because he wanted the comfort of curling up under the sheets rather than sleep. He tried not to think too much about the way things had been when he left, but he was pretty sure he wouldn't be hearing from Paul again. Why had he asked about that fucking photograph? Everything had been so good, and now he had screwed it up again. What was wrong with him? He seemed incapable of holding on to anyone's regard for longer than a few weeks. His self-pity was only reinforced by the thought of going to work in a few hours.

Eventually he dragged himself out of bed again and turned on his ancient laptop. Maybe it was time to go back home, or try somewhere else? He had very little savings left now, though. He decided to check his mail before searching for cheap flights back to Chicago. He only found the usual spam and junk mail, so he typed up a few lines to Brooke to let her know he was still alive and to check that she was okay. He didn't want to go into the situation with Paul, and he wouldn't have known what to say if he had.

After half an hour of scanning various websites and trying different search engines, he had to face that going home wasn't an option anytime soon. There wasn't much pulling him back, but finding out that he couldn't afford to return home made him feel even more alone. He looked around his empty flat. *No photographs here*, he thought drily. Maybe he could get Brooke to send some of her and the kids, or would that just make him feel worse? *You have really fucked it up this time*, he told himself.

BY THE time Friday came around, Paul was beginning to think he really had seen the last of Luke. He'd tried to call him on Tuesday and had been forwarded to voice mail. He left what he intended to sound like a casual but interested message, saying he hoped Luke was okay and did he want to meet up sometime? He'd had no response, so he'd called twice more. Both times the call had gone to voice mail, but he hadn't left another message. He was sure Luke was avoiding him.

He argued with himself over how much he cared. Luke was a fantastic fuck and could be great to be with, but he was also defensive, quick to take offense, and Paul wasn't sure how much he could trust what he said. Maybe he was better off without him. It was just that he couldn't stop picturing those sharp blue eyes crinkling up as he smiled, or remembering his desperate sounds as Paul fucked him. Luke had made him feel glad to be alive again, given him that buzz of excitement and lust that had only gotten stronger the more time they'd spent together. He cursed himself for being sharp with Luke after telling him about Craig, but, Christ, was it really such a big deal? He just wasn't ready to walk away without putting up some kind of fight. His final option was to go round and see Luke in person, and if Luke didn't want to see him, then that would be an end to it.

LUKE'S week hadn't been any better than Paul's. He missed Paul every day, but he had made a decision and he felt sure it was the right one. If it hurt this much to break away from Paul after a few weeks, it was certainly time to pull away. Listening to Paul's message, he ached to call him back, but he could imagine how it would go if he did. At first things would be good again and certainly there would be some intense make-up sex. But before too long Paul would get tired of him again, only by that time Luke might be completely hooked, maybe even as bad as he had been with Kit. In an effort to try and hold on to Kit, he had said and done things that now made his skin crawl. He could never undo that, but he could make sure he didn't sink that low again. Every time the wound caused by his separation from Paul tore at him, it reinforced his decision.

Now he had made it to the end of the week, and it was typical of his luck that he would have a weekend without any shifts to work, and no one to spend it with. He briefly considered going out to a club, but right now all he wanted was Paul, and anything else would just make it worse. He would shower, see if Brooke had e-mailed him, and watch TV until he knew he would fall asleep. Lying in bed waiting for sleep to come only gave him more time to think about being in bed with Paul, so that was something he avoided whenever possible.

When the buzzer linked to the building's main door rang in his apartment he jumped, and before he could stop it, the thought of Paul was in his head; Paul wrapping his arms around him, Paul kissing him and undressing him…. The buzzer sounded again, and he quickly pressed the intercom. Before he could speak, he heard a voice he knew.

"Hey, babe. I gotta say, you are taking 'hard to get' to a whole 'nother level."

Luke couldn't move. He had to be wrong. It couldn't be Kit, not here. He held his breath, as if he could stop time.

"C'mon. Let me in, or do I have to wake up the whole building?"

Luke considered not answering, but sooner or later someone would press the release for the front door and what could Luke do? He couldn't hide in the flat for the rest of his life.

"What do you want, Kit?" His voice sounded weak even to his own ears.

"I want to talk to you. I've come a long way and you've not been easy to find, so quit fucking around and let me in."

Luke hesitated, but then he pressed the release button. It had been his hope to avoid any kind of showdown with Kit. He wasn't sure he trusted himself to stand up to Kit, and he certainly didn't trust Kit to keep control of his fists if he didn't like what he was hearing. *Keep it quick and simple*, he told himself. He would not let Kit get his hooks into him again.

Luke opened the door before Kit had finished climbing the stairs. He thought he was ready for him, but when he saw Kit he felt as if he had been hit by a train. He looked straight into Kit's brown-black eyes and felt the ground tilt under him. The fear and despair of that last night, when he had finally realized that Kit was so out of control he could end up killing him, hit him, and, underneath it, the feeling that Kit had always bet on—that Luke would believe it was somehow his fault every time Kit lashed out. Luke put his hand out and steadied himself against the doorframe.

Kit wore the same sardonic smile he used so frequently as he walked toward him. His black hair was swept back from his face, and he wore a sharp, expensive-looking suit. At six foot one, he was taller than Luke's five foot nine, and the hours he spent lifting weights helped him to fill out his designer jacket. If he was sorry or ashamed of the way he had treated Luke the last time he saw him, he certainly hid it well.

"Well, aren't you a sight for sore eyes?" Kit leaned in to kiss Luke, who backed away quickly. That took him inside the flat, and Kit followed him, pushing the door closed behind him. Kit laughed. "I'm gonna think you haven't missed me in a minute," he said, as if talking to a naughty child.

"What do you want?" Luke asked again.

"What do you think I want? I want you. I've come all this way to bring you home, back to where you belong. I thought you'd probably have finished sulking by now, but it seems you don't think you've made me suffer enough yet."

"Made you suffer? I'm not interested in making you suffer. That's not why I left. It's over, Kit. I don't know how you could think I would come back to you after what happened."

"Because you always do. You know I love you, babe. And you know people aren't lining up to say that." He reached out to Luke again, this time succeeding in brushing his fingers through Luke's hair.

"You don't love me. I think you love having someone you can take everything out on. I know it's partly my fault. I stuck around and let you treat me like that. I wanted to believe all your bullshit. But that's all it was, so much bullshit." Luke crossed his arms. "I don't have anything for you now."

"You always did put yourself down, but trust me, babe, you've still got something I want." Kit let his gaze roll over Luke's body.

The intercom buzzed again, making Luke jump. "You expecting visitors?" Kit asked.

Luke shook his head. "It's probably just someone in the building who's forgotten their key."

"Well, answer it, then," Kit prompted.

Shit, Luke thought as he walked over to the door. *He's been here two minutes and I'm doing what he says like a trained dog.* He pressed the intercom. "Flat 4."

"Luke? It's Paul. Can I come up?"

Luke's chest tightened. He couldn't think fast enough to process everything that was happening.

Kit watched Luke closely. During their time together, he had learned to read Luke pretty well, and right now he read Luke's desire to keep Paul away from him. An unpleasant smile spread across his face. If Luke didn't want him to meet Paul, that's exactly what he would do. "Tell him he can come up. I'd like to meet your new friends." While Luke was still hesitating, Kit walked over and pressed the release button for the front door of the building. "Don't keep him waiting. That's rude."

"Kit, please… I don't want any trouble. Just let me tell him to go." He had never seen Kit become violent with anyone else, but Luke was suddenly afraid for Paul. He didn't want to bring all this shit into Paul's life.

Paul knocked on the door. Feeling sick to his stomach, Luke opened it and looked into Paul's eyes. There were few times in his life when he had felt so confused. Every cell in his body strained to press close against Paul, but he had to deal with Kit, and hadn't he decided to finish things, anyway?

Paul only had to look at Luke for a second to know something was wrong. He was just about to reach out for him when the door opened wider and he realized someone else was in the apartment. Paul and Kit looked each other over in a half second and both knew all they needed to know. Paul saw a hard young man in his midtwenties who was dripping with designer labels in a crude, obvious way that screamed insecurity. His face seemed set in a permanent sneer, looking down on everything around him before it could look down on him. Kit saw someone who had the confidence and poise he wished to exude himself, someone who had looked at Luke with warmth and concern.

Kit tried to keep control of the situation. "Hi. I'm Kit, Luke's boyfriend. And you are…?"

"I'm a friend of Luke's." Paul turned back to Luke, who looked like he was in hell. Luke's boyfriend? What the fuck did that mean? Had Luke been seeing him while he was with Paul? He had no reason to think they were exclusive after hooking up a few times, but he realized now he had imagined they were, had imagined Luke was looking for the same things he was. What an idiot. "I can see you're busy. Maybe some other time."

"Kit's just gotten here from America," Luke said, still struggling to think clearly. He didn't want Paul to leave thinking he was involved with Kit, but it was too risky to start arguing with him while Paul was there. He wished there was some way of explaining to Paul without Kit realizing, but that seemed impossible.

Kit put his arm around Luke's waist possessively. Luke flinched just a little, but he didn't want to trigger Kit's temper. Kit looked at him with blatant lust. "Yeah, it has been a while, so I'm sure you'll understand if now isn't a good time." He turned back to Paul and smirked lasciviously.

Paul kept looking at Luke. He had a horrible feeling about this, but he couldn't place the source. Was it jealousy? Was it Luke's awkwardness at being caught out? Or was there something else? "Luke?"

"I… I'll call you." Luke wasn't meeting Paul's eyes. He looked shifty and uncomfortable, and Paul was suddenly very aware of all the times he had thought Luke wasn't being honest with him, why he had gotten pissed off with him in the first place. A flash of anger ran through him. Luke had been jerking him around all the time, just filling the hours until his boyfriend got here. That was why he had never been honest with him; that was why he hadn't taken his calls this week. And he, stupid bleeding heart Paul, had been worried about Luke.

"Sure. When you've got time." He wanted to be out of there, and with a nod to Kit, he turned and left.

Kit closed the door behind him, smiling triumphantly.

"Well, you have been busy, haven't you? Of course, I'm not surprised. You've probably rolled over for half the queers in England by now." He moved very close to Luke and bent down to whisper in his ear, "I know what a little slut you are."

"Fuck off, Kit," Luke spat, pushing him back. Watching Paul's face change and seeing him leave gave him the courage to stand up to Kit and to hell with the consequences. "I don't know how much clearer I can make this. I left the country, for fuck's sake. I don't want you in my life anymore."

"Oh, so you think you've got a new stooge, do you? What's his name? Paul? I know his type. You're his bit of rough, something dirty and sleazy to have a few kicks with. Normally he'd have to pay for it, but with you he gets it for free. And you do it all for free, don't you, Luke? No one needs to pay you."

Kit wandered further into the flat, looking around as if he was considering buying the place. "It's not exactly a penthouse, is it? But I expect it feels like a palace to you, considering where you've come from." He sat down on the sofa, grimacing. "So how else have you been keeping yourself busy? Other than opening your ass, I mean. Are you running your own business? Got some high-powered job in management? Advising corporations on their next strategic move? Or are you still sweeping floors and picking up other people's garbage for a living?"

Kit shook his head and laughed to himself. Luke stood still, frozen to the spot. His stomach was cramping, and he wanted to run, to get away, but there was nowhere to go. He remembered that Kit didn't need to use his hands to locate Luke's weakest places and apply pressure until he felt Luke break.

"Come and sit down by me." When Luke didn't move, Kit frowned but continued talking. "You need somebody to look after you,

Luke, to hold your hand when it all falls apart, and let's face it, for you, it always does."

Kit stood up and walked back over to Luke, standing too close. Luke wanted to move away but didn't want to show Kit any signs of weakness. He looked up and met Kit's eyes and suddenly recalled all the times they had stood like this before Kit would reach down and kiss him. How easy would it be to let him do that now? To sink into someone who would make all the decisions, tell Luke what to think, what to do, and would never leave him alone. Just as long as Luke kept his place at Kit's feet like a well-trained dog and accepted the odd kick when the mood took him.

"Things are different for me now," Luke managed to say. His voice was quiet and hoarse, without conviction.

"You think he's gonna be your knight in shining armor?" He nodded toward the door, where Paul had recently been standing. "You think he knows you? You think he knows you like I do? You think he knows how rough and dirty you need it to get like I do?"

Luke couldn't meet Kit's eyes. Shame crept over his skin, but he fought to keep his voice level. "That was never about what I needed. It was about what you needed, what you wanted. I never wanted it to go that far."

"Well, you sure came like you did," Kit muttered into Luke's ear, sliding his hand down to his crotch.

Rage flashed through Luke's body, wiping out the fear and confusion. He pushed Kit away. "Fuck you! I told you I want you to leave. I want you to go. I want you out of my life!"

"Like everyone else, you mean? 'Cause I got to say, people really don't tend to stick around you, do they? Even your mom got herself put in jail to keep you out of her hair! You think this new guy is gonna stick around when he gets to really know you? Not just as a piece of hot ass with enough tricks to keep it fun for a week or two." Kit rubbed his thumb over Luke's lips. "Do you have any idea how embarrassing it is to listen to you talk? To hear all the dumb things that come out of your mouth? Shit! No wonder people can't leave you fast enough!

"You need to think about this," Kit continued, taking Luke's face in his hands. Luke tried to pull back, but Kit's large hands held him firmly. "I am the only person who has ever seen you for what you are and still stuck around. If I go, you'll spend the rest of your miserable little life whoring yourself to get a few crumbs of attention. I am the only one who will ever love you, and you want me to walk out that door?"

Luke could hardly breathe. His throat seemed to be closing, his heart was beating too fast, and acid tears burned his eyes. "Get out. *Get out!*"

Kit sneered at him and shook his head, but he was running out of ammunition. In the past, Luke had always caved before now, would do anything to make Kit stop slicing him into pieces with his words. He had planned this "reconciliation" carefully and had been certain Luke would soon be groveling for his affection again. For the first time, he began to think that Luke really wasn't going to come back to him. He gave it one last try.

"You really are pathetic. I tried to help you, but don't think anyone else will. This is your last chance. You know that black emptiness in you is just going to swallow you up if I'm not there to look after you. Is that what you want? In a few years' time, you'll be all used up and thrown away."

"I. Want. You. To. Go." Luke pushed the words out.

"Fine. You know, now I've had a look, I can see that you were right. There's nothing worth having here. You were always just a waste of my time."

Kit slammed the door, and the sound jolted through Luke's body. He just managed to get to the bathroom before he started throwing up, retching again and again. When he had finished being sick, the shivering and sobbing took over completely, and he curled up on the bathroom floor, pulling a towel around him for some kind of warmth. He had lost Paul and pushed Kit away, and now he was left with Kit's words echoing round and round his head. What if Kit was right?

CHAPTER
EIGHT

PAUL had driven back to his house burning with anger, mainly at himself. How could he have been so stupid as to let Luke get under his skin? He slammed the door behind him and dropped onto the sofa, flicking through the TV channels and cursing them all, finding nothing worth watching. Eventually he settled on the news channel and pretended to watch that, but really, all he could think about was Luke. The more he thought, the more his anger dissipated. Instead, the uneasiness returned.

He couldn't make Luke's words and actions add up to his version of things. There had been something, he was sure, just when the door opened but before Kit had made his presence known, something in Luke reaching out to him, needing him. And then the agony in his face when Kit had been talking… had he imagined it, or had Luke recoiled when Kit touched him? *You're just telling yourself what you want to hear*, he thought, but still it wouldn't go away.

Without making a conscious decision, Paul began to run through his options. Go back round to the flat? No, that held the possibility of too much humiliation. Phone Luke and see if he could get a better sense of what was going on? That was a strike as well. If Luke was in trouble, he had already shown he wasn't going to speak up in front of Kit.

Thank God for text. He could plan what he was going to say before he sent it, and he wouldn't have the embarrassment of having to speak to Luke when everything was really okay. After several attempts, he finally sent:

Just need 2 know U R O.K. Not stalking, just checking. Paul.

Over the next half hour, he looked at the time on his silent mobile phone again and again. No message, no call. Luke could be playing head games with him, but that just didn't fit with who he was. Luke had told him to go, but every time he remembered that Kit guy's smirk when he was leaving, his stomach contracted. Shit. There was no way round this. He was going to have to go back to Luke's and check he was okay.

He seemed to catch every red light on the way over to the apartment, and each time he could see how foolish he would look if everything was all right. In fact, they were probably too busy with getting-back-together fucking for Luke to have even noticed Paul had texted him, and now he was going to turn up looking like a complete idiot. He checked again. Still nothing on his mobile. He could still go home and retain a bit of his dignity. Yeah, and spend the whole night worrying himself sick. His dignity was just going to have to take a backseat on this one.

When he pulled up outside the building, he could see the light still on in Luke's living room. He rehearsed what he was going to say to cover his embarrassment and get away quickly when he found everything absolutely fine, then he got out and buzzed Luke's flat. No answer. He tried again, but still nothing. Wanting to get this over and done with, he buzzed a different flat.

"Yeah?" a man's voice answered.

"Sorry. I've forgotten my key for the main door. Can you buzz me in?" Paul was going to continue but the door was already released. Great security—he hadn't even had to lie about who he was.

Once inside, he took the stairs slowly, in no rush to meet the embarrassment he was sure was waiting for him. When he got to the door he stopped and listened, but he couldn't hear anything from inside the flat. He knocked three times on the door and waited. Still silence. No TV, no music, no voices.

Inside the flat, on the bathroom floor, Luke heard the knocking and his stomach contracted again. Was Kit back? He couldn't take any more. His head ached from the hard, cold linoleum. His body felt like he had run a marathon. His face was hot and swollen. Not for the first time, he wished he were dead. He heard the knocking again.

"Luke? It's Paul."

Luke slowly sat up. He didn't know what to feel. Putting thoughts together was beyond him. What could Paul want? He managed to stand up and hold on through a wave of dizziness, then take the few steps over to the door. He silently placed his hand against it, as if he could touch Paul through the wood.

On the other side of the door, Paul looked around for a clue as to what he should do. He thought he'd heard something, but he couldn't be sure. With every second, he became more convinced that something was wrong. Even though he knew he might be talking to an empty room, he tried again.

"Luke, if you're in there you need to let me know you're okay, because if you don't answer in the next minute I'm going to call the police and have them break the door down. I'll tell them you're a diabetic or something and that it's a medical emergency. If you want me to go away, I will. I just need to hear that you're okay."

Luke sighed. The police knocking down his door would just about complete his evening. He was going to have to speak to Paul. He scraped some words together in his head and managed to push them out. "I'm alright. You can go," he said hoarsely.

Paul's heart jumped and relief swept over him. Luke didn't sound good, but at least he was talking.

"Alright, I just need to see you and I'll leave you alone."

"I look like shit. I'm sick. I don't wanna see anybody. I just want to be left alone, please."

"Is Kit still there?"

Luke leaned his weight against the door. Standing up was proving too difficult. "No."

His voice was almost too quiet for Paul to catch, and he hoped Luke was telling the truth. One thing was for certain—he'd come this far, so he might just as well see it through. "I'm not going anywhere until I see you. And I mean it about calling the police; the clock's ticking." There was silence on the other side of the door. Paul waited, sending wordless pleas to Luke to just open it and let him in.

Luke was too exhausted to argue. Standing up was making him feel like he was going to be sick again and he still couldn't focus his mind. Paul seemed to know what to do, and maybe that was good enough. Finally, he reached up to the lock and inched the door open.

Paul pushed gently on the door, and Luke gave up, stepped back, and let him come in. One look at Luke made his stomach flip. "Jesus, did he hurt you?"

Luke managed a half laugh. "Not with his hands. I told you I'm alright. He's gone and I don't think he'll be back. So I don't need a knight in shining armor." Luke gave another of those sounds that might once have been a laugh.

Paul had no idea what to say. Instead, he slowly reached out and pulled Luke to him, wrapping his arms around him and holding him close.

A sob cut through Luke. "Don't. Don't do that," Luke whispered with a crack in his voice, but he did nothing to move away. The warmth of Paul's body and the security of his arms around him were unbearably good. If he gave into it, he wasn't sure he'd be able to pull himself back together again.

And then Paul knew what to do. He led Luke into the bedroom and sat him down on the bed, then knelt down beside him and took off his shoes and socks. Next, he removed Luke's T-shirt and then started on his jeans. Luke was like a lifeless doll in his hands, and Paul understood he was too drained to think anymore. He recognized something in Luke's shaken, fractured appearance that took him back to a time when he'd felt like he had nothing left to hold on to. Luke's skin was cold to the touch, and Paul was glad when he could get him under the duvet and pull it round him. He walked round to the other side of the bed, stripped down to his briefs and climbed into the bed beside Luke, spooning against him and holding the cold body against his skin to warm and comfort it.

Luke didn't speak again for what felt like a long time. Paul thought he was asleep until he heard Luke ask, "Why did you come back?"

"There was nothing on TV."

Luke managed a half sob, half laugh. "You should get a new subscription package."

"I'd rather have you."

Luke grimaced, as if Paul's words hurt him. "You don't even know who I am. I've told you so many lies."

"I know. I was kind of hoping you might stop at some point." Paul pulled Luke a little bit tighter to him.

"He just turned up. I didn't want to see him but…."

"Okay. But now he's gone for good?"

"Yeah, I hope so."

"Okay."

They lay quietly for a few minutes, each lost in their thoughts.

Paul was the first one to speak again, "I don't know what you want from me; I don't know what you need. I know I care about you. If you just want a friend, then I want to be that friend. But, Luke, I need to know if you want more than that, and if you do, I need you to start telling me the truth."

Luke lay still in his arms. He was so tired, but maybe that simplified things, because he didn't have the strength to second-guess himself. All he was left with were his bare emotions.

Paul changed position slightly, shifting the weight on his shoulder, and Luke blurted out a desperate, "Don't go!"

"Shh, I'm not going anywhere." Paul nuzzled against the back of Luke's neck and he felt Luke relax again.

"I want to be with you so much, but I don't have anything to offer you. I'm not like you. I'm not smart and I don't come from the same kind of place as you. I know how it would end and I don't think I could stand it."

Something Luke said triggered a response in Paul. "I've learned a couple of things in the last two years. The first is, trust me, you don't know how anything is going to end. You can be so sure, and all the time you really don't have a clue. The second is that there's no point trying to live your life by a set of rules, because there are no rules. All you can do is trust what's in front of you."

Paul sighed. "Why don't you tell me the truth now? You don't have to look at me, and if you say anything I can't deal with, I'll just get up and go. No arguments and no recriminations. But if I'm still here when you're finished, then you're going to have to start believing that I'm okay with it. You're going to have to start believing I'm okay with you."

Luke closed his eyes and tried to get his thoughts together. He was too drained to try and outthink Paul and spin him a new story. This was it. Did he have the guts to lay his cards on the table?

"I don't know where to start."

"Okay. What about your name? Is it really Luke Kearsey?"

Luke laughed. "Yeah. That bit's true."

"So why don't you tell me what you're doing in England?"

A deep breath. "I came over here to get away from Kit. To get away from everything, really. That whole thing about being a student at university and studying law was just to impress you."

"I kind of figured that one out, what with the lack of books and studying. Why did you think you needed to make something like that up?"

"It's not just college. I didn't even graduate high school. I got kicked out when I was sixteen and I got a job working construction. I don't have a part-time job at the burger bar—it's where I work, what I do, period."

Paul nodded slowly. "What about your family?"

Luke just lay there for a while, and Paul didn't rush him but he wasn't going to let him off the hook, either.

"That was all lies. My mom... she's in jail. My dad took off a few months after I was born. Somebody pointed him out to me once, so I've seen him, but I've never spoken to him. I know he's got some more kids, younger than me. Turned out he liked the name "Luke," so he called another one of his sons that too. I think he stuck around more with them.

"Mom found it hard… she was really young when she got dumped with me." A long pause. "Sometimes I got put in foster care." Such a short sentence, Luke thought. Could Paul ever understand what it meant? "I don't know… I think that's it. I mean, there's more, but… that's the main stuff."

Paul stroked Luke's chest. "I'm still here." Luke hadn't told him anything that he hadn't really been expecting, except maybe the bit about his mother being in jail. There were a lot of questions he could ask, but he felt like he knew who he was in bed with now, and that was what he had wanted.

Luke couldn't let it be. He turned over to face Paul. "You don't get it. I'm not some cute charity case for you to feel sorry for. I'm no good to be with."

God, those eyes. How could anyone have such open blue eyes? Paul made himself focus. "You're wrong. I do get it. You think I don't know how it feels to have a pity label stuck to you? His voice changed, imitating the people he'd overheard so many times. "'Oh, look, there's Paul, the one whose partner died. It's so tragic. He's so brave.' I know people are trying to be nice, but how long does it have to be before I get to be just 'Paul' again? I'm not just the shitty things that have happened to me. You're not just the shitty things that have happened to you." He saw Luke frown, thinking it over.

"But those things…."

"They are what they are. I think it's up to you, to me. I could become that person, the heroic, lonely widower. Or it can be something that happened, something important, but not who I am. You know, it was you who made me see that. I could never have planned on you, but you've made the blood pump in my veins again. I know this could end badly, but… I want to find out what happens next, where this is going to go. And while I can, I want to be with you."

Luke was so tired. He couldn't stop snatches of Kit's words from coming back into his head and he knew that was his nightmare, that one day it would Paul saying or thinking those things. But Paul's words made sense… he was so tired.

He let his head drop gently forward onto Paul's shoulder and whispered softly, "I want that too."

CHAPTER NINE

LUKE woke up first, felt Paul's body next to his, and breathed out. He was in this now, for as long as it lasted, and he decided to get things off to a good start. Very carefully, he slipped out of the bed, making sure he didn't wake Paul. He felt revolting after the previous evening and he set about turning himself back into a human being. He brushed his teeth before getting under the shower and scrubbing himself clean. Kit hadn't touched him, but he still felt better after washing everything away. He roughly dried himself off because he wasn't interested in getting dressed, but before he went back into the bedroom he gargled with the minty mouthwash for as long as he could manage. His mouth buzzed and tingled, and that was just what he wanted.

Back in the bedroom he carefully eased the duvet back a bit and maneuvered down to Paul's cock. Hard and warm, it was just waiting for Luke's mouth. Luke enjoyed the feeling of the so soft skin against his cheek and lips, the heat radiating from it, the smell of Paul's sex strong in his nostrils. Paul was right—enjoy it while you can, and fuck what the future might hold. He licked his lips repeatedly, getting them good and wet before stretching his mouth over the head and clamping his lips just under the ridge. A low, long moan slipped from Paul's mouth. Last night Luke had been like dough in Paul's hands, but now he wanted to be the one who was doing the giving and meeting Paul's needs.

Luke twisted his head to the right and left so his tight lips could rub against the edge of the glans and let his tongue flutter over the tip. Paul slowly rolled onto his back and moaned again, halfway between sleep and waking. Now Luke could get a better angle. Slowly, firmly, he pushed his lips down the length of the shaft, stimulating every nerve and maintaining a firm suck so the shaft pressed against the inside of his mouth and picked up the menthol from the mouthwash. He sustained the vacuum around Paul's dick and rocked his head back and forth so the softness at the back of Luke's throat massaged the tip of Paul's cock. This time the sound from Paul was more awake, and Luke felt the contraction in his hips as he stopped himself from thrusting deeper. Luke worked his mouth back up the shaft and removed his lips. He licked and kissed Paul's tightening balls, and Paul's hands found their way into Luke's damp hair, fisting and releasing. Luke didn't want to make him wait, so he returned his attention to the swollen cock, sliding his mouth up and down the length, swallowing when it hit the back of his throat so his mouth contracted around Paul even more tightly. His middle finger stroked Paul's perineum, and they both knew that when he came Luke would press down, taking Paul higher. Paul's ragged breath told Luke that wasn't going to be long, and he moved his head faster, wanting the bitter salt on his tongue, to feel the release coursing through Paul. When it came, Paul's hips jerked in rhythm with Luke's mouth, and Luke swallowed his come as it spurted into his mouth.

As Paul tried to catch his breath, Luke worked his way up his body. "That's one hell of a way to say 'good morning'," Paul sighed.

Luke grinned at him. "Last night you took care of me. Now I'm going to take care of you," he explained.

"I think you just did," Paul replied. "Where are you going?" he asked as Luke slipped from the bed. He was still naked after his shower, and Paul took in every curve and line, disappointed to see him pull on a pair of jeans.

"To make you breakfast. Stay there." And then he was gone. Paul considered following him but then sank back onto the mattress. After all, if it made Luke happy....

"How do you like your eggs?" Luke called to him.

"However they come," Paul called back, deciding that he could easily get used to this.

When Luke came back in he was frowning with concentration, carrying a tray containing juice, coffee, toast, and eggs. "It's not a proper breakfast," he said, shrugging. "I've got some cereal too, if you want some."

The tight, defensive expression he had seen so often on Luke's face was gone, leaving behind a shy openness that sent a hard pulse straight to Paul's dick. "It's the best breakfast I've seen for a long time. Come here." Paul's hand curled around the back of Luke's neck, strong and sure, pulling him down to kiss the soft mouth that had already made him very happy that morning. Their tongues stroked against each other, and Luke began to wobble before pulling away.

"Breakfast," he reminded Paul.

It wasn't a particularly big bed, but somehow they found room for Luke, Paul, and the tray. Between mouthfuls of scrambled eggs and buttered toast, Paul wondered why a man's torso always looked so good when a guy was just wearing jeans. Somehow the jeans emphasized the nakedness of the chest, and that faint line of hair running down from his navel and disappearing beneath the waistband of his jeans just made you want to see more. "This is really good," he told Luke honestly, and he didn't just mean the food.

He drank his hot coffee, and while his mouth was still warm, he started pulling Luke to it. Luke made him stop long enough to move the tray onto the floor before straddling him and letting Paul take control of his mouth and his body. Paul ran his hands up and down Luke's chest and back, enjoying every inch of him. When he started pushing his hand beneath Luke's waistband to get to his ass, Luke unbuttoned his jeans and fly to make it easier for him. He was in no hurry to push inside Luke, though. They had all the time in the world, and his hands stroked and squeezed his buttocks until Luke could take it no more and helpfully got some lube from the bedside table, saying, "For when you want it."

Paul could take a hint and soon he had a well-lubricated finger inside Luke's tight ass, which he swirled around while he swirled his tongue inside Luke's mouth. Luke sighed as Paul's finger found all the sweet spots inside his ass. When Paul replaced one finger with two, Luke had to pull his mouth away and press his forehead against Paul's shoulder, whimpering softly as Paul flexed his knuckles, pressing and pressing again. Waves of pressure and pleasure alternated through Luke's belly. He longed for a hand on his cock but couldn't remember how to coordinate his movements enough to make it happen. Paul loved Luke's sounds, loved knowing he was controlling the deep waves of sensation rippling through his body.

Gently, Paul slipped his fingers out of Luke's ass and rolled Luke onto his back, pushing the jeans down further until Luke kicked them off when they got low enough. He remembered where Luke kept the condoms and took one from the drawer before handing it to Luke to open and ease down over his cock. He wanted Luke to touch and think about his cock before it was inside him, wanted him to ache for it first. When he was ready, he stroked Luke's thigh. "Bend your leg," he murmured, and when Luke did, he hooked his hand underneath and lifted it over his shoulder. Luke lifted his other leg without needing to be told. Kneeling with his legs apart, Paul leaned forward, and using every bit of self-control, slowly pressed inside Luke. He felt Luke yield beneath him and held his cock just with the head inside, until Luke squeezed around him and he had to push in further. Even then, he stretched into Luke so slowly there was no burn, just a delicious giving way of his body until Paul was filling him up, his balls pressing against Luke's ass.

Paul's face was inches from Luke's, and Luke reached up to stroke his cheek, push his fingers into his hair and pull his lips down to his own. He wanted Paul all around him as well as inside him. With unhurried movements, Paul began to roll his hips in a circular movement, keeping his dick deep inside Luke. Luke's breathing matched his rhythm, both of them holding on for as long as possible to make it last. Sweat beaded on Paul's forehead but the look of slack arousal on Luke's face made him want to draw this out until he was begging for more. Luke's breath was ragged and tense when at last he made himself hold eye contact with Paul and whispered, "Please… please," in the voice of a man who was reaching his limits.

And then it started—the deep, long thrusts inside him. Every time his body had to yield all over again, and every time the pressure dragged over his prostate, pumping precome from his cock. Waves pulsed out from Luke's ass and balls, drawing short sounds of pleasure from his throat that made Paul push harder and further each time. Luke rode the waves for as long as he could stand it, but in the end Luke had to reach out and jerk the final strokes up through his cock, crying out loudly enough to shake the building.

With his remaining strength, he managed to lower one of his legs from Paul's shoulder, pulling his ass even tighter around Paul's dick. Just when he thought he was going to have to move again, couldn't take the ache, Paul bucked harder into him and reached his own climax.

It took a while for the throb in Luke's ass to subside, but he could live with that. His shower definitely wasn't built for two, so he lay in bed while Paul showered. Was this what it was going to be like from now on with Paul? *Don't think ahead*, he reminded himself.

He rinsed the smell of sex off his body when Paul had finished and then found some clean clothes. When he came out of the bedroom, Paul was looking at his meager collection of books. Luke took the breakfast things over to the sink and started washing up. He supposed Paul would be going soon, and he tried to think of something that would make him stay, but he'd already played his best card and there wasn't much in the flat to distract anyone.

Paul picked up one of the few books and read the title aloud. "*To Kill a Mockingbird.*"

"I know it's a kid's book," Luke said quickly.

"It's not a kid's book. It's a classic. Did you know Harper Lee never wrote anything else? Imagine being able to do that, saying everything you wanted or needed to say in one book."

"When I was a kid… I used to imagine Atticus was my father," Luke said hesitantly, waiting for Paul to laugh.

Paul looked up at him, smiling. "So did I! Which was a bit rough, because my dad is a pretty good guy. Atticus was hard to beat, though." And then it was Luke who laughed.

A beeping noise sent Paul off to look for his mobile phone. When he came back from the bedroom (the phone had ended up under Luke's bed), he was looking thoughtful. "That was a text from Henry, an old friend. He's having a barbecue tomorrow afternoon and inviting everyone round."

"I didn't know gay guys even had barbecues," Luke said, laughing.

"Well, it's pretty much like a straight barbecue, but with much better dressing on the salads," Paul told him. "Anyway, I just thought, do you want to come with me?"

Paul noticed Luke's frown, but carried on anyway. "You've already met Matthew and Jack, at the markets, remember? There'll probably be about six or eight more people there, and us and Henry. It'll give you a chance to get to know everyone."

Luke was still frowning. "I'm not sure Matthew and Jack liked me."

"Of course they did. Everyone will like you." He slipped his hands around Luke's waist and pushed away his own uncertainty about this. For queer guys, some of his friends were very straight.

Luke looked up at Paul and saw that this mattered to him. "Okay," he said with as much enthusiasm as he could dredge up.

"I'll text him back and let him know. I'm going to have to head back to my place and get some work done for next week, but I really want to see you tonight. Do you want to come over to my place, or go out somewhere?"

Luke started to say something, then bit his lip and turned away. "What?" Paul asked.

"You've got a pretty cool kitchen at your house."

Paul had to think for a minute. He had never considered that any kitchen could be thought of as cool.

Luke shrugged, going for casual in a completely unconvincing way. "I just thought, while you were working, maybe I could cook something for later."

"I have no idea what's in the cupboards," Paul confessed. "But real food? That would be something!"

"I can go shopping and bring it over. If you want."

"I want." A huge grin spread over Luke's face as he turned away.

"Look, why don't you bring over some stuff with you? Then you could stay tonight... what time are you working on Monday?"

"Eleven to eleven," Luke replied.

"Okay, so bring over what you need and stay for Saturday and Sunday night. I'll have to leave for work early on Monday, but that doesn't mean you have to go."

A frown flickered back over Luke's face as he considered. Paul made everything sound so natural and easy. Should he just trust and go with it, or keep hold of some of his defenses just in case? Maybe he was letting go of too much, too fast, but on the other hand, he didn't get many weekends without a shift to work. He turned to look at Paul and realized he was watching him, waiting for an answer. Perhaps he'd been letting down some of his defenses by asking Luke in the first place. He flashed Paul a smile. "That would be great."

LUKE knew exactly what he was going to cook for the evening, and what he needed for it, but his shopping trip was still descending into hell. After Paul left, he had gone into his bedroom and started looking for stuff to take with him, which would normally be straightforward as there wasn't much to choose from. Now, he couldn't help but notice how tight his T-shirts were, how bright and cheap everything looked (probably because it was). None of this would be right for a nice, middle-class get-together. He would look like something Paul was paying for. He was pretty sure he could get away with jeans, but maybe if he could buy something new to wear with them that was a bit more conservative, a bit more "Paul," he would be able to blend in a little better.

That had been over an hour ago. Since then he had looked at every permutation of "smart casual," and his head was swimming. Nothing was right—everything looked like shit as soon as he tried it on—he should never have agreed to go to this fucking barbecue in the first place.

He was looking through another rack of clothing without actually seeing any of it when he heard his name.

"Luke? Hi! I thought it was you." Luke turned to see Eddie, a guy he'd met at a club and then kept running into. They hadn't slept together, and they weren't exactly friends, but Luke had always found him easy to talk to.

"Hey, Eddie. How're you doing?"

"Not so bad for working on a Saturday. Making money so I can spend it at Crush tonight!" He winked at Luke.

"You work here?"

"Uh-huh. It's not the hottest place in town, but you'd be surprised the goods that come through that door. I wouldn't have thought it was your kind of place, though."

Luke only hesitated for a second. "I'm totally fucked. I'm seeing a guy and I'm supposed to meet his friends tomorrow, only they're kinda older and richer and I wanted to look okay, but I don't have a fucking clue what to wear and I know I'm gonna look stupid and wrong—"

"Okay, okay, just take a breath. I will be your fairy godmother! Only I'm not allowed to get my wand out; I got in trouble for that last time!"

Luke started to wonder if this was a good idea, but then it was too late and he had to admit the more Eddie talked the more it sounded as if he knew what he was talking about. Twenty minutes later, he was trying on an Alexander McQueen polo shirt that was just edgy enough to look right on Luke while making the blue of his eyes pop. The price made Luke's eyes pop too, even after Eddie used his staff discount to bring it down. He was just going to have to find some extra shifts to work.

Luke turned to Eddie. "Thanks. I really appreciate this."

"Just keep a look out and see if you can find someone for me while you're there," Eddie replied, although Luke really didn't think Eddie needed his help in that department.

LUKE arrived at Paul's just after four o'clock, which was plenty late enough for Paul. He couldn't help but notice how hard it was to focus on his work and not on the memory of Luke's hip under his hand, the sound of that lilting American accent, the way Luke's ass fit him so snugly…. He took a deep breath before he opened the door in the hope that his thoughts wouldn't be too easy for Luke to read, but when he saw Luke's uncertain smile, his dick pulsed hard enough to make further breathing difficult.

"Am I too early?" Luke asked, but Paul was already tugging him inside and pressing him against the wall, his hands in his hair as his tongue flicked into Luke's mouth.

Luke got a shot of the high that came from knowing someone wanted him and missed him when he wasn't there. He returned Paul's kisses, letting Paul know he felt the same way.

"I'm glad you're here," Paul murmured when he finally stopped kissing Luke.

"So am I." Luke kissed him once more before dropping his carryall in the hall and carrying the groceries through to the kitchen.

"Y'know, you don't have to cook something. We could always order in," Paul suggested, feeling a little guilty now.

"I want to. And anyway, it'll give me something to do while you're working."

Paul could vaguely remember the fact that he had a job. It just didn't seem so important when Luke was in the room. He soon found himself being pushed out of his kitchen, though, so he decided to get everything finished as quickly as possible. Once he was back at his laptop in the lounge, he thought how much more alive the house had become since Luke arrived. Somehow it felt more comfortable than when he had sat there alone all morning. Now that he could hear Luke unpacking things and looking for pans and utensils in cupboards, it seemed more like… a home.

Occasionally, Luke would call out to Paul to check something. "Is it okay if we eat around sevenish?" (yes), "Have you ever actually turned this oven on?" (no), "Is there anything you don't like to eat?" (aubergines, which it turned out was English for eggplant). Otherwise, Paul found it surprisingly easy to concentrate now Luke was there. He knew that he could go and kiss, touch, or talk to him whenever he wanted to and that took the edge off his yearning. He supposed it was the same need smokers displayed when regularly checking they had their cigarettes in their pocket. *I'm forming a Luke habit*, he thought.

After an hour, the smell of delicious things cooking tempted Paul back into the kitchen. Luke had several pans on the stove, but seemed more relaxed and confident than Paul had often seen him.

"It smells fantastic. What are we having?"

"Here, I'll show you." Luke picked up an old, stained cookbook and showed Paul a recipe for slow-cooked sauce with pasta. "And for dessert, we've got chocolate torte."

"You're going to make me very fat and then leave me, aren't you?" Paul grinned at Luke. "How did you learn how to do all this?"

Luke hesitated before remembering the "no more lies" rule. "One of the people who fostered me showed me how to do some stuff. She gave me the book." He gave one of his "trying to be casual" shrugs. "It's easy, really. You just do what it says."

"Maybe it's easy for you. I have to read the instructions on a microwave meal twice." He paused. "What was she called?"

"Shauna. She was okay. I was horrible, but she didn't do any of that 'trying to understand' crap. She just said, 'At least if I give you something to do, I know you're not getting in trouble.' She was right— it was easier if I had something to focus on."

"Are you still in touch with her?"

"God, no. They didn't encourage that. Once you were moved out you weren't supposed to have any more contact."

Paul wondered what it must have felt like to constantly have people entering and disappearing from your life when you were trying to work out who you were and how people saw you. He could have asked more, but Luke had turned back to the stove and he didn't want to push too hard. Instead, he stroked his hand down Luke's back. "I'll let you get on. Tell me if you need anything. Anything at all." He let his hand drift down over Luke's ass as he said the last bit, making Luke laugh.

As time passed, Paul opened a bottle of wine and tried to explain to Luke why its different notes would make it a perfect accompaniment to the food, but Luke's verdict was still a simple, "It tastes nice," and that was more than good enough for Paul. When the various pans could be left to simmer unattended, Luke sat with Paul and asked him about his work, and Paul ended up getting carried away, telling Luke all about the Roman invasion of Britain and the changes it brought. Later, Paul decided it was partly Luke's fault. His eyes had been so bright and intense, soaking up the stories and asking questions to find out more. Paul speculated about Luke as a boy and all the things he'd missed out on because he was too busy dealing with the shit the adults in his life created. Luke thought he was stupid because he'd struggled at school, but Paul knew there was only so much an eight-year-old could think about at once, and history would have lost out to where he'd be sleeping that night.

When the food was finally ready, Luke seemed anxious again, but he needn't have been. It was as good as anything Paul had eaten in a restaurant, with the flavors perfectly balanced. He kept telling Luke how delicious it was until he saw that it was making him uncomfortable—he wasn't able to hear that he was good at something yet, and so Paul made himself back off. The chocolate torte just melted on the tongue, and Paul silently pledged to spend some extra time at the gym in the hope that his earlier prediction wouldn't come true.

Paul insisted on clearing away while Luke made himself comfortable in the lounge. When he'd finished, Paul sat down next to Luke on the sofa and held his arm out to him. Luke curled into his side like he had been made to fit just there. Luke was tired—the past couple of days had been pretty intense, but for once he felt as if he'd ended up in the right place. They watched a film they had both seen before—*The Bourne Supremacy*—but the evening felt perfect. When they needed to, they could easily find each other's lips or slip their hands under clothing and rest them there, feeling the heat and closeness of each other's skin. Eventually, they watched the credits roll over the screen.

"Now you're going to take me to bed and fuck me, aren't you?" Luke whispered softly.

"Yeah. I am."

CHAPTER
TEN

PAUL woke up first on Sunday, so Luke missed the chance of waking him with a blow job again. Fortunately, Paul's walk-in shower was big enough for both of them, and it wasn't long before Luke was on his knees sucking like his life depended on it as the water hammered down on them. Paul gripped his hair and wondered how he had ever managed to get up in the mornings before Luke, until his brain was incapable of thinking about anything but the mouth on his cock.

Later, when they were getting breakfast, Luke started pumping Paul in a different way—this time he wanted the low-down on the people he was going to meet at the barbecue that afternoon. He had secretly wished for a typical British downpour of rain, but the sun was bright and the sky was clear so his chances of avoiding it were diminishing.

"Okay, so there's Henry. I've known him for years. It was his sixty-seventh birthday a couple of months ago, although he insists age is just a number. He can seem like a bit of an old letch, but he'd do anything for his friends and he's much smarter than he lets on. He likes to suggest that he used to be a spy, but really he was a civil servant, although he was pretty high up. He tells fantastic stories about his scandalous love life in his younger years, and I have the feeling most of them are probably true. Now he just likes to know all the gossip about other people. He can have a very sharp sense of humor, but I've never known him to be cruel. I guess he's a bit over the top, but he's the person you turn to when you're in trouble."

"Did you ever sleep with him?" Luke's blue eyes were like lasers.

"Henry? Oh God, no! He does tend to pretend he's madly in love with everyone he meets, though, so watch out." Paul looked over Luke's handsome features, just masculine enough to avoid the "pretty" tag. "He'll definitely like you."

Luke raised his eyebrows. He seemed to find any hint of a compliment dubious. "Let's sit outside and eat. You're so lucky to have a yard."

Paul realized guiltily that he had never really bothered to pay much attention to the outside of his house, but there was a metal table and some chairs out there amid the growing jungle. Once they were settled with coffee and toast, Luke wanted to know more, partly because he wanted information on the lions before he walked into the den, and partly because he loved listening to Paul talk.

"So who else will be there?"

"You've met Jack and Matthew—they've been together for a couple of years. I met Matthew through Steve about... six years ago. We've never been particularly close, but he's easy to get along with, and Jack's about the same."

"Who's Steve?"

You don't miss a trick, do you? Paul thought. Out of all the people who were going to be there, Paul had the worst feeling about Steve. Sure, Steve had been pushing him to get on with his life and to start seeing people again, but he had been close to Craig, and Paul really didn't know how he would react to someone as... different... as Luke. He wished he could just tell Steve about who Luke was under the young, defensive exterior and how he made him feel. Would that be enough to get Steve on his side?

Luke was waiting for a response, so Paul told him all about their friendship over the years and tried to convince them both that he would welcome Luke. Richard, or Rich, was an easier topic. He was the laid-back, unruffled counterpoint to Steve. Paul had never known him to get angry or agitated, which was quite an achievement when he considered that Rich had been Steve's partner for nearly six years. The other people Henry had invited were passing acquaintances of Paul's rather than friends, so there wasn't a lot he could tell Luke about them.

"It'll be okay, you know. It's really not a big deal." Paul reached out and covered Luke's hand with his own.

"I know," Luke answered.

LUKE was quiet in the car on the drive out to Henry's house, and Paul kept shooting glances at the deepening frown lines on his face. Yesterday Luke had been so open to him, and it had been easy to be with him. Now, he could feel Luke was on edge, and it was making Paul edgy too. Maybe this hadn't been a good idea; perhaps it was too soon? Too late now, he admitted.

"Y'know, that meal last night was fantastic. I still can't get over what a good cook you are."

Luke turned his frown on Paul. "You said that already. It was just pasta. I'm gonna start thinking you're impressed when I put one foot in front of the other soon." He managed to make Paul's praise sound like an insult.

Okay. So maybe a silent journey wasn't such a bad idea, Paul decided.

Luke fixed his gaze out of the window again. He knew he was being a shit, but he didn't seem able to stop himself. He had always been like this. Once his defenses were up, they were up for everyone. He didn't discriminate between friend and foe. Paul hadn't said anything about what he was wearing, and he couldn't tell if that was a good sign or not. Probably not. Probably Paul was regretting ever suggesting he came to this fucking barbecue, but it was too late now. He would see Luke through his friends' eyes and recognize what a ridiculous idea it had ever been that they could build a relationship together. They would most likely all be laughing about it together by next weekend. Fuck! How had he let himself be put in this situation? All that lovey-dovey crap had knocked the sense out of him.

Luke realized the car was coming to a stop and became more aware of his surroundings. Of course, they would be in the richest part of town, parking outside the kind of house that Luke had only seen in magazines. He felt Paul's hand on his arm. "You ready?"

"Yeah. Sure." He gave Paul a thin, tight smile.

They had to knock twice before anyone came to the door, which gave Luke's stomach time to start turning over. Then the door was flung open by a short, slightly overweight man who Luke guessed was Henry. He welcomed them both as though they were the most important people in the world to him and he hadn't seen them for years, although how he managed to get his hand on Luke's ass and give it a good squeeze in amongst all the greetings, Luke wasn't quite sure.

He found himself in an airy, light hallway with ornate tiling on the floor and a wide staircase leading upstairs. There wasn't much time to take in his surroundings, as Henry was leading them down through the house to the kitchen, with large glass doors opening out to a huge, manicured garden. Luke did his best to hide his wonder at the house. It wasn't just that it was obviously big and expensive—it was also beautiful.

On the grass outside were the rest of Henry's guests. Everyone seemed to have a glass in his hand and to be chatting comfortably with each other. Luke was glad for the opportunity to scope the situation out unnoticed, until Henry called out, "Look everyone, Paul's here with his new friend," and Luke really did want to die.

Paul shot a quick look at Luke, but there wasn't really anything he could do to help him now. Matthew brought Rich over to say hello and to properly introduce him to Luke, and Paul scanned the garden for Steve. He was sitting down with someone Paul didn't know, and after nodding a greeting at Paul, he focused on Luke. Although he was tempted to stay by Luke's side, Luke was a big boy and Paul couldn't hold his hand all day. Instead, he headed toward Steve to get their meeting over with.

Steve stood up as Paul came closer and then he hugged him warmly. "It's good to see you. And your friend." He raised his eyebrows as he said the last bit.

Paul didn't bite. "It's good to see you as well. I'm going to get a drink—do you need anything?" He soon returned with two glasses of white wine and found that Steve was on his own when he got back. "Thanks." Steve took one of the glasses. "So, tell me everything. When, where, how?"

"Well, we met at a club and it just kind of went on from there."

"So it's not serious." Steve's words were a statement, not a question.

"I… don't know. It's early… but I like him."

"I'm sure he has his attractions, but you don't want to get carried away. He's not exactly your type."

"I know he's not the type of guy I used to go for, but, Steve, I'm not the type of guy I used to be. Losing Craig changed me, and things are different now. Maybe what I need has changed too."

"There's nothing new about what he's offering." Steve nodded in Luke's direction. "I get it. You want sex, plain and simple, and he's certainly the kind of guy for that. It's just… this is the first guy you've introduced everyone to since Craig…. Just… take it easy."

Paul sighed and remembered how infuriating Steve could be. Everything he said made sense, and looking at him, Paul could see Steve was concerned about him. If he were in Steve's shoes, he'd probably be saying exactly the same things.

"Okay, I can hear what you're saying and I understand why you're saying it. I'll keep it in mind, if you'll at least consider the idea that Luke is more than a quick fuck to me." Paul looked at Steve for a response, and got a thin smile. *That'll have to do*, he thought.

"So how have things been with you?" he asked, moving the conversation on to safer topics.

Meanwhile, Luke was trying to hold his nerve as Matthew and Rich chatted with him and Henry. Fortunately, the main thing he was required to do was to look interested and nod a lot, as both Matthew and Henry were far more interested in the sound of their own voices than anyone else's. He watched Paul and guessed that the person he was sitting with had to be Steve. From the glances in his direction, he had the uncomfortable feeling that he was the subject under discussion and neither of them looked particularly happy. He found a glass of wine in his hand and drank it a little too quickly, but the warmth that came with it made him feel better. It was soon replaced with a new glass, but he forced himself to sip it this time in the same way he saw the others doing. *Just try to fit in*, he told himself. How hard could it be?

Henry took him to meet some more of the guests, letting his hand drift a little too low when it was around Luke's waist. However, Luke was grateful enough to him for not leaving him alone to overlook it. Part of him felt angry that Paul had deserted him, but on the other hand, perhaps it showed that Paul had faith that he could handle himself in this company. He tried to remember more names and who was with whom as Henry continued the introductions.

The scent of meat on the hot grill was getting stronger, and Luke admitted that despite his nerves he was hungry. He had noticed at some point that Henry had hired caterers to supervise the barbecue and keep the drinks flowing, and he had the feeling that he would have been more comfortable serving at a gathering like this than being a guest. He was now on his third glass of wine, and as it wasn't something he usually drank, he had no idea whether he was drinking too much. If nothing else, he could at least make sure he didn't make a drunken fool of himself.

Luke was glad when he caught Paul's eye and he came back over to him.

"Have you met everybody?"

Luke smiled. "Oh yeah, Henry's really been looking after me."

"Yep, I thought he might. Henry! How much longer until we get to eat this food? Your guests are starving!"

Henry laughed and looked askance at the caterers behind the barbecue. They nodded that they were ready, and people began lining up to collect their food. Luke realized that Paul's joke had been partially true and that compared to other "straight" barbecues he had been to, the food was much better here. But then, everything seemed much better in this part of town.

Luke found himself sitting at a table with Paul, Steve, and Rich. Steve was probably the only person there he hadn't been properly introduced to. He was talking to Paul about a holiday they had been on together to Thailand, and as the conversation went on Luke picked up that it hadn't just been Paul and Steve. Rich and Craig had been there as well.

"Have you ever been to Thailand, Luke?" Steve enquired in a friendly enough tone.

"No. It sounds great."

"Are you planning to visit Europe while you're traveling? You can't go back to America without seeing France or Italy—"

"Or Spain," Rich added. "Barcelona, Seville—you've got to see them."

"What about Berlin? You have to see Berlin! Before you go, you must let us plan an itinerary for you, leaving off all the boring places American tourists usually go to. We'll tell you the best places to see!" While Steve's enthusiasm seemed generous enough, Luke had to notice that it was all focused on him leaving. Had Paul said he was going back to America soon? He smiled and nodded as they continued to debate where he should visit, knowing all the while that he would struggle to pay his return flight to Chicago; a grand tour of Europe was something he couldn't even afford to dream about.

The food was delicious—there were no half-burned, half-raw burgers here, and Luke was relieved beyond words that he hadn't done anything clumsy like getting sauce on his clothes. When he looked at Paul, he seemed to be having a good time. The sun was shining but there was still a breeze to stop it from becoming uncomfortable, and the garden had been carefully landscaped to provide areas of shade as well as direct sunlight. Everywhere he looked, he saw examples of wealth mixed with good taste. He wondered if there would ever come a time when he would feel comfortable in this environment, but then decided to focus on getting through today first.

Paul and Rich got up to get some more food from the barbecue, leaving Luke and Steve at the table. Steve smiled warmly at Luke and leaned forward as if he had something to confide. Luke found himself mirroring his body language, so it was only him who heard Steve's words.

"Paul must seem like a very easy mark to you. But you're not going to find it quite as simple as you might first have imagined."

Luke leaned back, caught off guard. "I don't know what you mean."

Steve's smile hadn't changed. "Of course you don't. But I know your type. Paul's still grieving for Craig, someone whose shoes you wouldn't be fit to shine. He's got more money than you've ever seen, and it's just too good an opportunity for a boy like you to miss. I'm telling you now, the smartest thing for you to do would be to move on and find some other schmuck. Everyone will be very polite to you today, but you're really not welcome here."

For a moment Luke thought he was going to be sick. A cold mixture of rage and shame seeped over his skin. He wanted to punch Steve, but at least he could think quickly enough to know that would give Steve the advantage, not him. And then Paul was at his shoulder, laughing at something Rich had said, and Steve changed back to the easygoing person he had been previously. Luke focused on breathing evenly, controlling the impulses to throw up or tip over the table. People clearly fought differently here, and he was going to have to learn how it was done so next time it was him landing the blows, not Steve.

The conversation continued very much as before, only now Luke had to grit his teeth every time Steve smiled in his direction. Paul didn't seem aware of any change in the mood. Luke continued sitting at the table long enough to show Steve he hadn't scared him before getting up to find another drink and letting himself get drawn into a different circle. As Steve had said, everyone was being very polite to him, only now he couldn't get the thought of what they might really be thinking out of his mind.

Paul was looking around for Luke when Henry managed to corner him on his own.

"So, Paul, tell me, what first attracted you to that incredibly hot piece of ass?"

"There's a lot more to him than what you can see."

"Oh, I have no doubt you've been plumbing his depths!"

Paul had to laugh, despite himself. "You are terrible, wicked old man."

"You're so right. It's just that these days I only get to talk about it." When he spoke again, his voice was quieter, more serious. "You look happy, when Steve isn't raining on your parade."

He really didn't miss anything, Paul thought. "I am," he answered simply, and they both smiled.

"Well, just to be sure I think you should tell me in detail what's been going on between the sheets so I can make an accurate assessment." Paul shook his head in despair. "No? You are a cruel boy. Thank God I still have my imagination!"

"On that note, I think I'll go and rescue him."

Paul started wandering over to a table where Luke was sitting with Jack, Matthew, and Harrison. They were engaged in an animated discussion about the current government's suggested changes to health care, and Luke looked completely bewildered. Paul rested his hand on Luke's shoulder, and he looked up at him with his impossibly blue eyes. A relieved smile spread across his face, and Paul longed to kiss him, but it felt too stagey with everyone watching them out of the corners of their eyes. Instead, he massaged the back of Luke's neck with his thumb and hoped his eyes were telling him how he felt.

As the afternoon wore on, Luke increasingly felt as if he had been assessed and found to be of little interest. His job, his life in America, his academic career, and his hopes for the future had all been variously explored and it was found that they led to dead ends. He had no stories about traveling around Europe, or attending an American Ivy League university, or plans to change the world. His job, on the other hand, was clearly an embarrassment. Someone had helpfully mentioned that they knew someone who had worked as a waiter when they were at university, but that didn't really help. It wasn't that most of the people there weren't likeable; they just didn't have enough common ground to smoothly exchange small talk as a way of getting to know each other.

Adele was playing on a discreetly placed stereo, and he felt his fixed grin being pulled down with every sad song she sang.

He had begun to look around for something more to drink when he spotted Henry walking over to him. Out of everyone there, he probably had the least in common with Henry, and yet he had gone out of his way to keep Luke company and smooth over the lulls in conversation. Luke remembered what Paul had said about him seeming like a letch but actually being a good friend.

"And how are you, gorgeous boy?" he greeted Luke.

Luke knew it was just an affectation, but he was grateful for any kind words he could get. "I'm fine. You have a really beautiful home. Thanks for inviting me."

"The pleasure is all mine. It looks like you've tamed a few of the savages as well." He nodded to the other guests.

"Oh, I don't think so. I don't think they like me very much," Luke admitted. Steve's voice was still very clear in his head.

"Ah, but they don't know your secret."

Luke turned sharply to face Henry, but he was still smiling vaguely at the others. "What secret?" he asked, trying to keep the edge from his voice. Was Henry going to turn on him too?

Henry turned, and Luke caught how sharp and appraising his eyes actually were underneath his buffoon exterior. Luke swallowed, feeling cheap under his new clothes, but preparing himself for another attack. Henry smiled very gently. When he spoke again, his voice was just loud enough to be audible to Luke. "That you're in love with him, of course." Luke didn't know what he'd been expecting, but it wasn't that. *He's right*, he thought. *I love him.* He turned to look at Paul, drinking in the way he stood, the tilt of his head, the timbre of his voice. The air felt a little thinner.

"I can still remember how you have to feel to look at someone the way you look at him. Don't worry. They'll never guess, and your secret's safe with me. Although I might have to negotiate a price!" With his last comment, Henry's voice returned to its previous boisterous tone.

After that, all Luke wanted was to get back to Paul's house. For most of the day, he'd been uncomfortable to be the focus of so many judging, assessing eyes. He had worried that they would search out his lack of education and white-trash background. Steve had placed a magnifying glass over that and held it until it burned. Now he wondered what else he was giving away.

As soon as he had the opportunity, he whispered to Paul, "I want you to myself. I'm tired of sharing."

Paul turned to him with eyes that held a dark yearning. It was all Paul needed to hear. A few people had already left, and it felt as if the other guests were either settling down to make an evening of it or starting to get ready to leave. It would be perfectly natural to make their exit now, and Luke's soft words had reignited Paul's dick.

Paul caught Luke's fingers and entangled them in his own. When Luke met his eyes, he remembered how Luke would yield to him in bed, giving him whatever he wanted and loving the surrender.

"How do you do that?" Paul's voice was thick.

"What?"

"Look at me so that all I can do is want you."

It was what Luke needed to hear; he just wished they weren't in Henry's garden when he was hearing it. Paul seemed to have the same need and began leading Luke back into the house. Once they were inside the kitchen, he thought Paul would reach out to kiss him, but he kept going, leading Luke up the staircase and opening a door into one of the rooms. He glanced inside quickly before pulling Luke in behind him and closing the door.

"Get over here," Paul commanded. Luke glanced at the closed door and remembered the people downstairs who could come looking for them, but there was no way he could refuse that tone.

Paul grabbed the back of Luke's neck firmly, kissing his mouth deeply as Luke clung to him, swept away by Paul's yearning for him and his own need for physical reassurance. Paul wanted Luke's cock in his hand, wanted to feel Luke come, and he wasn't going to wait. He turned Luke around and wrapped his left arm across his chest, holding him tight. With his right hand, he undid Luke's jeans and started pushing them down, along with his briefs. Luke reached behind and held on to Paul's hips to steady himself and to increase the feel of Paul's dick against his ass.

"We can't do this here," he breathed. "Someone might hear us or come in," he said, but he had to admit the thought of some of those smug faces witnessing how hot he made Paul did nothing to stop his growing erection.

"I'm not stopping for anybody." Paul's voice was almost a growl.

Paul lightly stroked over Luke's hard, hot cock and fondled the balls underneath. He heard the breath catch in Luke's throat as he slowly, firmly, drew his finger up the line separating the two sacs. Paul caught up the fabric of Luke's tight shirt and pushed his left hand underneath it, still pinning him against his own chest but now able to pinch and tease his nipples without the fabric between his fingers and the hard nubs. He licked and nuzzled along Luke's jaw line, down to his throat, and then back to his ear. He brought his right hand up to Luke's mouth. "Lick it. Get it good and wet." His voice was husky against Luke's ear, and Luke eagerly lapped his tongue all over Paul's hand before taking each finger into his mouth then sucking hungrily. "That's it. I'm gonna fuck you so good when we get home, but I can't wait that long to hear you come so you're just gonna have to do it now."

Paul's big, slippery hand wrapped around Luke's cock and firmly worked the shaft, tugging up and over the head before twisting and pressing back down. Luke's legs nearly buckled, and Paul held him up as he worked his hand faster, sending electric jolts through Luke's pelvis.

Luke could feel Paul's hard dick pressing into his ass, fingers squeezing his nipple and pressing into his chest, mouth on his throat, and hand... hand pumping his cock and turning his whole body to liquid and heat and a pleasure that felt so good but still craved more and more. His breath came in short, hard gasps.

"Come for me, baby. Come into my hand," Paul urged softly, and something in Luke broke, sending come spurting from his cock and a cry of abandon from his lips.

Paul still held him firmly across his chest and Luke relaxed back into him, regaining his breath and sinking into Paul's strength. He knew Paul would never let him fall, that he was always going to be safe in those arms. He didn't want them to ever let go. When he could stand on his own again, he realized he had come on his shirt and groaned.

"Shit! What am I going to do? They'll all see!"

Paul laughed. "Here. Put my jacket on and do up the zip." Luke shook his head in disbelief at the situation, but Paul's jacket was only a little too big for him, even if it did seem odd to have it zipped up on such a warm day. He turned to Paul, who caught him up in his arms again and gave him a long, slow kiss.

"This whole thing has definitely been an experience. Can we go back to your place now?" Luke begged.

Paul laughed and took his hand to lead him out of the room and back down the stairs.

"Henry, we're off!" he called as they got to the door.

Henry came out into the hall, took one look at Luke's flushed, just-come face, and Paul's jacket and turned to Paul, raising his eyebrows. Paul held in another laugh and mouthed, "Don't," to him, and for once Henry was tactful.

"It's been lovely meeting you, Luke. You must come and see me very often," he said, shaking Luke's hand in both of his.

"Thanks," was about all Luke could think of to say in reply.

As Luke headed out toward the car, Henry pulled Paul close enough to whisper in his ear, "Take that boy home and fuck him until he sees stars."

And Paul did.

CHAPTER ELEVEN

PAUL tried to move around quietly and he nearly got away without waking Luke. When Luke did rouse, he leaned in close and whispered to him to stay in bed, telling him that he would call him later. Paul couldn't quite put his finger on why he liked the idea of leaving Luke sleeping in bed without him. Perhaps he had become aware of the stab of loneliness that tended to catch him when he closed the door of the empty house. He enjoyed thinking of Luke still warm and foggy under the quilt as he began his stop-start journey to work with the other traffic. In lots of ways, his life was the same as it had been before he met Luke, but now there was a warmer, exciting seam running through it.

Luke was too tired to wake properly as he heard Paul moving around, and he was grateful for the suggestion that he stay put. However, waking up alone in someone else's house still made him feel uncomfortable. He realized that it brought back memories of living in foster care, where you never knew where anything was and you were always so aware that you were in another person's home. He tended to fall into a pattern of putting things back exactly as he found them, as if he were trying to pretend he had never been there. Paul had said he could sleep in, but he couldn't shake the feeling of trespassing.

Would he have left Paul alone in his flat? He had to admit that he would have felt uncomfortable about it. What did that mean—that Paul could eat his ass and fuck him until he was crying out, but he didn't want him to look around his bedroom? It wasn't that he had a stash of stolen goods or dubious porn, or anything really that he wouldn't want

Paul to see. He worried about Paul seeing him, like the moment when he had picked up *To Kill a Mockingbird*. It was his favorite book, but he couldn't have let Paul know that without feeling ashamed, and he didn't even know why.

Conversely, Luke could see it hadn't occurred to Paul that he would ever need to hide anything about himself. There were things he might keep private, but by choice, not fear. He understood embarrassment, but not shame, not in the way that Luke did. Luke was always waiting to be caught out and brought down low, put back in his place. Maybe that would always be a difference between them.

He heard a crash downstairs, and his heart nearly exploded in his chest until he worked out that it was the mail hitting the mat. It helped kick-start him, though, and Luke decided to get out of the house as quickly as possible. He dressed without showering and headed downstairs, where he found a note from Paul telling him to make breakfast and stay as long as he wanted; just to put the latch on the door when he left. He'd signed it with a kiss. A sentimental, Paul kind of thing to do, but it put the smile back on Luke's face. He decided to take the note home with him and slipped it into his pocket.

Riding the bus back to his flat, Luke tried to process some of the events from the past few days. Now he had time to stop and think, he wondered if Kit was still hanging around or if he had gone back to America. He didn't like the thought of crossing paths with him again, and there was always the vague threat that he might cause trouble for Paul, although that seemed unlikely. Maybe Brooke would know if he was back in Chicago yet.

As he thought back over Kit's words, he remembered conversations from the barbecue and he was certain of one thing: he was sick of feeling like the most stupid person in the room. He decided to have a look on the web and see if there were any courses available that he could take. Maybe if he could do something by himself, slowly, at his own pace, without the pressure of classrooms and teachers, he might be able to learn some stuff after all.

He had one thing in his favor. He could read. Luke had come across children in the special ed classes who had still been sounding out letter by letter, even at high school, but Luke had always loved books. He had seen them as whole worlds he could disappear into when he was younger, and as people who spoke to him without judgment as he hit his teens. He didn't know why he had stopped reading and started to think books were a waste of time. Paul had loads of books, and now Luke regretted leaving so soon. He could have had a quick look and gotten some ideas. He wouldn't mention it to Paul, though, just in case. Luke didn't ask himself what "just in case" meant.

If Paul had changed his opinion of Luke after the barbecue, Luke had to acknowledge he had done a very good job of hiding it. When he thought about their hurried encounter at Henry's house, he couldn't help smiling. After arriving home, they had fucked, and it had been as good as it ever was, but it was the urgency, the can't-wait-got-to-have-you feeling of the hand job that made the blood drop to Luke's groin.

Instead of starting to get bored, the longer they were together the more Luke craved certain things that Paul did. He was starting to know the look in Paul's eyes just before Paul kissed him, the particular sensation of his cock filling Luke that now felt just right every time, the sounds Luke dragged from him when he took Paul's cock right back against his throat. And his hands—Paul's hands were big and strong, like they could scoop Luke up and hold him fast. When Paul's hands were on him, anywhere.... Luke felt the heat rising to his cheeks as he remembered where he was, and he looked around at the other passengers on the bus. No one seemed to be looking at him or guessing what he had been thinking about. *Who knows,* he wondered, *what they're thinking about themselves*, and the thought made him smile.

PAUL'S morning sped by in the usual rush of sorting out Monday-morning issues, assembly, organizing resources for lessons and introducing the new topics for the week to the class. He felt a little disorganized and realized that for the past eighteen months he had been thinking about nothing but his job. This weekend had changed that, and he was going to have to adjust to having different aspects to his life again.

At lunchtime he caught up with Helen, a teacher he had been working with for six years. Paul had always been out at work, and while he had the impression that a few parents didn't appreciate their children having a gay teacher, he had never experienced any direct issues from it. He was a good teacher who cared about the children in his class and at the school, and he'd found that that was a great deal more important to the children, parents, and colleagues than who he dated. Right now, though, his love life was exactly what he wanted to talk about.

After the usual "how's your morning been" exchange, Paul jumped in. "I'm seeing someone new. Well, for a few weeks now, but it feels more serious after this weekend."

Helen's face lit up, and she gave Paul her full attention. "Tell me everything," she said with a grin.

"Okay, umm... well, he's a lot younger than me, early twenties, I guess. I probably should know better—I know that's what a lot of my friends are thinking. But there's something about him... you know when you get that spark? It's not always with the person you expect or even want, but it's there, every time. I keep waiting for it to burn out, but if anything it's getting worse."

"Oh yeah, I remember the spark. That spark's got me into a lot of trouble, most of which I thoroughly enjoyed!" Helen grinned.

Paul returned the smile. "He's American, he's sexy as hell. He's... not had a great life. He understands things that maybe other people his age wouldn't. He dropped out of school, he works in a burger bar, he's defensive most of the time... but when he smiles.... He's different from me, very different, but then in some ways we completely get each other." Paul had no intention of going into the way in which they most "got" each other. Helen would have to fill in that blank for herself.

Helen raised her eyebrows. "He sounds pretty hot."

Paul remembered Luke's sleepy face on the pillow that morning, his soft mouth slightly open, gold and brown mixed up in his hair, and found his mind slipping back to the intensity of the previous night when Luke had been pushing his ass up to take Paul's thrusts, his face scrunched up with the force of the penetration. He cleared his throat. "Yeah, I think you could safely say he's pretty hot."

"Okay. You tell me that he's different from you. One question— do you want to change him?"

Paul considered this. "I want him to see what I see. I want him to see his own worth."

"But if he wanted to stay at the burger bar, whatever.... Can you accept that? Do you have a game plan to 'save' this guy? Because if you really want him to see what he's worth, you have to value him right now, not the 'new improved' version he might one day be."

Paul nodded slowly. "I get what you're saying. And, yeah, I think that the way he is now is just fine by me." He took a deep breath and came to the crux of the matter. "I don't know if I'm making a fool of myself."

Helen laughed. "Pride and love never make good bedfellows. Love makes us stupid; it's a fact. But have you ever tried to cuddle up to your pride on a cold night?"

"I didn't say I loved him," Paul corrected her quickly.

"No, but you sound like you're on the way. And it's the right way for you, Paul. You're a good man—probably one of the few! You have a lot of love to give. It would be the saddest thing, the most foolish thing, if you didn't let yourself take chances again. I don't know how things will go with this new guy, but I'm telling you, you should find out. And keep finding out until you do find the right one, however foolish you feel or look." Helen sighed. "It's that or the empty bed, my friend. After the divorce, I was certain that being alone was better than ever being hurt like that again. But you know what? However much it hurt, it didn't kill me, it's survivable. And I'll tell you a secret—I've joined an Internet dating thing!"

"Really? Why didn't you tell me before?"

"Y'know what? I didn't want to look foolish. Time to take my own advice, huh?"

DUE to their different work patterns, it was difficult for Paul and Luke to meet up during the week. Instead, they kept a steady stream of texts passing back and forth. At first Luke had been hesitant and guarded, carefully rehearsing his texts before sending them and weighing each word. As the exchanges became more frequent, he gradually let his guard down and was more spontaneous and relaxed. The short bursts of contact with Paul were something concrete and real that he could return to whenever he needed to. It wasn't that he was going to save them all forever—he just hadn't gotten around to deleting any of them yet.

Because of his shift pattern, Luke had two forty-five minute breaks—the first at 2:00 p.m. and the second at 5:15 p.m. When he went outside to the yard just after five thirty on Tuesday evening, he had planned to send Paul a text, but found himself dialing the number instead.

"Hi, Luke." Paul knew his number by now.

Luke got a shot of warmth from the tone of his voice. Paul never played it cool. He was pleased to hear from Luke, and so he let Luke hear it in his voice. "Hey," he answered. "Are you busy? I'm not interrupting or anything?"

"No, it's good to hear your voice. Are you at work?"

A big sigh from Luke. "Yeah, only another five and a half hours to go. They're building up to the six o'clock rush in there at the moment, and then it'll go quiet until we start getting people on their way home from the bars at ten." He sat down on the step and focused on the voice coming through the phone. "What are you doing?"

"I'm having a really exciting evening. We started converting decimals to percentages in math today, and marking the books is... quite emotional!" He gave a short laugh.

"They'll get it. They have a really good teacher."

"I hope so. How's your day been?"

"Pretty ordinary. There was a screwup earlier that caused some excitement. All the fries are cooked from frozen, right? Well, Brian, the idiot I told you about, forgot to put the latches back on the freezer room doors properly when he took a couple of bags out. Turns out, there's some automatic thing to save energy or something that stops the refrigeration when the door's open, so it's not pouring out freezing air. No one noticed for hours and all of the stock from that walk-in freezer has had to be thrown in the garbage." Luke laughed, then stopped himself. "I know it's not funny, but Brian's been sulking all day. He's too scared to even give anyone a dirty look, because he knows he's totally in the shit. And yeah, I know it makes me a bad person, but I have kinda enjoyed that."

"You're not a bad person. It's always good to see some universal karma in action."

"What *is* karma?"

"Well, the way people use the word in an everyday sense kind of means what goes around comes around. You dish out bad stuff, you get bad stuff back. You dish out good stuff and you get the good stuff back."

"I like the sound of that, but I'm not sure it's how life really works." There was a pause and then Luke spoke again. "Y'know how we're not going to see each other until Friday night?"

"Yeah."

"Well, do you ever... think about me?"

"Of course I think about you."

"No, I mean... think about me, when we haven't seen each other for a bit."

There was a pause, then, "Oh, I get it. Think about you. Hmmm. No!"

"You bastard!" They both laughed.

"Luke?"

"Yeah?"

"I think about you."

"Yeah? I think about you too. I'm gonna go now, and let you think."

They both laughed again.

"I'll see you Friday."

"Yeah, I can't wait." Paul ended the call, and Luke let out a long sigh. He'd never had this before. Every time he reached out to Paul, Paul was there. How long could something like this keep going?

Liam came out into the yard, frowning. "You okay?" he asked Luke.

Luke turned to him with a smile, not sure why he sounded concerned. "Yeah, sure."

Liam nodded. "I just wondered. Brian came out here a few minutes ago and he's just gone back into the kitchens looking like someone pissed in his coffee."

"Brian came out here?"

"Yeah. Didn't you see him?"

Luke had been sitting with his back to the door, caught up in his call to Paul. It would have been easy for Brian to have stood behind him, listening, without Luke realizing.

"Shit."

"What?"

"I was talking on the phone. I said something about Brian's screwup with the freezers." Luke looked at Liam, and they both grimaced.

"You better keep your head down," Liam advised unnecessarily.

WEDNESDAY night, quarter past eleven, and Luke was heading home. He'd missed the bus, but it wasn't cold and he sometimes found that walking home helped him cast off the day's drudgery. Earlier in the day, he'd found out the name of the college that Liam went to, and casually asked if they offered any adult courses. Now that he knew they did, he planned to have a look on their website tonight to see what was available. Trouble was, he didn't know exactly what he wanted to do. He wanted to feel smarter, but he didn't think there would be a "Get Smarter" course in the catalog.

Luke was glad his path and Brian's hadn't crossed much that day. Brian had been working a 6:00 a.m. 'til 2:00 p.m. shift, and some of that time he'd spent in the manager's office. Rumor was he'd had a formal reprimand, which would kill his chances of any pay raise in the coming year. Although Luke found it hard to feel sorry for him, he wished Brian hadn't overhead Luke talking about him. He'd been on the receiving end of that enough to know that it stung, and it felt like a cheap shot.

The next things happened very fast. Luke became aware of a group of men close behind him and automatically tensed. He heard someone mutter, "Get the fucker," but before he could react, he felt a fist smash into his back and found himself falling forward. He managed to break his fall with his hands only to come under attack from feet kicking him, seemingly from all directions. Luke knew enough about fights to understand the most important thing was to try and stay upright. On the ground, he was helpless. He pushed himself back up onto his feet and staggered a little, giving his opponents time to grab his arms while another pulled a bag over his head.

By this time he had worked out that there were three of them, and they were trying to drag him into an area of trees and bushes. Luke decided to save his strength and not focus on resisting them. The bag over his head was disorientating, but he could still breathe. They obviously reached a place where they felt more secure, because while his arms were still being held behind him, he was now being kept in one place, with the third man laying into him with more enthusiasm than skill. Luke forced himself to stop resisting and to go slack in the men's grip, readying himself to make a sudden break from them.

There came a pause in the fists striking into his torso, and he took his chance. He got one arm free easily enough and loosened the grip on his other. His first priority was to tear the bag off his head so he could see what was happening around him. The cold air gave him more energy, and his right fist connected with the person who was still holding on to his left arm. He turned to face the third person who had been so free with his blows and came face to face with Brian. Anger coursed through Luke, and his fist connected hard with Brian's jaw before the other two men attacked him from behind again.

The force of their weight drove Luke back down on the ground, and every way he turned to try and get up they were already there. His body was starting to melt with pain, and he knew he couldn't take much more of this when he felt a hand grab his hair, lift up his head, and smack it down to the ground. His forehead made contact with a rock and a stab of pain was the last thing Luke registered.

CHAPTER
TWELVE

As consciousness returned, the first thing Luke was aware of was the taste of blood in his mouth. Then he felt something pressing against his face and he tried to move. Pain and nausea swept over him, and he held himself still until it passed. He was starting to recall what had happened. Using his tongue, he carefully felt around his teeth and checked that none were missing. The blood seemed to have come from at least one cut on his lip, and an attempt to move his jaw was painful but a success. He listened carefully, but he couldn't hear anything apart from the traffic on the nearby road. From the frequency of cars passing, he guessed it was still the middle of the night, which meant he couldn't have been out for too long.

Luke knew he was going to have to move again but he wanted to put it off for as long as possible. He tried to work out what he was going to do. From the way he felt, he guessed he looked pretty grim. No taxi was going to pick him up, and the buses had probably stopped running. Even without moving, he was aware of a growing pain that seemed to encompass his torso. It was unlikely that he would be able to walk home, and if he tried, his appearance might attract attention from the police—something he definitely wanted to avoid. He had learned to be suspicious of authority figures, and talking to the police would only bring back memories of his arrest with his mother. He tried to think of somebody—anybody—he could call at this time of night to come and get him, and however much he wanted to avoid it, there was only one person.

Luke was pretty sure that Brian and his friends wouldn't have bothered to rob him, but his phone could still have been broken in the fight. He couldn't put it off anymore. He was going to have to move to get it out of his jeans pocket. He tested each part of his body as he slowly brought it to life. It felt like nothing was broken but everything was bruised. Once he had managed to roll onto his back, he got his hand into his pocket and pulled out the phone, still in one piece. His hands hurt and his fingers felt swollen, either from trying to defend himself or from finding themselves under someone's foot.

The little tune his mobile played when it came to life was the best sound he could imagine hearing at that point. By half lying on his side again, he managed to push himself up into a sitting position. He slowly inched over to a fence that he could lean against and then stopped to catch his breath. His ribs hurt, as well as everything underneath, and he let his eyes close for a couple of minutes. The air was cold, and the temptation to just stay there until someone found him was creeping up on him.

This wasn't the first time Luke had found himself dealing with the aftereffects of a fight. At school, he had been an easy target for bullies but he had finally realized that trying to stay out of people's way wasn't enough. He began to go looking for trouble, making it clear to anyone who might need to know that he always fought back, never backed down. On the whole, people had left him alone after that, whispering names behind his back when they felt they were at a safe distance. He didn't classify his clashes with Chris as fights, since eight-year-old boys can't really fight thirty-year-old men; they can only get beaten until the man wears himself out. For a long time, he had told himself that what Kit did wasn't the same, but in the end he had to face it—he had gone from fighting off bullies to living with one.

He slid a little further toward sleep before pulling himself back by clenching his fists so the pain would wake him up. He couldn't put off calling Paul any longer, although he heartily wished he didn't have to. He didn't want to have to ask for help, and he didn't want Paul to see him looking like a punching bag. Sighing was only making his ribs fire with pain. He managed to bring up Paul's number and pressed the button to make the call.

The phone rang long enough to make Luke think it was going to go to voice mail, but when Paul answered, he sounded alert. Luke knew that getting a call this late at night would have put him on edge.

"Luke? Are you okay?"

"Yeah, but I'm sorry, I need you to come and get me."

"You sound like something's wrong. Where are you?" Luke tried to remember the street name and described his location. "I know where you mean. Don't worry. I'll be there in about ten minutes. Luke? Are you really okay?"

"I'm hurt, but it's not that bad."

"Okay. I'll be about ten minutes, alright? Leave your phone on."

"Yeah, I will."

Luke ended the call and pressed his forehead against his hand. It hadn't been hard to hear the anxiety in Paul's voice, and he felt like a total shit for doing this to him. He tried to wipe at his face in the hope that he wouldn't look too bad, but he kept coming across swollen places and cuts. He decided to try to get to his feet and wait by the road, using the fence to support himself. A new wave of dizziness hit him, and this time he found himself vomiting as he clung to the wooden post. *Well*, he thought after it passed, *at least Paul didn't get to witness that*.

He gave himself a couple of minutes before moving closer to the road. He stayed in the shadows just in case a police car came past, and looked out for Paul. He breathed out with relief when a car started slowing down and he recognized Paul's license plate. Slowly he stepped forward and tried to look as "okay" as he could manage.

"Shit! Luke, what the fuck happened? I'm calling an ambulance!" Paul was pulling out his phone when Luke stopped him.

"No, no, really, Paul, no. I don't need an ambulance, I don't need the hospital. I promise you, I don't. Everything's working, it just hurts. Please. Please, could you just take me home?"

Paul looked at Luke uncertainly. "Let's get you into the car," he said, not prepared to rule out the hospital yet.

At the door, Luke hesitated. "Have you got a blanket or something?"

"Are you cold? Here, take my jacket."

"No. It's just… I'm gonna make your car all messy."

Impatience crept into Paul's voice for the first time. "Just get in the fucking car, Luke. I'm really not worried about the upholstery right now."

Luke let Paul help him duck into the car and tried hard not to groan with pain as he maneuvered his body. Paul helped him put his seat belt on before walking around to the driver's side and getting in. He stared through the windshield, his hands on the steering wheel, but not going anywhere. Luke knew he was deciding whether to take him home or to the hospital, but he didn't want to antagonize him any further so he kept quiet. The car was warm and the seat supported him. He let his eyes close. He didn't want to admit to himself how relieved he was that Paul was there. Paul started up the engine and pulled away.

After a couple of minutes, Luke opened his eyes to see what Paul had decided. They weren't on his route home, but he didn't think they were headed for the hospital, either. "Where are we going?" he murmured.

"I'm taking you home."

Luke worked it out. They were headed for Paul's house. "No, you don't have to take me to your place. Really."

Paul roughly pulled the car off onto the shoulder, flicked on the hazard lights, and turned to Luke. His face was tight with anger that Luke didn't understand. "You have a choice. You can come back to my place so I can clean you up, and I'll then decide whether or not I think you need to go to the emergency room. Or we can go straight there now. It's up to you."

"Okay. We can go to your place." Luke's voice was only just above a whisper. He would totally understand Paul being pissed off at him for waking him up and dragging him out in the middle of the night, but that didn't seem to be it.

They completed the rest of the journey in silence.

Once Luke was seated in the kitchen, he could clearly see the strain in Paul's movements as well as his face, but he didn't know how to make things better. He let Paul feel all over his head for any swellings or knocks, but the only one seemed to be on his temple. There was a painful swelling and a cut that had now stopped bleeding.

"Honestly, it's not that bad. Let me go into the bathroom and clean myself up."

Paul sighed. He knew that Luke was coherent and he didn't appear confused or to have difficulty with his vision. However, he had admitted to Paul that he had lost consciousness and that he had been sick, and Paul knew they were both warning signs that a serious head injury could have occurred.

He nodded to Luke to go, and watched him carefully as he walked back through the lounge and then up the stairs. He seemed coordinated and no longer claimed to feel dizzy.

"Leave the door open," he called up to Luke.

Luke did as Paul asked and understood more of his concern when he saw his reflection. He had seen himself looking worse, but still.... He lowered the lid of the toilet and sat down to remove his shoes and socks, then took off his jeans. There were a few nasty bruises on his legs but nothing too bad. His jacket was loose, so that was easy enough to slip off, but getting out of his T-shirt proved to be an act of endurance as he tried to raise his arms and stretched the muscles of his body. Brian and his gang had made up for their lack of fighting skill with their numbers and persistence. Luke could see red marks and developing bruises covering his chest, stomach, and back. He thought back to the blow he had landed on Brian's jaw and was glad to think that at least he was feeling some of Luke's pain. He hadn't recognized the other two men and was relieved that they weren't from work. That at least suggested they didn't have anything personal against him. Maybe they were just idiots Brian had convinced to come along. He knew he was going to have to think about what to do next at some point—go back to work as if nothing had happened? Have a private "chat" with Brian? Resign and find another job? All of that would have to wait for another time. His head already hurt enough.

As he turned on the shower and adjusted it to the weakest water pressure, he could hear Paul talking to someone downstairs. It sounded like a one-sided conversation, so he guessed he was on the phone. He hoped Paul wasn't calling an ambulance. Luke was so tired all he could think of was curling up in bed. He washed the dirt out of his hair and let the water do most of the work before halfheartedly drying himself off and towel-drying his hair. His face was still swollen in places, but at least he had washed most of the blood away.

When he came out of the bathroom, Paul was sitting on the top step, waiting for him. He looked so sad and worried that it made Luke's heart ache. He wanted to be the one who made Paul happier than anyone else. Instead, he had brought a pile of misery to him.

"I'm so sorry about this."

"I've put some clothes out for you on the bed. I'll wait for you. I don't want you coming down the stairs on your own."

Luke ached to lie down in a warm bed, but he nodded to Paul. In the bedroom, Paul had put out a thick, soft sweater and jogging pants with a thin waistband that wouldn't dig into Luke's bruises. Luke pulled them on and followed Paul downstairs.

Paul sat down on one of the armchairs and Luke sat on the sofa. "While you were cleaning up, I called the medical helpline. I went through your symptoms and described how you are now, and they said you would probably be okay not to go to hospital tonight, although you should see a doctor in the morning. And I have to sit up with you until at least two hours have passed since you were sick to check you don't develop any further symptoms."

Luke felt wretched. "What time is it now?"

Paul looked at his watch. "It's just gone quarter past two. I picked you up about half-past one, so you need to stay awake until half three."

"I'm so sorry," Luke said again, only this time his voice was breaking.

"Hey." Paul got up and came and sat next to him. "I want to hold you but I'm scared I'll hurt you."

"I don't care," Luke whispered, leaning into him. He could take a beating, but knowing he had screwed up Paul's night and seeing him upset was killing him.

Paul draped his arms around Luke and pulled him as close as he dared. He kissed his damp hair. "Do you want to tell me what happened?"

Luke gave Paul a shortened version, leaving out the fact that he had worked out who one of his attackers had been and had a pretty good idea why the attack had taken place. As he spoke, he felt Paul becoming tense again.

"Those fucking animals! Really, we should call the police now, but I guess you want to leave it until the morning."

Luke knew there was no way he was going to the police. In his experience, the police meant trouble and he didn't need any more of that in his life. But he also knew he didn't have it in him to argue with Paul now, so instead he said nothing.

"Are you warm enough? If you're in shock, you'll feel cold."

"I'm fine, thank you, doctor," Luke answered, managing a half smile. He couldn't get a fix on Paul. Sometimes he seemed angry and completely pissed off at Luke, and then he seemed as though he wanted to take care of him. Luke was too tired to work it out and he let his eyes close for a moment.

"Hey, no, you can't fall asleep. You need to stay awake. You need to talk to me about something."

Luke groaned. "Can't we stay awake very quietly with our eyes closed?" he whispered.

This time Paul smiled. "I think that's called sleeping. We need to find something easy to talk about. Okay, what's your favorite film?"

"My what? I don't know."

"C'mon. Tell me a film that you really like."

"I don't know. *E.T.*?" Luke regretted it as soon as he said it. Surely he could have thought of something more impressive than a kids' film.

"Excellent. *E.T.* So tell me what it's about."

"What? You haven't seen *E.T.*? Everyone's seen *E.T.*!"

"Maybe the American version was different from the British one. They might have taken bits out or put extra bits in."

Luke looked very doubtful. "I really don't think so."

"Look, you need to stay awake and I need to know that you're not getting confused or anything, so this way I get to hear a story as well."

"Fuck. Well, it starts at night, and there's this UFO that's visiting Earth...."

Luke managed to retell the story of the film with the help of occasional interruptions from Paul and a brief disagreement over how many boys were on their bikes when they took flight. When he finished, Paul finally agreed they could go to bed.

Once they were under the covers, Luke whispered, "I think I'm beyond tired."

"You know, you scared me tonight," Paul said.

"I know. I'm sorry." Luke was beginning to realize how feeble the word "sorry" was. He kept saying it, but it didn't make anything any better.

"I know. Just... just promise me you'll try and take care of yourself, okay? You'll try and keep safe? I don't want shitty stuff to happen to you."

"Okay," was all Luke could manage, and even that choked in his throat.

"I've set the alarm to wake me up at seven so I can call the head teacher and say I won't be in tomorrow... today... you know what I mean. If you hear the alarm, just go back to sleep."

Paul waited, but there was no response apart from Luke's slow, regular breathing. He desperately hoped that he was right not to take him to the hospital. He had never seen someone so badly beaten before—well, he had never known anyone who had been in a proper fight before now, and he felt ridiculously helpless. What he really couldn't understand was Luke's casual attitude about what had happened to him. It was almost as though he thought it was acceptable, and yet it enraged Paul that anyone could think they could put their hands on Luke like that and get away with it. He was determined they would go to the police in the morning.

Paul closed his eyes and tried to push away the images of Luke's bruises and focus on the feel of him next to him in the bed, but it took him a long time to get to sleep.

CHAPTER THIRTEEN

THE alarm woke Paul from a thick sleep, and he shuffled downstairs to call the head teacher and explain he wouldn't be in work today. Apart from being tired, he felt too mixed-up to face a class of children and he was still worried about leaving Luke alone. Fortunately, his work record was good and no one was going to give him a hard time about missing one day. Then he thought of something else—what about Luke's job? He hesitated briefly, knowing he was probably overstepping a boundary. However, if the call had already been made, there was no way Luke could play the hero and drag himself into work. Paul justified it to himself by thinking how employers always liked to know as soon as possible if someone wouldn't be in, so he found the number in the phone book and called. He spoke to the manager, who sounded as if he was in a bad mood already.

"Just what I need. I've already had another guy say he's not coming in. What the hell are they all playing at?"

Paul bit back his response, which was along the lines of telling him where to stick his job if that was his attitude toward his employees, and managed to placate him a little by sounding sympathetic to his complaints.

On the way back to the bedroom, he found some ibuprofen and a glass of water, which was the best he could think of for Luke. He was tempted to let him sleep, but also anxious to make sure he was okay, so he decided to be a bit noisier than he needed to be when he returned. He was rewarded by Luke rousing, and he immediately felt guilty.

Paul went round to Luke's side of the bed. "How're you feeling? I've got some painkillers if you want them?" Luke made a noise that sounded like agreement and he managed to sit up enough to take the pills. Although the swelling had gone down, the bruises had developed, giving him a multicolored skin tone. At least he didn't have a black eye.

Paul climbed back into bed and lay on his back, wondering if he could go back to sleep. Luke rolled over and rested his head on Paul's shoulder, slipping his arm over Paul's chest.

"You want me to go?" Luke murmured.

Paul grimaced. How could Luke think that he would chuck him out like this? But this wasn't the time to start an argument, so he managed a simple "no" instead.

He felt Luke slowly relaxing against him as his breathing grew slower and more regular. He clearly had no trouble getting back to sleep, and Paul was left with his thoughts. He remembered his talk with Carol and the question she had asked "Do you want to change him?" Right now the answer would be a huge yes. Paul wanted to change him into a person who was shocked when someone beat him up, who knew Paul would want to look after him for as long as he needed, who expected to be cared for when he was hurt. Paul was starting to see that breaking down those barriers and trying to show Luke that there were different ways to be in a relationship with someone, different from the dysfunctional relationships of his past, was going to be exhausting. Did he really need this in his life?

The answer had to be no. He didn't want or need hassle and emotional strain, now or ever; he wasn't a drama queen. Paul told himself he wanted a quiet, easy life and there was very little about Luke that was quiet or easy. Maybe he should bring the whole thing to a halt now. Only… did he really want that? He remembered the jolt in his groin when Luke's eyes met his, the driving desire that made him feel so alive, the joy of being with someone who could challenge or surprise you because they were different. Well, Luke had challenged and surprised him last night, no doubt about that. He closed his eyes and concentrated on the rhythm of Luke's breathing and the warmth of his body.

Paul drifted in and out of sleep for the next hour or so before deciding to get up and fix breakfast. He showered and shaved, and was digging out some clothes when Luke awoke again.

"I should get up," he murmured to no one in particular.

"Stay in bed. It's still early. Get some rest." If Paul were completely honest, he could do with breakfast by himself. Luke didn't take much convincing after he tried to roll over and groaned in pain.

After Paul left, Luke tried to get back to sleep, but it just wasn't happening. The tablets he had taken had started to wear off, but he knew it was too soon to take more. He couldn't get Brian's face out of his head. The sneaky little shit hadn't had the guts to take Luke on by himself, but he bet that wasn't the story Brian was going to be telling. Were they on the same shift pattern today? Luke couldn't remember. That was if he could make it in to work in the first place, and if they would want him there with his battered appearance. He hoped the blow he'd landed had turned into a good bruise for Brian, at least.

The other problem he faced was where he stood with Paul. Luke loathed having to ask anybody for anything. He preferred to be seen as someone who didn't need any help and didn't show vulnerability, but that just didn't seem to be happening when he was with Paul. Last night he had needed Paul's help—the one person he didn't want to see him as weak, the person he wanted to impress. He couldn't shake the feeling that things had changed between them, and not for the better. He needed to get things back to how they had been, and lying in bed wasn't going to do it.

Before he hit the shower, he opened Paul's wardrobe door and surveyed the damage in the full-length mirror. His legs were okay apart from a couple of pretty deep bruises on his thighs, and although his shoulders and arms were stiff and aching, he couldn't see any damage. There was a large swelling on his forehead that was painful to the touch, and his right cheekbone was swollen and badly bruised. He tried to work out if this gave him a rugged, sexy look. Maybe to some, but he was pretty sure Paul wouldn't read it that way. The worst bruising was around his stomach and sides, where it was hard to find a patch of normal-colored skin.

He showered but didn't have anything with him to use for shaving. Unshaven, he looked even more of a wreck, so he eventually took a new razor from Paul's cabinet and used his shaving gel—some kind of luxury brand that he had to admit felt really good. Before going downstairs, he experimented with wrapping the towel higher around his body to cover more of the bruises but it ended up looking weird so he went for full-on sexy and kept it very low instead.

Luke took a breath before walking through the lounge to the kitchen, and plastered on his best "fuck me" smile.

"Hi," he called to Paul.

"Hey, you didn't need to get up already," Paul answered, getting up from the table and taking his cup and plate over to the sink.

Not exactly rushing into my arms, Luke thought, *but I can deal with that.*

He moved to stand closer to Paul, but when he turned, Luke didn't get the response he wanted.

"Jesus! You look terrible. I really should have taken you to the hospital last night."

"It's not that bad, really." Luke leaned in for a kiss, but Paul was backing away again.

"I don't want to hurt you."

"I don't mind."

Paul gave one of those laughs that really wasn't a laugh at all and shook his head. "No, I'm not sure that you do."

Luke suddenly felt pathetic, stood there in a towel trying to get Paul hard, when Paul seemed to be viewing him with disgust. He wanted to disappear or at least find somewhere to crawl away to and hide. He quickly changed his plans.

"I just wanted to know if I could borrow some clothes to get home. I'll get them right back to you." He made his voice hard so the weakness couldn't break through.

"Fine. Take what you need," Paul answered. Luke nodded and went back upstairs, focused now on getting out of there as quickly as possible.

Paul let out a long sigh. He didn't want Luke to go, and the last thing he wanted was to make him feel even worse. He wished he could separate his anger at the situation and his feelings for Luke. Now he wished he had kissed him when he had the chance. He followed Luke upstairs and found him wearing the jogging pants he'd borrowed last night and putting his sneakers onto bare feet. He dug out some socks for him.

"Here. Put these on."

"I'm okay."

Paul reached out and stroked his arm. "I'm sorry."

Luke shrugged and carried on lacing up his shoes. "Don't be. For what? You helped me out and I'm really grateful. I'm sorry you had to miss work."

"Don't freeze me out," Paul said quietly.

Luke paused. "I don't know what to do. I don't know what to say. You're mad at me and I don't know how to make it right." Luke took a deep breath. "I have to get ready for work anyway."

Shit. Even before he said it, Paul knew this was not going to go down well. Had he really thought it was a good idea to phone Luke's boss? "No… um, actually I called in for you this morning. I told them you weren't well."

Luke kept still for a moment, then turned to Paul with unmistakable anger in his eyes. "You did *what*? Who the fuck asked you to do that?" Luke spat the words out.

"I just thought…."

"Thought what? That I needed you to sort everything out for me just because I needed one fucking ride? This is my job, Paul. I know you think it's shit, but it's how I eat, how I pay the rent. I am totally disposable to them. If I let them down, they fire me—it's that simple."

The pain in Luke's head was reaching critical point and he was glad he was sitting down so Paul wouldn't see him sway.

"Well, that's why I thought I'd call for you, so they knew you wouldn't be in with plenty of time to sort something out. The person I spoke to seemed fine about it. They said to call them later to let them know when you'll be able to go back." Paul told himself it wasn't that big a lie.

Luke held his head in his hands and told himself he couldn't be sick because he hadn't eaten anything. He could just about make out what Paul was saying.

"I'm sorry for the way I was before. I just feel so angry about what's happened to you and I don't get why you're so calm about it. It's like you think it's okay. I care about you, and it's not okay to me." He stroked Luke's back, and Luke felt the band of pain in his head ease a little. He tried to sit up and looked at Paul.

"You're so pale. Come on, lie down." Paul pulled him gently, and Luke had little choice but to let himself slip back onto the bed, curling up his legs and lying on his side. Paul spooned behind him and Luke was reminded of the night when Paul had come around after his argument with Kit. He'd been a wreck then too. No wonder Paul thought he could take over his life when half the time he was falling apart.

"I was wrong to call your work. I know that and I'm sorry. I just wanted to help, and you seemed like you needed it."

Luke formed at least five good answers to this that would teach Paul not to be so goddamned smug. Only he didn't want to argue, didn't want to move, let alone storm out and try to get back to his flat. He knew now that there was no way he could work today; he was exhausted already. He was behaving like the angry brat he'd been when he was in foster care.

"I'm such a fuckup."

"Yeah, but you're my fuckup." Paul worked his body even closer against Luke's.

Luke gave a weak smile. "I think that's one of the nicest things anyone's ever said to me."

"Now I've softened you up with flattery and endearments I'm going to push my luck," Paul warned him. "I really want you to see a doctor today, just to get checked out."

Luke managed to sigh instead of snap. He knew what the brat would say, but if he stopped fighting the world for a minute what would actually be sensible? But there was a problem. "I don't have a doctor. I never registered."

"You could go to the drop-in center," Paul suggested a little too quickly for him to have only just thought of it.

Luke fought back his smile. "You know what? I think that's a really good idea."

"You do?"

"Yep. See what a good influence you are on me?"

Paul grinned and pressed on. "I think I know what you're going to say to this next one, but let's get it over with. I want you to go to the police."

Luke tightened against Paul. "No." He turned around and faced him. "No police. I know you don't get this, and I know it would be different for you, but it's not you—it's me. I don't want anything to do with the police, and that's not changing."

Paul could tell this went deeper than just standing his ground or not doing what others wanted him to. This was a deal breaker for Luke.

"Okay." He pushed the hair back out of Luke's eyes, avoiding his bump. "You know, I do respect what you've done. I know you've looked after yourself for a long time, and I happen to think you've done a pretty good job—a much better one than I would have done in your shoes. And if some of your decisions are different from what mine would be because of that, then I guess I just have to suck it up."

"At least you're very good at sucking." Luke's smile was back, only this time it had turned wicked, and in his eyes there was a glimmer of the Luke who held Paul's heart. He leaned forward and kissed him until he felt Luke reaching for his cock.

"Oh no. I'm not having you exerting yourself until you've been checked out by a doctor. So, if it's okay with you, I'm going to make you some breakfast while you stay here and rest, and then we'll go to the drop-in center."

Luke drew breath to argue, but Paul was up and out the bedroom door before he could stop him.

THERE was a lot of waiting around at the drop-in center, and Luke tried not to complain and fidget as he waited to see a doctor, was sent for X-rays, and then waited again to see someone else to discuss them. Finally he was given the all clear—kind of. Due to the still impressive bump on his head, he was signed off work until the end of the following week.

When they got back into the car, Luke was quiet, and for the first time he looked worried. Paul had been thinking too, and he turned to look at Luke. "I know you can take care of yourself, that's not why I'm going to say this, but… if you wanted, you could come and stay with me until you're feeling better. I'd really like you to. After all this, I'd like to have you close for a bit."

Luke managed a smile as he met Paul's eyes. "You think you could put up with me?"

"Well, I know it'll be tough, but I think I can take it."

Luke's old patterns told him to keep to himself, and to depend on himself. If he went to stay with Paul and something went wrong, it would be another thing to deal with, something else to get over, and he didn't need anything else. However, that would be him alone. If he wanted to be in a relationship, he knew things needed to be different. "Okay," he answered. "Thanks."

Paul put his seat belt on, eager to get going before Luke had another attack of independence. "Let's go to your place now. You can pick up anything you need, and then you can rest when we get back to mine."

"That sounds good."

Maybe he was tired, or maybe he was in pain, but Luke still seemed distracted.

"What is it?" Paul started the car and began to make his way to Luke's apartment.

"It's just… my job. I don't know what to do. They'll take it out of my pay if I'm not there for a week, and I don't know if I can take that hit."

It took an act of supreme self-control on Paul's part not to offer to lend Luke the money to make up the shortfall. It seemed so obvious, and the easiest thing in the world, but he also knew Luke would have a complete meltdown if he made even the slightest suggestion of it. Literally biting his tongue, he tried to think of something else that would help and might be more acceptable to Luke.

"Do you have any holiday due?"

"Umm, well, I haven't taken any since I started working there. I guess I should have some."

"Look, I could give you a whole talk about workers' rights and employment law, but I'm going to be very self-controlled here. If you don't want to lose the money, you could ask to take the days as holiday. The worst they could say is no." *And then maybe you'd get a job somewhere with basic human rights*, Paul thought, but managed not to say out loud.

"Yeah, I could do that. That would work." Luke sighed and looked like a weight had been taken from him. "Thank you." He gave Paul a look of gratitude that made biting his tongue worthwhile.

At his flat, Luke insisted on wiping down all the surfaces and "tidying up" before he was willing to go, although Paul couldn't see anything that needed cleaning. Luke was definitely showing signs of exhaustion again, and several times Paul caught him closing his eyes or raising his hand to his head. In the end, he picked up Luke's bag in one hand and curled his other arm around Luke's waist, nudging him toward the door.

Just before they left, Luke turned to Paul, slipping his hands around Paul's waist. "You know, there will be some advantages to having me stay with you." He glanced up at Paul and gave him a look he instantly recognized. "I'll earn my keep."

"No, you won't," Paul answered, making Luke frown. "The doctor said rest, no exerting yourself, and that's what you're going to do." He kissed Luke's puzzled forehead and led him back out to the car.

"You make my head hurt," Luke complained. He couldn't work that one out—why would Paul want him to stay if they weren't going to fuck? But he wasn't lying about his head and he sank back into the seat.

Back at home, Paul sent Luke up to bed to lie down before he dropped. He was very pale, but Paul wasn't so worried now he knew all Luke needed was to take it easy. Later, he made him a sandwich for a late lunch and realized they would have to order something in for the evening—his choice of microwave meals for one was a little too depressing. Luke had new painkillers now, and they seemed to help more than the over-the-counter stuff he'd used earlier.

The mixture of the food and the tablets gave Luke the lift he needed to call his work and ask if he had enough holiday time to take him up to the following weekend. He was a couple of days short, but the bulk of the time would be covered. His boss didn't sound as relaxed about it as Paul had implied earlier, although Luke was fairly sure he would keep the job open. He got some interesting news too—Brian had also called in sick that day, and later called back to quit his job. He hadn't given notice or any real reason, so most of his boss's resentment was focused on him, and an experienced worker like Luke suddenly had a bit more value.

Luke wondered what had made him do it—was he ashamed of what he had done or just panicking because he knew Luke had recognized him and could inform the police? Luke didn't like to think of Brian getting away with it, but he didn't want to waste his time and energy dwelling on it either. What was it Paul had said—karma? Maybe life would pay Brian back and leave Luke to get on with his.

Paul made him lie on the sofa for the rest of the afternoon watching daytime TV and old movies, and although he couldn't face a week of it, right now it felt great. He had to admit it—he was being looked after by someone, and he loved it. He loved it when Paul put a throw over him in case he got cold. He loved it when Paul made him a cup of coffee. He loved it when Paul looked over at him just to check he was okay. *This*, he thought, *was definitely worth getting beaten up for.*

CHAPTER FOURTEEN

PAUL went back to work the next day, leaving Luke in bed with strict instructions to take it easy. He had cleared some space for Luke's things, and when Luke did get up, he couldn't deny the butterfly feeling in his stomach as he unpacked some stuff. Obviously, he hadn't needed to bring much with him, and it was only for a week, but it still felt important somehow.

A check in the mirror showed that the egg-sized bump on his forehead was slowly diminishing; only now his cheekbone hurt more than it had yesterday. He was still puzzling out Paul's "no sex" statement. One thing was for sure, he wasn't going to be able to give a good blow job for a couple of days, not while his cheek ached with every movement.

After a shower, shave, and breakfast, he booted up his laptop, brought from home, and e-mailed Brooke, leaving out the bit about getting beaten up but telling her more than he meant to about Paul. It was hard not having anyone to talk to, although he'd never been a great one for confiding. He did tell her about Kit turning up, though, and asked her to see if she could find out if he was safely back in America.

It was then that a thought hit him, and it just wouldn't go away. Was Paul seeing other people? They had never talked about being exclusive, and Luke knew lots of guys didn't think it was important, even those in long-term relationships. Luke had never felt that way, but Kit had, and maybe Paul did too. It would explain why he thought no sex with Luke for a week wasn't a big deal when it definitely was for Luke.

For the rest of the day the idea kept coming back to him, until he knew he would have to broach it in some way with Paul, although he had no clue how. If he was honest with himself, it would hurt like hell if Paul was still fucking around, but no, it wouldn't make him walk. Sometimes it felt as if Paul were a drug that Luke couldn't get enough of, and he knew it wasn't going to last so he wanted to get as much as he could before his supply was shut down. Every time Paul stroked his waist or kissed his lips, he got a hit, but each hit left him craving just a bit more. If he had to share Paul to get it, he would just have to deal with that.

Paul finally got in just after six, by which time Luke was certain that he'd found something good to do in the time between school finishing and getting home. Paul wrapped his arms around Luke, and yeah, he spent at least five minutes kissing Luke hello, but Luke was sure he was only semihard. *Shit*, he thought, *I'm like a fucking jealous housewife and I've only been here one day!*

Paul insisted on ordering a pizza even though Luke offered to cook something. While they were waiting, Luke curled into Paul on the sofa and felt Paul relaxing against him. Maybe now would be a good time.

"Y'know, I think sometimes it's better to be up front about things. Sometimes something's not a secret, exactly, but someone might not know it, and it's better to know, right?"

Paul thought back over what Luke had said several times. Nope, he still couldn't figure it out, but Luke was looking at him like he was expecting an answer so he smiled and said, "I guess so."

This seemed to be the right answer, because now Luke was nodding. "So I just thought maybe we should say if we're seeing other people."

Paul's brain came sharply into focus. Where the fuck had that come from? "Are you seeing other people?" The question was out before Paul had thought through whether he wanted the answer.

"No. No, I'm not. But that doesn't mean you can't."

"Me? I'm not seeing anybody. You're definitely all I can handle. What's brought this on?" Paul sat up and turned to face Luke.

"I just thought... maybe we should say, y'know." Luke gave a casual shrug his best shot.

Paul frowned at him, certain there was something else. "If you want to see other people...," he began but then stopped, because he had no idea how he was going to end that sentence.

"No, I don't want to see other people, but I know that some people do, and if you did, well, it would be okay, but I think I'd rather know."

Now that he was getting over the unexpectedness of the topic, Paul could see that this was a conversation they should probably have had before. It was just that he'd always felt that once he was in a relationship with someone, he was faithful to that person and he expected it from his partner as well. He was undeniably out of practice at this dating stuff. Had he ever even had this conversation with Craig? He couldn't remember; they had just known.

Luke was looking intently at an invisible spot on the carpet. Paul took Luke's face in his hands and brought it round toward him. "I'm not seeing anyone else. I don't want to see anyone else. And I don't want you to see anyone else either, okay?"

The anxiety melted from Luke's face. "Okay." In a heartbeat they were kissing again, and Paul thought it was all finished with until Luke's hand started rubbing at his cock through his trousers.

"That's what this is about!" He pushed Luke back, half amused and half infuriated.

"What do you mean?" For someone who didn't understand Paul's meaning, Luke was doing a good impression of someone who had been caught out.

"This is because I said we wouldn't be fucking. Christ, Luke, it's only because the doctor said so."

"But don't you care?"

"Luke, I like fucking you. Hell, I *love* fucking you, and maybe we won't last the whole week, but it's not like the only thing I want you for is fucking. Jesus, I could just get a blow-up doll for that. Life would be one hell of a lot easier!"

Luke ducked his head down, trying to hide his smile. "Paul?"

"What now?"

"You'd never really get a blow-up doll, would you? 'Cause that is kinda gross."

Paul looked at Luke and couldn't help laughing. "I promise I will never get a blow-up doll. Happy now? Is that it?"

"Yeah, but I think we needed to clear that last one up. That could've been a deal breaker." Luke took Paul's arm and wrapped it round his shoulders again, nestling back into his spot at Paul's side.

OVER the next few days, Luke started to feel a lot better, and not just because his head had stopped pulsing with pain. He had even found a way to make himself useful. After deciding to cook a meal for the evening, he had discovered that the only groceries in Paul's cupboards were the things leftover from when Luke had stayed there the last time. He had hit the local supermarket and returned with enough bags to take up half the bus, buzzing with ideas for things to cook. He then spent ages making a lasagna from scratch, cooking up all the sauces, although he did use ready-made pasta. There was never any real point in going to all that trouble for one person, but staying with Paul gave Luke permission to indulge in his love of cooking to the max.

He also spent some of his time looking at adult education courses on the Internet. In the beginning, he'd been thinking about something that would help him build his writing and math skills, but he kept ending up looking at the different catering courses available. Could he really turn something he loved into his job? When he thought about the way that Paul talked about his work, it made him ache. He wanted that—the sense of achievement and passion for what he was doing. He didn't want to spend the next forty years of his life serving fries and burgers, but when he started reading through the lists of entry requirements and what he would need to learn on courses that interested him, he felt like an idiot for even considering it. In the end, he sent off for some prospectuses to be sent to his flat. After all, he wasn't committing to anything; he was just interested.

Luke was trying to find recipes for Chinese food that wouldn't require him buying up a whole spice shop when the doorbell chimed through Paul's house. He had been starting to feel more at ease as the days passed, but he still had to work not to feel uncomfortable as he went to open the door. He imagined that anyone who found him alone in the house would be able to tell he didn't belong there, and in his worst imaginings, they ended up calling the police. When he opened the door it was even worse than that. It was Steve.

"Well, aren't you a delightful sight," Steve said, taking in Luke's multicolored bruised appearance.

Luke's eyes narrowed. "Fuck off." He slammed the door. He hadn't had any choice about the physical beating he took, but he wasn't going to lie down while Steve gave him a verbal one.

Luke waited until Steve rang the bell for the third time before opening the door again.

"Paul's not here." Luke had no intention of getting into a conversation with Steve.

"Obviously. He's a teacher and it's the middle of the week. I came to see you."

"I don't think we have anything to say to each other. You've already made your feelings pretty clear, and I don't need to hear any of them again." Luke started to shut the door.

"I'm here to apologize, if that makes any difference."

Luke stopped and looked at Steve. He might not have aced school, but he wasn't entirely stupid. "I don't know what game you're playing, but I'm not interested."

"Look, this isn't exactly easy for me. Is there any chance I could come in or are you going to keep me on the doorstep?"

Luke sighed, torn between not wanting to give Steve another chance to burn him and doing the right thing by Paul. "I'll give you five minutes." He walked away from the open door, back into the lounge.

"Well, thank you so much," Steve muttered, but he followed Luke in and watched him sit down on one of the armchairs. "Good to see you're making yourself at home."

"Four and a half minutes."

Steve sat down and took a deep breath. If he was going to do this, he'd better get on and say it before he kept coming out with stupid remarks that were only going to make things harder.

"Paul's been one of my best friends for a long time. We grew up together. I was there when he met Craig. Craig was... he was perfect for Paul, and over time we became close, maybe as close as I was with Paul. When he died... well, of course it was terrible for Paul. I wanted to be there for him and to help him as much as I could." Steve looked down for a minute and took a breath.

If he wasn't being genuine, he deserved an Oscar, thought Luke.

"Someone's pointed out to me that it was a lot easier for me to worry about Paul than it was to grieve for the friend that I lost. When I saw you with Paul, all I could think about was Craig. You see, every time I see you, I don't see him. And I miss my friend."

Luke didn't know what to say. Steve's voice had lost its arrogance.

"I wish I could change things, get shot of you and get things back to how they were. But getting rid of you won't bring Craig back, will it?"

"No."

Steve shrugged.

Reluctantly, Luke had to respect Steve for having the guts to put himself out there. "I'm not as bad as you think," he offered.

Steve's face relaxed and he laughed. "Well, that would take some doing. Anyway, I already know you're not as bad as I thought, because you're here alone and you haven't robbed the place. Okay, okay," he added quickly as he saw Luke scowling again. "I know I've been unfair. I've said that, haven't I? I am trying."

Luke's scowl diminished a little.

"I just... I can see that it would be best for Paul if there wasn't any awkwardness while you're around."

"You don't think I'll be around for long, do you?"

"I'm trying to keep my opinion to myself." Steve got up. "So... a truce?" He held his hand out to Luke. Luke hesitated, but figured he could play along and see how this panned out.

"Truce." He shook Steve's hand.

"Well, I'll be seeing you, then," he said as he headed toward the door.

"I'm sorry you lost your friend," Luke said as Steve was leaving.

Steve stopped and looked a little surprised before answering. "Yeah. So am I."

After he left, Luke made coffee and sat out in the garden. He didn't completely trust Steve, but he also thought it was unlikely that Steve would have another go at him, and maybe that was something. He hadn't wanted the situation with Steve to escalate because he didn't want to do anything that might make it awkward for Paul—maybe Steve really did feel the same. He just wished Steve hadn't been so sure Luke was only going to be a short-term problem.

That same evening found Luke needing more than just Paul's arm around him on the sofa. It had been days now, and while he understood the need for some restraint, he was convinced if something didn't happen soon it could only be bad for his health. The trash on the television was only making it worse. He turned to Paul and cupped his cheek, leaning up for a kiss. Very slowly, he let his tongue slide in and out of Paul's mouth until he felt as well as heard his groan.

Before Paul had a chance to start being sensible, Luke straddled him, planting one knee on either side of his hips and resting his ass on Paul's lap. "Luke...," Paul started to say, but it was hard for him to talk when Luke was sucking on his lips. And yeah, Paul had to admit that it was getting more difficult to not walk around with a permanent hard-on, and kissing, that was okay, right?

Once Luke was confident Paul wasn't going to say anything to stop his fun, he started working his mouth along Paul's jawline. He swirled the tip of his tongue over the faint stubble, loving the roughness against his mouth. Paul tipped his head back and then Luke licked up over his Adam's apple and back between Paul's lips. He undid a couple more buttons on Paul's shirt and slipped his hand inside, squeezing and rolling the nipple between his finger and thumb with just enough pressure to make Paul's breathing change.

"I take it you're feeling better," Paul managed.

"No. I have a terrible ache. Let me show you where it is." The smirk on Luke's face got a lot harder to keep in place after he'd guided Paul's hand to his cock, which was trying to rip through his jeans. He placed his own hand over the hot bulge in Paul's trousers and kissed him deeply until he felt Paul grab the back of his head and start pushing his tongue back into Luke. *Now I've got you*, he thought.

Paul pulled at Luke's belt and got his jeans undone, briefly noting the dampness coming through from the tip of his cock before he reached into Luke's briefs and pulled out a cock that felt as swollen and hungry as his.

Luke's eyes closed as he felt Paul's hand wrap around the pulsing need between his legs. Cool and dry, Paul's hand encircled most of the shaft while his thumb rubbed against the tender spot under the ridge. Luke tipped his head back and groaned softly.

"You look so beautiful, so hot," Paul whispered. "I'm not going to fuck you, but I am going to make you come."

Luke swallowed hard. "I think you need some attention here too." He unbuttoned Paul's trousers and pulled down the zipper, and yeah, it was corny, but he'd missed the feel of that cock in his hand—the weight, the ridges and veins, that full swollen length. Okay, not just in his hand, but that would do for now.

"Take off your jeans so I can get to you better," Paul told him, and while Luke did that, he pushed his own trousers and briefs down. "Not your T-shirt. Leave it on." When Luke straddled him again, he positioned himself so that their cocks were rubbing against each other, red and demanding between them. Somehow, by still wearing his T-shirt, Luke's thighs, cock, and balls seemed more naked, more illicitly exposed than if he'd been wearing nothing. Luke used one hand to steady himself against the sofa near Paul's head, which pulled his T-shirt up higher, and intertwined the other with Paul's around their cocks. He watched the heads press together as they pulled their hands up the shafts as one, saw the milky precome squeeze through their slits and run together.

When he lifted his eyes back to Paul's, he was flushed and breathing harder. "We're gonna get come all over us."

Paul didn't think he had ever seen such a dirty smile as the one Luke was wearing. "Yeah, I think we are."

"Bet I can make you come first."

"Oh, I bet you can't," Paul shot back. He was pretty confident too—he was sure being a top required a lot more control than a bottom.

Luke brought his hand up to his mouth and licked it slowly, keeping his eyes locked on Paul's. He kept going until it was good and wet, and until he had seen Paul swallow twice from watching his tongue at work. He placed his slick palm over the head of Paul's cock, and using the precome to add extra slip, he rolled his palm round and round. He couldn't keep it up for long, though, because Paul was making sure Luke kept catching his own dick, and then he had to keep thinking about how their cocks were pressed together and he was touching Paul and touching himself.... No, he needed another strategy. It was hard to think with the scorch of Paul's dry hands hurting in just the right way to get him chasing the buzz, though.

He had to try to get Paul's cock isolated from his, and maybe if he could get to his balls a bit too.... He twisted his hand around so the thumb and index finger were at the bottom of his fist, giving his finger a chance to stroke the line between the two balls before dragging up smooth and hard. Luke saw Paul's eyes grow heavy and knew this could work. He started building a strong, steady rhythm, always taking time to rub down to Paul's balls on each stroke and sliding the precome back down with his hand. He could feel his own balls tingling with the building tension, but he could hold it, he was sure.

Paul couldn't believe it, but Luke was doing it, taking him right to the edge. Fuck. If only he hadn't told him to keep that T-shirt on, if only he didn't have to look at him biting down on his lip. He needed something to rebalance the playing field, and fast, and then he knew exactly what it was. He took one of his hands from Luke's cock, maintaining his rhythm with his other hand, and sucked on his index finger.

And Luke knew exactly what Paul was going to do. He knew he could tell him no, but then he wouldn't, and Luke really, really wanted him to.

Paul reached behind Luke and found his tightly closed ass. It was such a little hole, really, and he watched the penetration reflected on Luke's face as he worked his finger way in. He slid along the front wall inside Luke until he felt the swelling and caught Luke's "aahhhhh" of pleasure.

"Cheating," Luke managed to whimper.

"I could always stop."

"No, please, uh, can't... uh." Luke looked at Paul, trying to hold his eyes as Paul's finger thrust and rubbed, thrust and rubbed, and when his gaze dropped, it fell onto their two swollen cocks pressing together under their hands, the heads milky with come. Then his eyes closed as it was too much, too good, wouldn't stop, couldn't stop, and suddenly it was ripping up through him and his balls were exploding, sending thick strings of come onto Paul's chest and shirt. When he was empty, he tried to keep his now trembling hand on Paul's cock to finish the job right for him.

Luckily, Paul's hand was still a bit steadier, and feeling Luke's ass spasm around his finger while Luke shot come over him meant a few more strokes was all that was needed before Luke was spattered as well.

Impervious to the mess, Luke slumped forward against Paul's chest, and Paul held him close as he dropped his forehead to Paul's shoulder. "Oh, God, that feels better," he murmured.

LUKE was still thinking about Paul's hand on his cock when they were in bed a couple of hours later. "Did you use to jerk off like that when you were a kid?"

"Not quite like that," Paul said with a smile. "But yeah, God, I remember those teenage years. I'm surprised I don't have an overdeveloped right arm!"

"How old were you, you know, when you first had sex with somebody?"

"I was eighteen. It was shortly after I got to university. I was convinced I was the oldest virgin on the planet. I had been desperate to do it before I went, but I wasn't confident enough to be out at home. So I got to university with one thing on my mind. Luckily, so did pretty much every other gay guy on campus. There was a freshers' fair, and one of the societies was for gay students. I remember feeling so daring when I signed up! Anyway, I went to a meeting and there was this guy there who I thought was sex on legs. I couldn't believe it when he spoke to me. He was a couple of years older than me, and it turned out later that he and his friends liked to try and spot virgins in the first few weeks. I think they practically had a competition to see who could get the most. It all worked out well for me, though. At the time, I thought I was doing a great job at seducing him, playing it really cool. I was so nervous, but he didn't give me a hard time—I think he thought it was kind of cute. From what I remember, I was terrible—he had to keep giving me hints and directions. I should have bottomed first, really, to get the hang of it, but it never really occurred to me. And after that there was no stopping me!"

"Do you ever bottom?"

"Not very often. I have—never say never, right?"

Paul reached out and stroked Luke's face, then pushed his fingers through Luke's hair. He could just see him in the dark.

"What about you? When was your first time?"

Luke frowned, like he was trying to remember. "Oh come on, don't pretend you've forgotten!"

"No, it's just, well, there was this guy who I always think of as my first, but we didn't actually fuck. Then there's the first time I got fucked. Which one do you want?"

"Both."

"Nope. That's not fair. I only got one, so you only get one."

"Hmmm." Paul considered. "Tell me about the guy who didn't fuck you."

Luke took a deep breath and rolled over on his side, turning his back to Paul.

"Hey, where are you going?"

"I can't talk about stuff with you looking at me. Right. It was when I was sixteen, when I was still in foster care. I was being fostered by this family who had older kids, but they had either left home or were away at college. Well, they had this son—I saw him in their photos, and he was gorgeous. I knew I was gay by then, of course, but I never could have told anyone. I didn't know anyone who was gay—in my world, the only time you heard the word was in a joke or an insult. I was pretty sure it was going to be my secret for the rest of my life. But when I was on my own... well, I spent a lot of time thinking about the guy in the photo and jerking off. As long as no one knew I thought it wouldn't be a problem.

Luke took a breath. "So, it comes round to the holidays and he comes home from college. And he's even more fine in person than in the photographs. Now I know it's hard to believe, but I was hideous at the time." Paul laughed softly but pulled Luke a little closer at the same time.

"I had my hair long and dyed black, and most of the time it was over my face so I could hide behind it. I think my whole vocabulary consisted of the words 'fuck' and 'off'. Apart from when Joe was around. When Joe was around, I couldn't talk at all. I never knew why, but he was really nice to me. He'd talk to me like I was a normal person, and all I could do was make grunting noises occasionally. He never gave up, though. By the end of the second week, I was like his shadow, following him around everywhere. I remember his mom saying what a good influence he was on me and how much nicer I was when Joe was home. I didn't actually do anything nice, of course; I just abused everyone else a bit less."

"I bet you weren't really that bad," Paul argued.

Luke thought about it. "I wish I could agree with you, but there were witnesses that would definitely disagree."

"Anyway, one day he was talking to me about college and he just mentioned that he was gay. I couldn't breathe. He was a normal guy, and he was gay? He went on talking and told me about how he was out at college and had gay friends and straight friends, and that it wasn't a big deal. Then he said that the reason why he was telling me this was because he really wanted to kiss me and he wanted to know if it would be okay. I managed to nod, and he kissed me so softly on the lips." Luke moved his hand to his mouth at the memory, and for a moment Paul felt a stab of ridiculous jealousy.

"I remember my heart was beating so hard. I just kept really still. I wanted him to do it again so much. And he did. A lot."

"After that we did a lot of kissing and petting, and that progressed on to hand jobs, and when he gave me my first blow job—which ended very quickly—I thought I was gonna die. That someone would want to do that with me? I couldn't believe it. I adored him, would've done anything for him. When he left... *fuck*, that was hard. I missed him so much. I wrote him a letter, but I was stupid, I left it open because... well, I wanted to check the spelling and stuff. His mum found it. She went insane—she didn't know he was gay, and thought that it was all some crazy obsession in my head. I was 'relocated', and I never got to see him again. Even after I'd stopped pining for him, I always wished I could have seen him again, just to thank him, because he changed everything for me."

There was silence as Luke slowly came back from remembering. He became aware that Paul hadn't said anything for a long time.

"Are you still awake?" he whispered.

"Yeah, I'm awake." And the words were right there. *"I love you."* So why did he swallow them back? "If you ever do see him, say thanks from me too. I'm glad somebody made it better for you."

Luke smiled and tangled one of his legs back into Paul's, skin stroking against skin.

"Y'know, I think it's probably going to be safe for us to start fucking again tomorrow, and if you don't agree, I'm going to go back to that doctor and make him sign something that says it is."

"You don't have to do that. I'll just make sure I fuck you very, very slowly."

"Promises, promises."

Luke felt Paul rest against him. Usually he fell asleep first, but now that he wasn't working, it tended to be Paul, and he liked holding out for that moment when he knew Paul had drifted off. Tonight it took longer than usual, but he was just awake when he caught the change in Paul's breathing, and he fell asleep with a smile on his face.

CHAPTER FIFTEEN

LUKE sat down at the table and closed his eyes. All his insecurities seemed to be hitting him at once. What the fuck was he doing? Staying with a guy who was out of his league (and probably still in love with his dead partner) and trying to play house by cooking stuff that was obviously way beyond him. He tried to focus on his breathing, but the thoughts just kept flashing up in his head, his mother's betrayal, his failure at school, Kit…. He knew he had to hold on, couldn't let these feelings sweep him away to fuck knew where. He had to get a grip, make himself do something, and when he looked at the state of the kitchen, it was pretty obvious what needed doing.

Although his body felt like wet cement, he got up and started slowly sorting out what needed to go in the trash, what needed washing up, and what could go back in the cupboard. Everything felt like a huge effort and thoughts kept trying to knock him back off-balance. He couldn't ignore how much food he'd wasted in his first, then second attempt at cooking a French recipe to surprise Paul that evening. What had ever made him think he could pull it off? Then he heard the door and realized Paul was home.

He looked again at the mess everywhere, and a new wave of hopelessness swept over him. Now he would have to explain the whole thing to Paul on top of everything else.

"Whoa! You've been busy!" Paul exclaimed as he walked toward the kitchen.

Luke couldn't look at him. It wasn't just the recipe not working out, it was the way every little thing got to him so much. It made him feel so pathetic. If he could just pretend everything was okay, then at least Paul wouldn't know how low he felt.

"Yeah. It went a bit wrong. I'm gonna clean it all up."

Paul caught something in Luke's voice and looked around again, starting to imagine how much work it would have taken to make all this mess and then noticing the lack of any end product.

He walked over to Luke, but Luke kept moving away until eventually Paul managed to corner him against one of the units.

"Hey… hey… come here," he whispered, putting his hands on Luke's hips and leaning into him. "What's up? Talk to me."

"It's really stupid," Luke blurted, hating the break in his voice, hating that he was going to have to tell Paul and look ridiculous.

Paul kissed the side of his throat. "It didn't work out, right? Do you know what went wrong?"

For the first time, Luke thought back over each stage of the recipe. "I think it was when I put the eggs in. I should've let the mixture cool more first."

"Okay, so you can try again."

Luke shook his head. "There isn't enough stuff left. I've wasted everything."

"Well, it's a good job there are things called shops where we can buy some more." He squeezed Luke closer to him, and Luke found he had to give a half smile. Looking at it through Paul's eyes was putting things back into perspective.

"Let's make a list of what you need from the shop. I'll go and get it while you sort out this, and by the time I get back you'll be ready for a second go."

"Third," Luke admitted, but he was feeling more tempted by the idea. The more he thought about it, the more likely it seemed that it had only been a small error that had spoiled everything. But did he really want to try again? Paul's certainty made it too difficult to say no. "Okay, I'll make a list. But it still might not work."

Paul shrugged. "I'll get a pizza that we can stick in the oven if it doesn't work out. Then, it doesn't really matter either way."

So Luke made a quick list of the ingredients that needed restocking, and Paul hoped he was leading Luke in the right direction. He knew it was a risk to encourage Luke to try again, but he also knew that anything else would leave Luke feeling like a failure, and that had already happened too many times in his life. He didn't know much (or anything, really) about cooking, but he had eaten at enough restaurants to know that Luke's food was better than most. Luke had good instincts and an excellent palate, but limited experience.

He tugged Luke close to him again, enjoying the closeness of his body before he had to go get back into the car. Luke moved in for a kiss, and Paul was glad to oblige before grabbing the list and heading toward the door.

Once he was gone, Luke took a deep breath and tried to get his brain back on track. He cleaned the kitchen with more enthusiasm and purpose now, before going back over the recipe step by step, making sure he understood what to do at each point. By the time Paul came back, he was ready to make a new start. Paul left him to it, spreading out his evening's grading in the lounge area so he was close enough if Luke wanted help but far enough away to give him space. He let Luke get on with the cooking as if he had no doubts that Luke would pull it off, but he still felt a little relieved when delicious smells started to reach him.

After nearly three-quarters of an hour, Luke finally felt confident enough to tell himself it was working. He looked over at Paul, engrossed in marking his class's books, and his heart ached. Somehow, Paul had gotten him back on his feet again without the humiliation of explanations and soul-baring. He had been able to see what Luke needed when Luke wouldn't have been able to say himself. And nothing he gave had a price attached. Was this what love felt like? This mixture of lust and respect and wanting to kiss and hold him and never let him go? He wanted to do something, say something to show how much Paul meant to him, but he didn't know how.

Then he had an idea. It would have to wait until after they had eaten, and it would take a little organizing, but he knew what he was going to do.

Maybe Paul sensed Luke looking at him, because he glanced up from his work. "All okay?" he asked casually. Luke smiled the smile that turned Paul's interest from one to ten in a heartbeat.

"Yep. Everything's fine. It's gonna be ready in about fifteen minutes."

Paul kept the disappointment from his face. That smile had suggested a lot of different things to him, but they would all take longer than fifteen minutes, so he was going to have to wait.

"I was wondering… could you run me round to my flat when we're finished? There's some things I need to get."

"Sure," Paul replied. *And then I'm going to fuck you senseless*, he added in his head, as that smile spread over Luke's face again.

The meal was delicious, although if Luke was honest, he was so sick of the recipe by that point he had lost his appetite. He managed to eat it, though, as it would have seemed a little bit suspicious if the cook wouldn't eat his own food. He had to admit it had come out right in the end, and while he was always tempted to push away Paul's compliments, he seemed genuinely impressed.

Paul would've liked to get Luke on the sofa and concentrate on eating him, too, but Luke was insistent about going over to his flat, so they were soon in the car.

"I won't be a minute. You don't need to come up," Luke said as he quickly got out of the car and ran over to the door of his building. By this time, Paul was certain Luke was up to something, but from the way Luke's eyes were shining, he was pretty sure he was going to enjoy it so he played along and waited in the car.

When Luke unlocked the door to his flat and turned on the light, he felt an unexpected hit of sadness. Perhaps he had forgotten how barren and empty his home, and for that matter, his life, had been. He knew he couldn't stay with Paul forever, as that had never been the deal. It was Friday night, and he should be moving back to his flat this weekend. He wasn't going to think about that tonight, though, he reminded himself.

Refocused, he went through to the bedroom and opened the bedside drawer. He hesitated for a second, his confidence wavering. What if Paul didn't like the idea or wasn't into it? Fuck it, he decided. He couldn't think of another way to show Paul how much he trusted him and wanted to give him. It was worth the risk. He grabbed a carryall and chucked a couple of T-shirts and pairs of jeans in on top, and after a last glance around, he left the flat and headed back to Paul in the car.

He leaned over and kissed Paul's lips as he pushed the carryall onto the backseat. "You finished all your grading for tonight?"

"Yep. You finished all your cooking?"

Luke grinned. "Oh, yeah."

"What will we find to do?" Paul asked mischievously.

"Oh, I think I've got something that will help pass the time. Get driving," Luke said, pulling on his seat belt as he eyed the bulge in Paul's lap. Not for the first time, Paul was grateful that the distance between their homes wasn't too far.

As soon as they were inside the door, Luke started tugging on Paul's shirt as he led him toward the stairs. Paul was happy to go along with his urgency and let Luke lead him up to the bedroom. Luke peeled his T-shirt off and flicked off his shoes before starting to unbutton Paul's shirt. Paul felt it too—the need for skin against skin—and ran his hands up and down Luke's back, feeling the muscles move under the tight skin. Although his bruises were still visible, their sensitivity was fading, which Luke proved by pressing tight against Paul's chest as soon as his shirt was open. There was none of the gentle slowness that had set the tone between them lately.

Paul enjoyed the sensation of Luke's tongue moving purposefully in his mouth while Paul stroked the dip in Luke's back, following the curve of soft flesh. As Paul pushed his tongue deep into Luke, he felt him sink a little against his chest. He loved it when he felt that, Luke giving in to the feelings, giving himself over to Paul. He pulled his mouth away and moved one hand up to caress Luke's cheek. "I'm gonna fuck you so hard tonight," he told him, and he turned his head slightly to continue kissing him.

"No."

Paul raised his eyebrows. Luke never said "no" and he didn't usually try to take charge when they were fucking. "I want... I thought maybe we could play with this tonight." Luke's breathing was quick and shallow as he unzipped the bag and brought out the inflatable dildo. Uninflated, it looked pretty ordinary, with a thickly veined shaft and a rigid center. It was about nine inches long with a circumference of roughly five inches. Closer inspection revealed that the head would extend further as air was pumped inside, taking it up to fourteen inches in total with twelve available for penetration. Paul held out his hand for the pump, and Luke gave it to him. Slowly and purposefully, he inflated it to its full expansion and took in its now nine-inch circumference. Luke could feel his ass getting tighter and his cock getting bigger with every second.

"Have you played with this before?" There was unmistakable interest in Paul's voice.

"Once. I bought it when I was feeling really horny and I didn't really think about how big it could get." He gave Paul a slightly embarrassed smile. "I couldn't take it all, but it was still... really good. I always thought it would be more fun with another person, but I never met anyone who...." He left the last bit unsaid. He had never met someone who he could trust to have control over something like this when it was inside him.

Paul was watching him intently. Luke took a breath before speaking. "I want to suck you... I want to suck you 'til you come, then I want you to put this inside me and pump it until I can't take any more."

"And you trust me to stop?" Paul asked softly.

"Yes." The word was almost a breath.

Paul's fingers slid into Luke's hair before fisting there and pulling him in tight. "Well, aren't you full of surprises," he breathed out against Luke's lips before kissing him deeply on the mouth.

Paul lay back on the bed and undid his trousers, watching the smile on Luke's face grow in confidence. He watched Luke undress, something he thought he would never get tired of. Each time felt like unwrapping a present, and he knew it was all for him.

Luke stood at the edge of the bed and leaned over to hook his fingers inside the waistband of Paul's trousers and briefs. Slowly, he pulled them off and then climbed onto the bed, licking his lips as he looked at Paul's erect cock. He lay down on the bed, positioning his head near Paul's cock, and reached out to stroke it so he could feel its swollen heat. From experience, he knew that Paul loved it when he focused on the head, and so he used his hand to keep the base and shaft happy while he covered the top with soft, wet kisses, rubbing his lips against all the ridges and especially the slit. He made his lips very wet before working them over the head, giving Paul the sensation of pushing into Luke's mouth again and again and making Paul thrust up to him.

Paul knew that Luke had learned enough about his body to keep a blow job going indefinitely and he was usually in no rush to spoil that, but today he had something else on his mind. He kept reaching out to touch the inflated dildo at his side, and when he watched Luke bobbing his head and working his tongue over his cock, he didn't want to wait to get things moving.

"Take it," he whispered hoarsely. "Take it and let me fuck your mouth. Don't try to save that tight little ass of yours with delaying tactics." He noticed the corners of Luke's mouth curling up, but then he could only think about the tight lips up and down his shaft, the tongue dragging up the line underneath, the pace quickening in time with his breathing. Paul leaned into the mattress and let his body climb higher and higher, felt the drag in his balls and relaxed into it instead of trying to hold on. His back arched and he cried out with the first hard spurt of come, feeling the rocket go off in his cock as Luke sucked him all the way through it.

Paul focused his mind again as soon as he could and looked at Luke. He was lying on his back, stroking his nipples, waiting patiently for Paul. Paul smiled. Now it was Luke's turn.

Paul took his time spreading lube all over the dildo while it was still inflated, to make sure the whole surface was as slippery as possible. Luke watched, feeling the throbbing pulse in his prick and wondering how he was going to stop himself from coming as soon as it was inside him. His cock burned to be touched, but Paul was in charge now.

Finally he released the valve and let the dildo return to a more manageable size. "Get down on all fours, right here." His voice was husky as he indicated where on the floor he wanted Luke. Luke obeyed. "Move your legs slightly further apart, that's it. Lean back just a little." He opened the wardrobe door so he could see Luke reflected in the mirror. "I want to watch your face when it's inside you, every second."

Paul knelt behind Luke and began to stroke his balls, hearing the catch in his throat. He bent his head down and began lapping at the sensitive crack, making Luke's ass as wet as he could before beginning to tease at his sphincter. Eventually Paul eased his suffering by spreading his ass cheeks open and thrusting his tongue through the resistance, pushing it back and forth and swirling it around before returning to licking the entrance again. He repeated this again and again until Luke was swaying and moaning with every breath. Paul removed his mouth and replaced it with a lubricated finger, which began a maddeningly slow exploration of Luke's ass, rubbing in soft circles against the thin walls until every nerve was sensitized but giving only fleeting attention to his prostate. One finger was replaced by two, and now Paul focused on stretching and preparing Luke's ass for the deeper penetration that was coming. Luke looked up and met Paul's eyes in the mirror, and suddenly everything grew more intense.

"You want me to touch your cock now, don't you? And I'm going to, but not yet, not until that dildo's right inside you. You're going to need something then, something to help you, and you'll understand why I've made you wait."

"I want it so much," Luke breathed.

"I know, baby, I know," Paul said, and then he slipped his fingers out of Luke's ass. Luke could hear Paul slightly inflating the dildo and found himself licking his lips again. He dropped his chin down onto his chest, his body supplicant and waiting. Finally, he felt the shaped head of the dildo against his muscle.

"Here we go, babe," Paul whispered, and he began very slowly easing it inside him. Paul had learned how Luke curved inside and knew how to tilt the dildo so it kept slipping smoothly in. He loved watching it pass through Luke's sphincter; it was intoxicating to see it moving into his body. When it was about halfway, he stopped and held it there with one hand, fingering Luke's balls with the other. "Now push yourself back onto it, slowly. Keep your eyes on the mirror. Stop when you need to. Take your time."

Luke made himself hold Paul's gaze. He could see how aroused Paul was, that he was getting off on this as much as Luke was and was with him each step of the way.

Paul held the dildo firmly as Luke worked his ass back and took the pressure deeper inside him, frowning hard and stopping to let his body adjust before taking more. He could feel the sweat on his face and back, and he was panting lightly when the hilt reached his sphincter.

"That's it," Paul murmured. He finally let his hand slide from Luke's balls onto the base of his cock and then slid his hand up the shaft to find the head wet with precome, hot and demanding. Sliding on the precome, he brought his hand back down, dragging a long cry from Luke's lips as he tipped his head back. "Now the fun starts." The first few pumps pushed the head deeper inside him as the dildo began to extend to its full length before it would expand. It felt like it was pressing right into his belly, and the next four pumps made Luke wonder if this was going to be over before it had really begun. But then Paul's hand was pushing back up and down his cock, and all the strain turned to want. He had to see if he could take a little more.

"Again," he managed to breathe, and Paul sent three more squeezes of air into the dildo. It must have become fully extended, because he no longer felt it pushing in like it was aiming for the back of his throat. Now it was starting to swell. Luke had never felt anything like it as it pushed against his inner walls. As Luke's body adjusted, Paul worked the base of his cock, knowing that if he applied too much pressure or moved too high, Luke wouldn't be able to stop himself from coming. He held Luke's gaze in the mirror and squeezed once…

twice… three… four times. Luke fought to keep his eyes on Paul as his lids flickered with the intensity. Very gently, Paul rocked his hand against the base of the dildo, and Luke's head dropped forward with a long moan.

Paul dipped his head down to Luke's balls. He opened his mouth wide, took the whole sac in and sucked softly, sending sensations all the way through Luke. When Luke was rocking slightly in time with the sucks, he squeezed the pump again, four more times. He raised his head to watch Luke in the mirror again, to see him trying to catch his breath, sucking on his lips. The blue of his eyes seemed darker, and the muscles of his body were more defined from the inner tension. Paul had paid careful attention to the way each pump had altered the dildo when he had tried it out, and he was counting the pumps now so he could picture how big it was inside Luke. While the base expanded against the inner and outer rings of muscle, it grew widest around the middle. He knew it would have extended to its full twelve inches, pushing deep inside him, and he guessed the circumference was at about eight inches—a big stretch for Luke's tight ass.

"Now that you've had a warm-up, let's start from the beginning again." Paul released the valve, and a deep, long groan came from Luke's lips. It was almost like the relief of an orgasm as the pressure was released and so much tension left his body. Now, though, there was nothing to distract him from the tension in his balls and cock. He fought against the desire to come and nodded to Paul.

The second time should have been easier, but the first expansion had sensitized his ass so much that the inner skin seemed to twitch with every pump. Paul gave him less time to get back up to the same stretch but then waited when he got there. In the mirror, Luke could see Paul's hard cock, could see the intensity on his face, could feel the electricity between them. He couldn't have begun to explain how this was more intimate, felt closer even than fucking, but he knew he could take more to keep it going for a little longer. He nodded to Paul and closed his eyes.

Small moans slipped from between his lips as his body tried to stretch itself further than ever before. The dildo felt huge inside him, and he realized he could no longer move—the penetration was too deep and it held him, impaled on the dildo. Sweat was running into his eyes, but he couldn't raise his hand to wipe it away. He felt Paul's hand on his cock again and heard himself whimpering, "Yeah, yeah, yeah," with every stroke. Then Paul placed his other hand on the base of the dildo and started rocking it inside him, and the sounds he made then were no longer coherent. His body cried that he couldn't take it, but he wanted to, wanted to hold on just a little longer, and he bit down on his lip, then on his tongue, to try and distract himself with the pain.

"Look at me." Paul's voice was harsh and commanding, pulling Luke back. "One more? Two more? No more?"

Luke looked at those dark eyes. He couldn't take it. Couldn't stop it. Couldn't stand it. He licked his lips slowly, tasting the salt of sweat on them. "Two," he pushed out, and he watched Paul swallow before nodding. The first pump convinced Luke that there was just nowhere left inside his body that wasn't already stretched beyond endurance. He found Paul's eyes in the mirror again, felt the connection between them, so strong, and dropped his head in a nod.

The final pump pulled a sound from him that grew from a mixture of suffering and pleasure too complicated for him to understand. And then Paul's hand was on his cock, wet and slippery with so much precome and sweat, and it was tight and swollen against Paul's hand. Luke knew coming was going to hurt, had no idea if it was even physically possible anymore, but release—release was all he craved, more than the air in his lungs. His arms and legs were trembling with the strain as Paul's hand pulled hard and fast up the shaft, over the head, then back down to the base, again and again. He could hear sounds from his throat but he couldn't control them, couldn't control anything. Paul controlled everything now. He tried to lift his head, but even that was too much. But Paul's voice still reached him.

"Let go, baby, give me everything, give me everything."

And he was crying out now with each stroke of Paul's hand. Just when he thought he was going to go mad with it all, lightning ripped through him and come shot out onto his chest. With the second spurt of come, Paul undid the valve, and the release was complete as he shuddered again and again, unable to stop as his body spasmed to its completion.

Luke slumped onto the floor, dripping with sweat and come, in an exhausted heap. Paul began using his hand to reach his own climax, but when Luke realized what he was doing, he moaned, "Stop. In me. Please."

"You can't come again. It'll only hurt you."

Talking took such a huge effort. He pushed each word out. "Don't care. Want you. Please."

He rolled over onto his back, his eyes beseeching Paul, and there was no way Paul could resist.

Paul only just remembered to grab a condom before he started fucking into him. Luke scrunched his face up as he squeezed his stretched, swollen ass around Paul. He tried to reach up to touch Paul's face. Paul had been right—it did hurt, everything hurt, but he had to have it, he had to have Paul. Nothing in this world mattered to him except Paul.

Paul grabbed Luke's hips because for once coming quickly wouldn't be a bad thing. He thrust and thrust, and everything that had been building inside him forced its way out. He tipped his head back and he cried out Luke's name as he shuddered again and again.

Moving off the floor was a distant idea for Luke, too far away to really contemplate. Paul pulled the duvet from the bed and covered them both with it where they lay. He pulled Luke's head against his chest, but he wasn't sure if he was already asleep until he heard his soft voice.

"Love you."

Paul smiled. "I know. I couldn't not know now." And then he paused—was Luke waiting for him to say it back? Could he say it back? Then he realized Luke was asleep, and the question didn't need an answer. Yet.

CHAPTER SIXTEEN

IN THE morning, Luke felt uncomfortable. It wasn't just because they had spent half the night sleeping on the floor, before they both awoke from the discomfort and relocated to the bed. It wasn't just because his ass had taken more than he had ever thought possible and now ached dully in protest. It was because he couldn't remember if he had thought or actually said the words "I love you" to Paul. To make it worse, he couldn't remember if Paul had said anything back.

Maybe he had said it and Paul hadn't heard. Maybe he hadn't said it at all, just thought it, as he'd found himself doing before when he was coming. Maybe Paul had heard, and had said it back. Maybe Paul had heard, and had said nothing. One thing was absolutely certain, there was no way in hell he could ask.

Luke slipped out of bed and headed for the shower. He could feel the remains of last night's sweat and come still on him and he knew it was not a good sign when you smelled bad to yourself. He had to admit he had finally come to feel at home at Paul's and now enjoyed all the little luxuries it offered instead of feeling guilty for using them. The shower was definitely one of his favorites. The head was huge, you could adjust the temperature to get it exactly right without jolts of hot and cold, and there was a selection of settings, from dynamic "full power" to gentle "rainforest," to go with your every mood. After a good dose of "full power" and some vigorous lathering, he switched to "rain storm" to rinse off and then plucked a towel from the heated rail (heated towel racks were another unheard of luxury to Luke).

He heard the radio come on in the bedroom and figured Paul must have woken up. He knew that Paul liked to listen to the news station in the morning and he'd been trying to pay more attention, too, as part of his "get smarter" plan. He still found it hard to keep track of the different political stuff, but that was so different from America he let himself off the hook. He glanced in the mirror and wondered if he could get away without shaving. He didn't want to delay seeing Paul to see if he could judge if Paul'd heard him, so he decided to leave it.

Back in the bedroom, he lay down on his stomach next to Paul, on the top of the duvet.

"How are you this morning?" Paul traced his hand down Luke's back until it rested on his ass.

Luke grinned. "Fucked," he replied honestly. Paul's hand, just there, was setting off all the nerves again, and he tried unsuccessfully to convince himself that he could take Paul fucking him.

Paul pulled Luke's mouth over to his so he could kiss him. "You were incredible. You *are* incredible." He kissed Luke again, and warmth flooded all the way through Luke, not just the burn in his ass. Paul pushed his fingers against the towel, applying gentle pressure to the crack there. "Can you still feel it?"

"Yeeaahh." Luke couldn't work out if Paul's fingers felt good or bad, but, God, he could feel it. "But you can fuck me again if you want." The words were out before he was sure he could live up to them.

Paul shook his head. "No, we're not playing that game today. You need to recover. Then I'll fuck you, I promise." He kissed Luke again before he pushed him over onto his back and undid the towel, peeling it back to unwrap him.

Luke played it up, parting his lips slightly and resting his arms over his head, watching Paul's eyes slowly take in every inch of him— the definition of his arms, the curve of his pecs each topped with a hard, pink-brown nipple, the faint indents caused by his ribs, the line leading down to his belly button and smooth flat stomach now with only the faded hints of bruises, the ridges of his hips leading down to his (increasingly erect) cock, the muscular thighs and calves.

"You are so fucking gorgeous," Paul murmured slowly. A hand curled around Paul's heart when he caught Luke's blush.

Paul let his knuckles drag over the inside of Luke's thigh and heard Luke suck the air into his lungs at the touch. Yeah, he knew what he was going to do. He tugged gently at Luke's legs until he had them hanging over the edge of the bed while Paul knelt on the floor between them. He spread Luke's thighs with his hands and started covering his balls with the lightest of kisses, then took the right sac into his mouth and rolled it with his tongue, gradually increasing the pressure until he heard a sound from Luke. He kept it right there, cradled in the warm wet of his mouth, and gave it soft pulsing sucks until he could feel Luke rocking with it. Paul slipped his mouth off, but only to take the other sac and repeat the whole process again—finding just the pressure Luke needed and then working it. When he took both balls into his mouth, Luke breathed out his name, dragging over the vowel sounds for the longest time.

Paul didn't want to tease Luke, just give him the most pleasure he could. He switched his focus to the rock-hard cock swelling above Luke's balls, using his hands on the shaft and his tongue to work all around the head. He lifted his head up just long enough to get two of his fingers very wet, then started to take more and more of Luke's cock into his mouth.

Luke shivered as the wet fingers played around his asshole, feeling himself contract in anticipation. He wanted them inside so badly, and yet he wasn't sure what it was going to cost him. When one finger very slowly moved past the first ring, he knew his need was stronger than his doubt and he pushed against it, easing it in deeper. Paul's mouth was sliding up and down in a steady rhythm, and he used his tongue to flicker against the vein underneath. Luke bunched the sheet underneath him in his fists as all the good chemicals flooded his brain.

He gave a soft moan of disappointment as Paul's finger withdrew, but might have regretted that as it returned with a second. Although it was only two fingers, Luke was sure he could feel them at the back of his throat—his ass was so raw and tender everything felt a hundred times bigger. If Paul was going to fuck him with them he wasn't sure he could take it, but Paul wasn't interested in pushing Luke today, didn't want him to find his limits—just pleasure. He moved his fingers just enough to find the rubbery swelling and used the lightest touch to brush against it, drawing a long moan from Luke's lips.

Paul felt the tension pulsing through the engorged cock in his mouth and worked it faster, trying to focus enough to keep his fingers light and controlled inside Luke while increasing the pressure on his cock. He could hear the sound of Luke's breathing in time with the movement of his mouth and felt Luke's cock tremble against his tongue. He pressed his fingers just a little more and concentrated on sucking the come right up out of his balls.

Luke practically levitated off the bed as he spurted into Paul's mouth, the burn in his ass taking him higher with each contraction.

"Absolutely. Fucking. Gorgeous." Paul kissed Luke between each word, and Luke hungrily found traces of his come in Paul's mouth. He held onto Paul until he pulled away with a smile and headed for the shower. Luke slumped back onto the bed and decided he would wait until tomorrow to go back to his own flat. He didn't seem to have worn out his welcome just yet.

SUNDAY came too quickly, and Luke asked if Paul could run him back to his flat that afternoon. Did Paul look disappointed? Luke wasn't really sure, but he didn't suggest Luke stay any longer, so that was that. Luke wasn't even sure what he would say if Paul did ask; he just wished he could live the past week all over again.

Luke resisted the temptation to leave a few things behind, as if he were marking the territory, and packed his stuff up after lunch. Paul kissed him in the car before letting him go, and it became harder to keep his lighthearted act going. Part of him ached to grab Paul and tell him again that he loved him, that he wanted to move in with him, and that he wanted it to be just them forever. Fortunately, that part wasn't in control of his mouth because he wasn't certain he *was* ready to move in with Paul; he just didn't want to not be living with him, either.

A pile of junk mail and some sour milk awaited his return. It was strange how quickly a place could feel unlived in. He tried to change the mood by plugging in his iPod and blasting out The Killers *Hot Fuss* album. In among all the junk were the prospectuses and applications he had requested from the local colleges. Luke hesitated, then sat down on the sofa and started to look through them. The courses sounded like something he would love to do, but he wasn't sure he had the academic skills to manage. He turned to the application forms and then his heart really sank. Question after question about his school qualifications, relevant experience, and, worst of all—a full page to complete as a personal statement, explaining why he should be given a place in the course. Just looking at it made Luke feel physically sick. He grabbed the packs together and chucked the lot in the trash before taking some deep breaths. The whole idea had been stupid, but it was done with now. He needed to do something, so he decided to clean the flat from top to bottom. If anything was going to numb his mind, it was that.

IT WASN'T that Paul didn't like talking to the parents of kids in his class—most of them were intelligent, friendly people who cared very much about their children's education. It was just that talking to over half of them in one evening after teaching all day got to be a bit much. Whoever invented Parents' Evenings was no friend of his. His face was stiff from endless smiling, his brain whirled from trying to think of tactful ways to suggest a little more reading and a little less Xbox might be a good idea, and after finishing with one of his most difficult parents, he felt frustrated enough to scream out loud.

During a short break, he'd sent a text to Luke—*Can I come over 2nite? NEED 2 c u xx.* Now he read the reply—*Be waiting 4 u babe xxx*—and couldn't get there fast enough. He just hoped Luke didn't want to talk.

Luke buzzed him in straight away and already had the door open while Paul was still climbing the stairs. Christ, that smile—like he'd just seen his presents on Christmas Day—had Paul taking the last stairs two at a time and then wrapping his arms around Luke like he was going to lift him up and carry him to the bedroom. His mouth was hot and eager against Paul's—exactly what he needed.

Luke half dragged him into the bedroom, pulling at his clothes, and Paul wanted in him, now, had to make himself slow down. "I missed you," Luke breathed against his neck, "I want you."

Paul yanked Luke's T-shirt off and got his mouth all over that chest, kissing and sucking and biting. Luke had started undoing and pushing down his jeans, then he caught Paul's wrist and guided his hand to his ass. When Paul touched the hard base of the plug, all his insides flipped over. It was a lot smaller than the dildo they had used at Paul's house, but it was enough to stretch Luke so he was ready to take Paul straight away.

"Want you now. Need you in me," Luke urged.

Fuck. The pulse in Paul's dick went into overdrive. Clothes were removed in whatever way got the job done quickest, and then Paul pushed Luke down onto the bed on his stomach before getting his hand back on the plug and twisting it just to hear Luke moan. With shaky self-control, he slowly withdrew the butt plug until the widest part was stretching against Luke's muscle, then thrust it all the way back in sharply. Luke gasped through the burn, tilting his hips until the plug found the sweet place again. Paul couldn't wait and realized his hands were practically shaking as he ripped the condom packet and slid it down his cock. He pulled the butt plug out, watching Luke's hole drag against it.

Luke brought his right knee up to his side so he could open himself further just before Paul slammed into him. The air was forced from his lungs, and he had a second to wish he owned a bigger butt plug before Paul started dragging back and then slamming in again and again. The burn was gone, and now there were just the waves of sensation pushing him up and up with every thrust. Paul leaned forward so his dick pressed against the front of Luke before he began shorter, faster movements. Luke used his bent leg to push himself up slightly and reached underneath himself to get a hold of his cock. He barely had to move his hand himself—he let the force of Paul's lunges jerk his cock back and forth against his palm until he couldn't catch up and felt his body racing ahead of him.

Paul felt the flutter around the base of his cock as Luke's muscles contracted in waves and heard the groan that came up from deep inside him. For a moment he was slack under Paul's hands. Then he lowered his raised leg and pulled both legs in together, making it so tight around Paul that he only managed another couple of thrusts before shooting off inside him. Carefully, Paul let himself drop down over Luke without taking out his cock.

A small moan slipped from Luke's lips, but then he had Paul's weight on top of him, Paul's arms over his arms, his hands covering his own hands, and it was so good Luke wanted it for as long as Paul would stay there.

Paul could only risk it for so long, though, and then he had to grip the condom at the base and carefully ease out of Luke, wrapping it in a tissue before chucking it in the trash. He lay down next to Luke and let his fingers drift down his spine, but he knew he couldn't relax.

"Babe, I hate to fuck and go, but I've got to be up early tomorrow."

Luke turned his face to Paul with a sleepy, well-fucked smile. "It's okay, I guessed you would. Don't guilt-trip. I'm glad you came over."

It was so obvious to Paul now—he'd missed Luke so much after he moved back to his flat, he should never have let him go. So why didn't he say so? Why did he keep holding back? Luke hadn't when he'd said that he loved him, although he also hadn't repeated his declaration of love, and remembering the wrecked state Luke had been in when he made it got Paul wondering. They needed to sort this out, but he needed to know what Luke wanted first.

"Come over Friday night again, stay the weekend," he urged as a way to find a middle ground.

"Can't. I'm working late Friday and Saturday. I'm off on Sunday, though."

Luke was still smiling at him like that would be okay. Was that enough for Luke? He realized he was too tired and too fucked out to try and work out anything trickier than a light switch tonight. He kissed Luke. "Sunday, then. But call me before that."

"Okay," Luke murmured. Paul got up and pulled the duvet over Luke before he gathered up his clothes and quickly got dressed.

"I'll put the latch down as I go out, okay?" he said quietly, but Luke's breathing already had the steady, slow rhythm of sleep.

Paul stopped by the door to put on his jacket and throw away some old receipts. He wasn't looking, but something in the bin caught his eye. Glancing back toward the bedroom door, he reached in and pulled out an information pack with an application form on the top. He didn't like the feeling of spying on Luke, but it seemed an unlikely thing for him to have. A quick look showed him it was an application pack for a catering course, and he couldn't help but smile. Then he remembered he'd found it in the bin. Did that mean Luke had given up on the idea before he'd even started? Remembering Luke's reaction when he had phoned his boss, Paul dropped the pack back into the bin. It was Luke's call, but that didn't stop him from feeling it was the wrong one.

PAUL needed someone to talk to—someone who he knew wouldn't judge him or have their own agenda, and that someone was Henry.

Now he sat in Henry's lounge drinking some kind of fancy tea, and there was expectancy in the air. They had done the whole catching-up thing, and Henry didn't take that long to spot when something was wrong.

"You looked so happy at the barbecue. I'm a very good listener, you know. You should probably make the most of it before I start going deaf."

"He told me he loves me."

Henry smiled. "Well, that's good, isn't it? You clearly adore him. Of all the troubles in the world, being loved by someone you love is probably the best to have."

"I don't know if I do love him. I don't know if I want to. I know what you're going to say, but it feels wrong. It feels disloyal to Craig. Something should have happened because of his death; there should be some change, something in the world should be different, and instead, the Earth keeps turning and everyone carries on with their lives as if he was never here. I pick up my life and love Luke like he never even existed. He should be missed! There should always be an empty space where he was, but that space is closing over."

For once, Henry looked his age. His face was serious and tired. "I know. We can walk on the moon and split the atom, but human beings haven't quite mastered the basics of life yet, like grieving." He sighed, and they were both quiet with their thoughts for a minute. When he spoke again his voice was low but clear. "I can tell you all the things you already know—about how Craig wouldn't want you to turn your heart to ice, about how safe it would be to grow old with a memory rather than the excitement and frustration and danger of sharing your life with another person. I can tell you maybe it's too soon or maybe Luke just isn't the right one. You're right—the world does just keep on spinning around, and whether you or I or Craig or anyone else happens to be on it is really far less important than we like to believe. You have to look inside yourself and decide if you're going to live your life or freeze it. But be honest with yourself, because in the end, whichever you choose, you are choosing for yourself. Don't tell yourself it's for Craig—he's not here; for all I know he may not be anywhere anymore. You can only decide for yourself."

They sat quietly for a while. "I'm afraid I haven't been much help after all, have I?" Henry apologized.

Paul let out a long sigh. "Actually, you have. You just haven't told me the answer. I guess that bit's down to me."

As Paul was leaving, he hugged Henry tighter than usual. "You're a good friend, Henry. Thank you." When he let Henry go, he saw that his eyes were bright with emotion.

"Get away with you. Just… choose carefully, Paul. We all die; it's the living we do that really counts!" and something of his usual mischievous grin returned.

CHAPTER
SEVENTEEN

THE next few weeks settled into a rhythm. Now that Brian was no longer organizing the schedules at work, Luke managed to get more daytime shifts, which meant that he could spend some evenings with Paul. He even managed to talk Paul into going clubbing with him a few times. Paul complained that he was too old, but Luke loved it when Paul watched him dance, and even Paul had to admit that there was a definite payoff when he got a hot, sweaty, pumped-up Luke back home again.

The summer teaching term was creeping on, and now it was July; the time until the long holiday could be counted in weeks. A conversation in the staffroom had made Paul realize he didn't have anything planned, and he had hit the travel agents on the way home, grabbing a range of brochures. The thought of taking Luke away somewhere new and sharing it with him made the idea of travel exciting again. He remembered the conversation they'd had at Henry's barbecue and couldn't decide whether they should start by exploring Europe or travel further. What would Luke think of Asia, or Africa?

But when he showed the brochures to Luke, the now familiar frown creased between his eyebrows. They were relaxing on the sofa after enjoying a particularly fantastic herb-crusted rack of lamb from a recipe Luke had found on the Internet. "We don't have to go to any of these places; they were just the ones I picked up," Paul offered.

"Paul… I can't afford this. I'm sorry."

Paul opened his mouth and then closed it again.

"That doesn't mean that you can't go," Luke told him. "You don't have to stay home just because of me. You should definitely go somewhere. You've earned it."

"No."

"No?"

"No. I work hard and I want to go on holiday with my boyfriend at least once a year. I don't think that's a lot to ask. Now I know that you don't want any handouts, and you want to do everything by yourself, and mostly I respect that. But not if it means I don't get my holiday."

Now it was Luke's turn to do his fish impression. Paul didn't usually take Luke on like this, and he was being so blunt about it that Luke was struggling to see how he could stick to his guns.

Paul carried on talking while the silence lasted. "We don't have to go anywhere expensive, and we don't have to go for weeks and weeks. We just need to go somewhere. Anyway, when you build in all the 'single occupancy' additional charges, it won't cost that much more."

"It feels wrong," Luke finally managed.

"Maybe it just feels different," Paul suggested. "You're just used to doing everything by yourself, but that's not how it is now, is it?"

"It's exactly what your friends expect from me. They think I'm after your money."

"That's because they don't know how good I am in bed," Paul said with a wink. "Hey, you're not supposed to laugh."

"What if we break up? Then you'll regret wasting your money."

"No, I won't. I want to go on holiday with you. Although I will be pretty pissed if you go off with another guy while we're actually on holiday, but I think that would be the case even if you were paying."

"You're not taking me seriously," Luke complained.

"You take things seriously enough for both of us. Come here." Paul pulled Luke over to him until he was sitting straddling Paul's lap, and kissed his mouth. "Do this for me. I'll choose where we go and I'll make sure you don't have any fun at all. How's that?" He cradled Luke's head with one hand while he stroked the seat of Luke's jeans with the other.

"You think I can't say no to you when you've got your hand on my ass."

"I *know* you can't say no to me when I've got my hand on your ass."

Luke scrunched up his face. "Okay, okay. Nothing expensive. Somewhere you want to go. And I'll pay for drinks and stuff."

And then it just seemed right.

"I do love you, Luke Kearsey. You know that, right?"

Everything just fell away from Luke's face, and Paul had never seen him look so defenseless, so young. He couldn't help but think of the child Luke had been as well as the man he was now. How many times had Luke been told he was loved? Not many, he guessed.

Luke's lips moved but no sound came out. "You know you're not actually speaking, right?" Paul told him.

Luke swallowed, tried again, and then buried his head against Paul's shoulder. "Fuck... I just... I didn't think you'd ever say that."

Paul managed to pull Luke's head up so he could force him to make eye contact. "I love you; I'm in love with you. You mean the world to me." Luke's eyes shone, and Paul let him hide his face against his neck again. He held him there, still and close, until he was ready.

When he sat up again, his eyes were still bright but he was back in control. "You love me."

"Yeah."

"You really love me."

"Yep."

Luke's smile was so bright it made Paul's heart hurt.

"You can't take it back."

"I don't want to take it back."

"I'm just saying…." But Luke was still grinning wider than any Cheshire cat had ever managed.

"You know, it's traditional for you to say something around now," Paul prompted.

"Maybe I don't have anything to say?" Luke teased.

"Oh, I think it's a little late for that."

"What do you mean?" Luke felt the blush coming up to his cheeks.

"I seem to remember, in the not too distant past, a guy who looked a lot like you lying in my arms on the rug in my bedroom telling me he loved me."

Luke dropped his eyes. "You did hear me. I wasn't sure afterwards."

"It's too late to play cool and aloof now."

"I don't want to play cool and aloof. I want to love you. And I want you to love me. And you do." Luke's voice wavered just a little on the last bit, and there was only one thing Paul could do.

Ten minutes later Luke was lying on his back on the bed with Paul's finger in his ass and mouth wrapped around his cock. He fisted his hands in the sheets as Paul pushed a second finger in and stretched and stretched. "Fuck me now. I'm ready. Please."

Paul pulled his mouth off Luke's cock long enough to tell him, "You are so pushy," before swirling back down the length again.

"You want me to beg? I'll beg. Please, please, please fuck me." It wasn't that Luke couldn't normally spend a whole day with Paul's mouth on his cock. It was just that right now he needed to be able to look into Paul's eyes as he squeezed his cock inside his body, and Paul's fingers, however long and skilled, just weren't enough.

There was no way Paul could resist that pleading tone and he slipped his fingers out, giving Luke a few last sucks on the head of his cock. Once he had the condom on, he sat down on the bed with his back against the headboard, pushing the pillows out of the way. "Come here. I want you on my lap. I want to kiss you the whole time I'm inside you."

Luke didn't need to be told twice. He pulled his knees up close to his body and slowly lowered down onto Paul's cock, Paul helping to steady his weight as he slid inside Luke's ass. The stretch felt so good, and then his arms were around Paul, and Paul's arms were around him, holding on tight.

"Tell me." Paul's voice was hoarse, and Luke knew exactly what he meant.

"I love you," he whispered, managing to keep his eyes on Paul's the whole time.

Paul's mouth found his, and they clung to each other while their tongues stroked and their hips rocked. Paul couldn't thrust into Luke like this, but this wasn't about an athletic workout—it was about taking things deeper and closer than they ever had before. His tongue found every part of Luke's mouth, tasting and stroking him, feeling his own heat coming back at him.

Paul had promised to kiss him the whole time, but there was only so much Luke could take without sinking into a swoon. He curled one hand around the back of Paul's neck and rested the other on the bed behind him to take some of his weight and help him balance. Leaning back a little pushed the pressure right up against his prostate and the rub felt so good as he lifted his hips up and down the shaft of Paul's dick.

Paul stroked the hair back out of his face and pressed his thumb against Luke's lips until they parted and sucked him in. He watched the sensations from deep in Luke's body play out across his face, caught every sweet moan from his lips. He slipped his thumb from between Luke's lips and placed his hand over his mouth. "Lick it, so it's wet on your cock," he instructed. He watched and felt Luke's quick and obedient tongue as it went to work. He didn't care how he did it—how Luke seemed to turn on every part of his brain as well as his body, because Luke was his, he was Luke's, and there was no need to analyze it anymore.

When Paul first reached out to touch Luke's dick, he felt it twitch under his hand and he knew it was tight with need. Luke's breath was coming in quick pants now, and he was sweating from the exertion of moving up and down Paul's cock. Like most tops, Paul didn't mind Luke doing some of the work for a change, but he was happy to give him a hand—literally. He began stroking up and down the shaft in time to Luke's own movements, and the sound of Luke's whimper shivered through him. He was biting down on his lip now, opening himself to Paul as he pushed down and squeezing hold of him as he raised his ass back up again. As Paul rubbed his thumb up over the ridge and along the slit, precome oozed out and Luke tipped his head back.

Luke worked his body faster even as he gasped for breath, and he could feel his climax building inexorably, pushing up through his thighs and his ass until it all centered in his tightening balls and shot out through his cock onto Paul's chest. His ass clamped around Paul's cock, and he held himself perfectly in place to feel it press right into his prostate as his body jerked, and his climax seemed like it would never stop.

Paul somehow managed to stay still as Luke rocked with ecstasy until his cock gave a final shudder, but then his control gave out. As Luke's come dripped down his torso, he pumped his hips up into the ass that just didn't seem to know how to stop gripping him, even after Luke had come.

The muscles in Luke's thighs burned with exertion, and he tried not to bite through his lip as he pushed the muscles harder, rocking his ass up and down on Paul's cock. Paul cupped his hand behind Luke's head and guided it forward, then pressed his forehead against Luke's as his groans turned to desperate, breathless cries.

They both sank down onto the bed and lay together, gradually getting their breath back. "I've got to start going to the gym with you," Luke mumbled. "My legs are gonna kill me tomorrow."

"C'mon." Paul pulled at Luke's arm. "It's too early to go to bed. Let's grab a beer and look at holiday brochures."

"I can't stand," Luke complained. "Bring them up here."

"Oh, so is this how it's going to be now? I tell you I love you and you think you can turn into a princess?"

Luke beamed up at him.

"Okay, okay, I'll go and get them. You stay here—don't wear yourself out by rolling over or anything," Paul teased as he walked to the door.

Later, sitting up in bed nestled against Paul, drinking beer, eating potato chips, and looking at holiday brochures, Luke didn't think he'd ever been so happy. He wasn't agreeing with Paul about everything because Paul was paying. It was just that he didn't care where they went as long as they got to do this.

QUARTER past nine on a Saturday morning felt too early for the phone to be ringing, but neither Luke nor Paul could pretend it wasn't. They'd been awake for a while, but Paul curling into Luke and fucking him on his side had been the perfect way to start the weekend and there was no rush for them to move after that.

Paul sighed before reaching for the phone and checking the display. "Henry," he murmured to Luke before connecting the call. "Hi, Henry."

Luke closed his eyes and listened to half of the conversation.

"Calm down and tell me what's happened."

Luke opened his eyes again and looked at Paul, but he looked only mildly concerned so Luke relaxed again.

"Are you sure you can't get anyone else? ... Well, I'm sure they'll understand. You'll just have to reschedule it. ... Henry, have you thought that maybe you could be overreacting? ... Okay, okay, I understand. ... Henry, I really don't know. ... I know, but... Henry, let me talk to him and I'll call you back. ... Alright, I'll tell him. ... No, I'll talk to him and we'll call you. ...Yes, we'll call you soon. Bye, Henry."

Paul didn't move for a minute, and Luke's anxiety started prickling. He couldn't outwait Paul and turned to him, eyebrows raised.

"That was Henry."

Luke got the feeling that Paul was stalling. "No, really?"

Paul shoved him and smiled, but it didn't last. Finally, Paul took a deep breath. "He's got a problem. He's got some people coming over tonight, and the person who was going to cook for him has let him down. He says it's too late to get anyone he would normally use, and he's probably right." Paul stopped and looked at Luke. "He wanted to know if you could do it."

"Me? Why on earth would he want me?"

"Well, I might have told him what a fantastic cook you are, and how you've been making all these great meals for me...."

Luke sat up. "You have to set him straight. You have to tell him I'm not a proper cook. I work at a fucking burger bar—is that what he's planning on serving? 'Cause if it is, I'm his guy. Otherwise...."

Paul looked away. He didn't want Luke to feel pressured into doing something that made him uncomfortable, but he didn't accept Luke's reasons, either.

"Surely it would depend on what it is he needs you to cook." He put up his hands quickly to ward off Luke's hot response. "I know you're not a professional, but there are lots of things that you can cook really well. I've been to Henry's dinner parties before and I know that the food you cook is as good as what he serves his guests. If it wasn't, I would let you know. I'm not going to set you up for a fall."

Paul tried to find any opening in Luke's expression, but he was shut down tight and wouldn't meet Paul's eyes.

"Fine. You don't want to do it. I'll call Henry and tell him, and that's the end of it." Paul picked the phone up again, but waited to press Henry's number when he heard Luke sigh.

"It's just that he thinks I'm better than I am. I like Henry. I don't want him to be embarrassed in front of his guests, that's all."

"Maybe you should talk to him." Paul held the phone out to Luke, half suggestion, half challenge. He wanted to take care of Luke, but he saw no reason why he should help him to shortchange himself, and he didn't relish saying no to Henry when Henry had only ever said yes to him.

Luke's frown darkened and he bit his lip, but he took the phone. A challenge was a challenge, and he'd trained himself to always step up. Now he sat on the bed looking at the phone.

"I'm going to have a shower." Paul longed to hear how the conversation went but knew he had to step back, and physically removing himself from the situation seemed the safest route.

By the time Luke came into the bathroom, Paul was out of the shower and had nearly finished shaving. He caught Luke's reflection in the mirror and saw it was just as tight as before. Luke turned the shower on and stepped in. Okay, so Paul might have spent longer finishing up than he needed to, and he might have spent more time looking at the water running down Luke's back and ass than he did looking at his own face in the mirror, but he still resisted the temptation to be the first to reach out, and when he had delayed as long as he thought he could get away with, he went back into the bedroom to get dressed.

He was downstairs, eating toast and drinking coffee, by the time Luke came down and sat across the table from him. Luke looked at him for a minute, but Paul just smiled so Luke had to go first.

"So I called Henry."

Paul nodded as though there was nothing more to say.

"He's really hard to say no to."

Paul put down his toast and looked at Luke, waiting, but still saying nothing.

"He wants me to go over. He said we can talk about the food and keep it simple."

Paul was trying so hard, but his face just wouldn't play along. He could feel the grin curling up his lips and crinkling his eyes.

"I haven't said I'll do it."

Paul nodded.

"Fuck you!" Luke burst out, his own face breaking into a smile as well. "You knew I wouldn't be able to say no to him. I can't believe I've gotten myself into this."

Paul reached over to him. "You've gotten yourself into this because you know that if you keep to recipes you know and give yourself plenty of time, you can do it."

"Apparently there'll be a girl there to help with serving and washing up. I've never done anything like this. I tried to tell him, but…."

"When are you supposed to be going over?"

Luke shook his head. "About an hour. Oh, Paul, we were supposed to be going out tonight. We never get a Saturday night."

"We'll get plenty of Saturday nights. I'm going to make you some breakfast, which you are going to eat, and then I'm taking you round to Henry's."

Luke flopped down over the table. "It would be kinder to shoot me."

After Paul dropped Luke at Henry's house, he realized he now had a long empty day ahead of him. He'd made Luke promise to text or call if he needed anything, but other than that there was nothing for Paul to do but step back and let things happen. He tried to think about the day as he would any other Saturday, but it was hard to focus at the gym when he kept checking his phone every five minutes, and when he got to the supermarket he could only think about what Luke should choose to cook and whether he needed anything to be picked up. *Back off*, he told himself, *stop trying to play the hero. He doesn't need rescuing.*

He was just starting to think about getting some lunch when Luke called.

"Hi, babe."

"Hi. I thought I'd just call you while I've got a minute. Henry's gone out to get some stuff—that guy can really talk."

Paul smiled to himself. He could hear it in Luke's voice—he was on top of things, working it out and staying calm.

"I'm glad you called. I've been thinking about you. So what are you making?"

Luke went on to tell him about the simple salad with tomato and mozzarella he was doing as a starter, pork roasted with balsamic vinegar for the main, and the chocolate torte he'd made previously for Paul for dessert.

"The thing is, Henry's got all the best ingredients, so I don't need to fancy it up. I just need to put them together right."

"You sound like you've got everything under control," Paul offered.

"Well, in theory. I'm just prepping the vegetables now. I don't know what time I'll be finished here, probably about ten. We could still go out."

"Just come back to mine when you're done, and we can decide then. I think it's great that you're doing this for Henry. He's helped me out a lot of times, and it's not often he needs help himself."

"Okay." There was a pause and then, "Paul?" Luke's voice was quieter but urgent.

"Yeah."

"Tell me again."

"I love you. And I'm going to show you how much when you get home tonight." Paul could swear the warmth of Luke's grin was coming through the phone.

"I love you, Paul. See you later."

On either end of the finished call, Paul and Luke sat and thought the same things for once—how good they felt and how much they wanted the other's body to show them.

IT WAS more like eleven o'clock when the taxi dropped Luke off at Paul's house, and although he was buzzing and high on his success he didn't want to go out. Instead, Paul got to hear a blow-by-blow recount of the night told at a million miles an hour, which slowly dropped to a hundred as Luke ate a toasted sandwich and unwound.

Paul had known things were going well when he received a text from Henry which read: *I am in love with your man. I don't think I'll be able to give him back at the end of the night. We may have to duel!* He'd heard nothing from Luke, which again he took as a good sign, and although he found it hard to keep up with the details of Luke's story, there was no doubt it had been a success.

Luke was still restless after eating—he'd been too busy cooking and worrying to have anything himself during the day, and he collected up his dishes and started washing them. Paul came and stood close behind Luke, not touching, until Luke couldn't stand it and pressed back against him. Then Paul slid a hand round Luke's waist, over his flat stomach and up over his chest to press down on his heart. He moved his other hand over Luke's hip and covered his cock.

"All mine," he breathed into Luke's hair.

"All yours," Luke murmured back. He went to take his hands from the sink but Paul stopped him.

"Don't move."

"You do like to be in charge, don't you?" Luke smiled, but did as Paul said because he liked it too.

"I want to fuck you like this, standing up."

"Yeah." Luke's word was just a soft breath.

"I'm gonna go and get the lube. You're going to take off your clothes, and when I come back downstairs you're going to be standing here like this, waiting for me."

Luke's chest grew a little tight. "Okay."

Paul took his time upstairs so Luke would have a chance to be ready for him when he came back down. He wasn't disappointed. Luke stood with his back to him, legs slightly apart, and his hands resting on the counter in front of him. Paul couldn't help noticing that Luke had folded up his clothes neatly.

He went and stood behind Luke and rested his hands on the tops of Luke's thighs, hearing Luke's intake of breath at the touch.

"How are those thigh muscles today?"

"Not as bad as I thought. I think they just need regular work."

"I can arrange that." Paul stroked his hands down over the skin and then brought them back up to entwine over Luke's hard cock. Luke turned his head to find Paul's mouth, and they kissed, long and slow. Paul pressed his body closer against Luke, and rubbed his cock against Luke's ass as their tongues moved against each other.

"Give me your hand." Paul pumped lube over Luke's fingers. "Now, open your ass up for me."

Luke reached behind him and pressed his index finger against the ridge of muscle and through the resistance. The knowledge of Paul's eyes on him was making his cock drip with precome, and his breath was ragged. It wasn't like he'd never fingered himself before, but with Paul watching….

"Look at me." Paul's voice rasped with want.

Don't come, don't come, Luke told himself over and over, but it was so much harder when he turned his head to look over his shoulder at Paul and saw him leaning against the table slowly jacking his hand over his cock.

"Two fingers. Really stretch it open—show me inside. C'mon."

Paul watched as Luke bit down on his lip and closed his eyes, pulling at the entrance and softness beyond to spread it wider. There was no way he could keep his hand on his cock and not come, so he moved in close again and gave in to the urge to slip his index finger in beside Luke's.

"Oh, God, Oh, Paul," Luke whimpered as their fingers rubbed against each other inside him.

Paul's tongue licked so lightly over his ear lobe it sent lightning through Luke's nerves. The skin on his dick was too tight. His breath came in ragged gasps.

When Paul slid his finger out, Luke could breathe a little easier, but then he heard the tear of the condom packet and his cock swelled even more. He kept his fingers in his ass until Paul told him to remove them and place them on the counter next to his other hand. His back felt damp with sweat, every nerve straining as he felt Paul stand behind him and then gently lean forward.

Paul eased the head of his cock through the muscle and held still. "You do it," he told Luke. "Push yourself back onto it."

Standing upright made it harder to open himself up, and the angle was difficult, but pushing back with his hips helped. He felt the tight burn as his body was forced to stretch over Paul's long cock. He bit down on his lip to silence his body's protests until the pressure hit his prostate, and then his mouth fell open in a long gasp of pleasure. He pushed back further and further, taking the burn deep, until his ass was pressed against Paul's hips. Paul wrapped his arms around Luke's waist and pressed his whole body against him, and it was so good the hurt was worth it. Luke remembered Paul's words—*I love you*—and felt skin pressed to buzzing skin everywhere.

Paul slowly swiveled his hips in a circle, finding every sensitive place inside Luke and earning him the sweetest sounds from Luke's lips. Luke ground against him, and Paul kept him tight by gripping his hips so he remained in him to the hilt. "So good," he whispered against his ear. "So tight, so good." His tongue stroked along Luke's jaw and flicked against his throat.

The need for Paul to fuck him hard was crowding in on Luke, but he wanted to hold on to this for as long as he could, so he pressed his hands harder into the wooden surface, until he almost expected them to sink into it.

When Paul took one hand from Luke's hips and stroked it up and down his thigh, Luke reached his breaking point. "Please, please," he begged hoarsely, and he squeezed down tightly on Paul's dick to reinforce his need.

Paul caught his breath at the added pressure and started to withdraw from Luke's ass, giving him the space to pound back in hard enough to force a sharp gasp from him. "Is that what you want? That what you need?" Paul growled.

"Yeah." Luke's voice was high and thin. "Oh yeah." Now he was holding on to the surface to keep himself upright as his legs shivered with the hard, fast thrusts. Each time, Paul caught his prostate and set off a whole new bunch of fireworks that reverberated through him. It felt as if Paul was fucking right into the base of his cock. He could hear Paul panting with exertion and would've sworn he could feel his dick swelling inside him. Luke's own cock was too heavy, too tight for him to stand it, but he didn't think he could keep his balance if he used one hand to jerk himself off. He closed his eyes, pushed away the thought of coming, and just focused on the hot ripples pushing out from his ass through his balls, his cock... his whole body. He wasn't expecting it—had never come just from a guy's dick before, so when he felt his balls grip and explode he gasped with surprise before the first wave hit him and sent come over his chest and the counter. He had to depend on Paul to hold him up as he shuddered and lost control of his legs.

Paul felt him come, and it only spurred him to fuck harder into that hot, sweet ass that was pushing back onto his cock like he still couldn't get enough of it. Luke took his weight as Paul groaned into his shoulder and wrapped his arms around Luke so tightly he couldn't breathe.

There was only one small thing in all this that stopped it from being perfect. When Paul had his breath back, he said to Luke, "I want to fuck you and come in you with nothing in between us. I want to be able to stay inside you, just for a minute, without worrying about the condom. Let's get tested and ditch them."

Luke's smile was the right answer. "Okay."

"You look like I just promised to take you to Disneyland."

Luke kissed him again and again. "I think you just did!"

CHAPTER EIGHTEEN

THE following weekend, Henry invited them over for lunch to thank Luke for his help. He greeted them enthusiastically at the door and led them into the living room. Luke's smile became a little tighter when he saw Steve already sitting there, but he felt more relaxed in Henry's house and in his company after cooking for him. "I've invited Steve along too because he's missing Rich. Where did you say he's gone?"

"Bournemouth. It's a conference for work. I did say he was only going to be gone for two days, but I seem to remember you deciding I was too lonely to be left on my own," Steve teased as he got up to hug Paul and nod to Luke.

"Well, whatever, we're all here now."

Once Henry had made sure everyone had a drink and sat down, he turned to Luke.

"Do you remember when I said I would find a way to repay you for coming to my rescue? Well, I have. I am a genius! I've called Ralfe, who's the head chef at La Perfection, which just happens to be my favorite restaurant. He's prepared to give you a tryout for their apprenticeship position. Isn't that fantastic?"

Luke tried to remember how to breathe. He hadn't wanted Henry's money and hadn't really given any thought to his promise to find another way to repay him. He definitely hadn't expected this. His first reaction was terror at any kind of test, and his second was that this felt like another handout. How could he say no as politely as possible?

Paul saw Luke's confusion and bit his tongue so he didn't start speaking for him.

In the end, it was Steve who spoke first, and perhaps he was trying to help Luke, but when their history got put together with that slight tone in his voice, Luke read something else.

"Maybe that's not the kind of thing Luke's interested in. I mean, you like the job you have, don't you?"

And that was it. Luke went from panic-stricken to never-back-down in a heartbeat.

"It sounds fantastic," he managed to say and hoped he looked convincing.

"I knew it! I knew it!" Henry came over to Luke and hugged him. "You'll be wonderful and soon you'll be head chef in your own restaurant!"

"I don't think it's quite that easy," Steve suggested. "Won't there be other people trying out as well? I know you go there a lot, but Ralfe isn't going to take someone on based just on your recommendation."

Henry met Steve's eyes and held them until he shrugged and looked away. "I know Luke will be wonderful. He's perfectly capable of getting it on his own merits, and I'm sure you don't disagree."

The silence pressed down on Steve until he managed a muted, "Of course," with a tight smile.

"Paul, what do you think about all this?"

All eyes turned in Paul's direction, and now it was his turn to present a fake smile, but for different reasons. He'd caught Luke's reaction before Steve had spoken and he'd seen happier-looking rabbits in his headlights. He had the feeling that Luke was just trying to keep Henry happy, but at the same time he agreed with Henry—it would be a fantastic opportunity for Luke. The only question was whether he was ready to take it.

"It sounds great," he offered.

"YOU'RE really quiet." Paul was taking Luke back to his flat after leaving Henry's, and he hadn't said a word since he got in the car.

Luke shrugged. "Just thinking."

"About the apprenticeship?"

"Mmm."

"It would be a great way to start a career, if that's what you want."

Luke turned to face him. "You think I can't do it."

"Oh no. You're not going to get away with that. *You* think you can't do it. That's the problem. Don't stick it on me."

Luke stared back out of the window. Now that Steve was no longer there to bait him, he had to face the mess he was in. He'd only ever worked at fast-food places or bars before now, not fancy restaurants. Yeah, he liked cooking stuff from a recipe book after he'd had a chance to think it through, but he was no chef genius. It wasn't even the fact that he wouldn't get the job—it was the humiliation of being seen to fail in front of everyone.

When they pulled up outside Luke's flat, Paul tried again to come up with the right words. "You know it doesn't matter to me what job you do. I just wish you were spending your time on something you enjoy more."

"Yeah, well, not everybody gets to do a job they love like you do." He turned to get out of the car, but Paul grabbed his arm.

"No, they don't. But you could. You love cooking. You're not afraid of hard work and long hours. You could make it happen for you. You just have to try."

"And if I don't get it?" Luke wouldn't look at him.

"Then you try again and again and again until you do. You want me to believe you're some kind of princess who expects everything to go their way the first time?"

"No, but...."

"Why is it so much harder for you to believe that you're good at something than it is to believe you're shit at everything?"

"Because it's easier to take if you say it yourself first."

"You never struck me before as someone who would settle for the easy option."

"Yeah, well, I'm full of disappointments. Stick around and I promise you'll get more."

"Oh, I don't know. You have to leave some room for all that self-pity."

Paul got a reaction from that. "What the fuck do you know?" Luke snapped.

"I know there's a thin line between doubting yourself and feeling sorry for yourself."

"Fuck you!" Luke slammed out of the car and was inside his building before Paul could draw breath for a response. He remembered Luke saying that he had been hideous as a teen, and right now that didn't take much imagining. Paul had a pretty strong feeling that going after Luke would only result in more of the same. Reluctantly, he started the car and drove home.

A couple of hours later, Paul's mobile vibrated into life, and a quick look at the display told him it was Luke.

"Hi."

"I'm sorry. Do you hate me?"

"Not quite." Paul couldn't keep the smile from his voice.

"I don't know what to do."

"I know. But that's okay. You'll figure it out. Whatever you decide, you'll make it the right thing."

Luke made a sound halfway between a laugh and an exclamation. "Where do you get all this blind faith from?"

"From you. Luke, you never think about what you've achieved. You've kept yourself sober, off drugs, out of jail, and paying the bills since you were sixteen years old. You even managed to get yourself out of a destructive relationship and start rebuilding your life in a new country. Do you have any idea how many people who've been through the care system manage that? And you've done it all on your own without anyone to back you up."

Luke was quiet for a minute. "Y'know, when I see you next I'm gonna make it up to you."

"Yep. You are." They both laughed.

"I love you. Please don't give up on me."

"Babe, I'm a long way from that."

"Okay. I'll call you tomorrow."

"Luke? I love you too, babe."

When Luke hung up, Paul knew he'd done all he could to help, but he was pretty sure Luke had a sleepless night ahead of him.

A FEW days later Luke received a pack of information from La Perfection and freaked out again. After Luke promised he wasn't going to take his anxiety out on him, Paul went over to Luke's flat to look through it all with him. A quick glance over the paperwork told him that, yeah, it looked daunting, but these things always did. When you sorted through it, it wasn't so bad.

"Okay, so you've got a basic application form which you need to send in before your interview. Then on the day you've got to make something up to cook based on the ingredients they give you, follow a recipe they give you, and have an interview. It's pretty straightforward."

Paul looked at Luke's face. "Alright. I said it was straightforward, not easy. Just take it one step at a time. We can fill in the application form now, and then think about the rest later."

"I don't need you to do it for me," Luke snapped, before remembering their deal.

"I'm not offering to do it for you, but usually it's helpful to have someone to talk to when you're filling in these things. That's how I've always done it. If you want my advice, write it out in rough first and check it through."

Luke looked at the paper in front of him, and he couldn't have looked more unhappy if he were going for a root canal treatment.

"I'll tell you what, you get it filled in, and I'll sit here and read your newspaper. And when you're done, I'll suck you all the way to heaven."

Luke's face crinkled up into a smile, and he reached for the pen.

The next two hours dragged, and Luke tried several times to get an advance on Paul's offer, but there was nothing happening there. Once he got started, it did get a bit easier, and although he hated asking for help, Paul made it seem natural to discuss how to answer some of the questions, especially since he wasn't always sure how to fit his American life into the English form. Finally, he signed the declaration, dated it, and pushed it away from him.

"Done! Now get over here!"

Paul kissed him deep and slow, letting his tongue know what his cock was going to get.

"C'mon. I want you on the bed, because you're not going to be able to stand."

Luke grinned. "Oh, you better be able to back this up."

Paul could back it up. Once he had Luke on his back with his trousers and briefs off, he set about fulfilling his promise. He knew Luke's body now, knew his sounds and could read him better than any book. He could tell when the pressure was teasing and when it was just right, when Luke wanted him to move and when he wanted it in just one place, when Luke was sliding toward coming and when he was dropping back. Paul took him up to the brink and then eased him back down again until he was pretty sure Luke wasn't thinking about forms or interviews anymore. With three fingers in Luke's ass up to the knuckle, it occurred to Paul that they really should do some online shopping—the inflatable dildo was strictly for occasional use, but he could think of some other purchases that could be fun. He had to offset that against losing the feeling of Luke's ass around his fingers, so soft, hot and tight. Remembering that they had both had their first tests, and that in three months he would be able to feel that hidden skin against his cock gave his now aching jaw extra enthusiasm.

Luke had wads of pillow in both fists, and his hair was damp with perspiration. He couldn't hold on, but Paul wouldn't let him go, so he writhed there with Paul controlling him completely. When Paul turned his fingers or pressed deeper, Luke heard himself making sounds as if they were coming from someone else, and when Paul tongued at the slit in his cock, his back arched, straining for more and more.

And then Paul seemed to sense it, seemed to know want was turning to desperate need. His fingers eased out a little so the tips rested against Luke's prostate—stroking and stroking. Paul's other hand gripped the base of Luke's cock firmly and worked in time with his mouth so he could keep a regular rhythm that pulsed up through Luke's body. Luke surrendered to it, let the waves build higher and higher until he convulsed with ecstasy. Paul kept working him right through it up to the point where it became unbearable and then he pulled off.

Luke lay on the bed, trembling slightly as he tried to pull the pieces of himself back together. He felt Paul lay down beside him. He couldn't reach out for him—not yet, but he knew he would be right there waiting for him when he wanted to, and that was the best thing of all.

LUKE had ten days until the interview and he was determined to put them to good use. Whenever he wasn't at work he was either cooking, reading cookbooks, or perusing food halls and markets. He taught himself how to make basic sauces and to recognize different cuts of meat, then tried to memorize recommended cooking times and methods. He tried to develop his knowledge of classic combinations so he knew what went with what. He looked at online menus from every restaurant he could think of until his head was ready to explode and he'd completely lost his appetite. Luke had to admit it—he wanted this.

He couldn't stop himself from imagining a different life; one where he could feel confident around other people instead of shifty and unsure. Maybe he could have something he was good at too. He would be able to join in conversations with Paul's friends instead of smiling blankly and hoping no one asked him anything, earn enough money to pay the bills without working out what he would do without that week, and be proud of where he worked.

The apprenticeship consisted of two days a week at a local college and four days working in the restaurant as a line chef or commis. He would have the opportunity to gain experience in a professional kitchen and see how all the other chefs worked. Henry had told him that most of Ralfe's previous apprentices were still working at the restaurant and had progressed to being responsible for different stations, which made Luke think Ralfe couldn't be too bad a boss. The chances were he'd probably had worse, anyway.

The only time Luke stopped thinking about the interview was when he finally heard from Brooke. At last he knew that Kit was back in Chicago. Brooke had sounded apologetic when she wrote that she had seen him with a new guy, but Luke felt a heaviness leave him. If Kit had found someone new, he wouldn't be bothering Luke anymore. It was finally over.

As the day of the interview got closer, the nauseous fear in his stomach grew stronger. Paul tried to help him rehearse for the interview and think up questions they might ask, but Luke ended up shutting down or storming off, overwhelmed by anxiety. He just couldn't cope with the thought of people judging him, and crumbled. Paul tried to take Luke's mind off the tryout using every trick he could think of, but nothing worked. Their sex life had become practically nonexistent, with Luke distracted and tense. Whatever the outcome, Paul just wanted it to be over.

However difficult Luke was, Paul wasn't going to leave him to his thoughts, and he insisted that Luke stay with him the night before his interview. He had a growing suspicion that, left alone, Luke would end up talking himself out of even turning up. He wouldn't let Luke cook anything, despite him claiming that he still needed the practice, and instead ordered his favorite pizza. He even dragged Luke around a nearby park to get him some fresh air and exercise. When Paul got him into bed, he sucked Luke's cock as if he could pull the tension out of him that way; he wanted to fuck him and hold him and make him feel it was okay. Paul could feel the tightness in his ass just from fingering him, though, and he suspected Luke just wasn't going to be able to relax enough for that, so he had to settle for a blow job. That took the pressure off enough for him to fall asleep, and Paul hoped he would stay that way until morning. He wasn't surprised, though, when he awoke in the early hours of the morning and realized Luke was already awake.

"You okay?" Paul whispered.

"I'm sorry. I didn't mean to wake you. I just keep thinking about what they might ask, or what could go wrong. This is so stupid. I have a job. I don't even remember why I'm doing this."

Paul stroked Luke's chest. "I could tell you all the sensible reasons, but I don't think they'll help right now. You know why you should go in there today? If you do, at the end of the day it's over, done. You get offered the job or you don't. If you don't go, you are going to spend weeks, maybe months, maybe longer, thinking about it—how it might have gone, how things might have turned out, but you'll never know. So, you can either wrap it up in a day or dwell on it for months. Which would you rather do?"

"You think you're pretty smart, don't you?" Paul could make out Luke's smile in the darkness.

"Yep. It's an advantage of getting old."

Luke kissed him. "I'm gonna go downstairs and watch some TV. I don't think I'm going to be able to sleep."

"No, stay here. Put the TV on in here. I think there's a DVD in there."

"Then you won't be able to sleep." Luke kissed him again. All his instincts and old habits pulled him to retreat into himself when he felt anxious, but Paul was there and almost challenging him to not back away, to lean on him.

"It's Sunday. I can sleep all day. I can even sleep with the TV on. It's another advantage of getting old."

"Okay, but I'll turn it down." Luke climbed out of bed and turned on the television, feeling around at the side for the remote. "Do you remember what DVD it is?"

"Put it on and find out," Paul mumbled.

Luke found the button and slipped back into bed while the DVD loaded. When he'd nestled back into Paul and pushed the pillow around for a bit, he heard a familiar soundtrack starting up. He closed his eyes for a second and swallowed.

"You really are pretty fucking wonderful, aren't you?" was the best he could manage.

"You're fucking wonderful. Now shut up. I want to watch *E.T.*"

AT BREAKFAST, Luke was quiet and edgy. Paul made him eat a banana to go with his coffee, but other than that tried to keep out of his way. Dropping him off outside the restaurant, he caught him for a kiss. "I love you," Paul told him and saw that it still put a spark in Luke's eyes. Luke took a deep breath and got out of the car.

The interviews were taking place on Sunday so the restaurant would be closed and could be used to try out the applicants. Luke was shown through the guests' dining area and into the kitchens by the headwaiter, who was helping to organize the day. It helped Luke's nerves a little when he caught the interest in the way Josh was talking to him—not that he was looking, but it couldn't hurt.

The kitchens contained a lot of gleaming steel and three other applicants—two men, both of whom looked younger than Luke, and a woman who was probably a few years older. They could see that individual stations had been set up for them but they had to wait together until everyone had arrived and there were two more people yet to come. At least everyone was as nervous and awkward as Luke, shuffling and fidgeting, glancing at the stations and trying to work out what had been set out for them and what they might be asked to do. They all seemed to breathe out together when the final applicant arrived and they knew they could get started.

Ralfe, his sous chef, Marianna, and a selection of chefs de partie who had come in for the day were all introduced, and Luke tried to remember their names and specialties. They would be watching the applicants during the first practical task and giving feedback to the interview panel, Ralfe explained. He added that they would use the first task and the interview to eliminate at least two candidates, but perhaps more. Those remaining would then be given a selection of ingredients and asked to create a dish as a final challenge.

Luke wished he'd skipped the banana as he felt it churning around in his stomach. If nothing else, he was determined not to throw up in the spotless kitchens. But then he had no more time to think about that, because they were starting the first challenge. Each applicant had his or her own workstation, the necessary ingredients, and instructions —to cook and present chicken breast wrapped in Parma ham with a pesto sauce and a medley of vegetables. Ralfe emphasized that this was a simple dish and that he and Marianna would be looking for each component to be completed to a high standard.

White panic hit Luke as the clock started to count down their hour. He took some breaths and remembered what Paul had said—"Just imagine you're cooking for me and forget everything else." He looked around and familiarized himself with the equipment and ingredients and got started.

The hour passed in fits and starts. At some points, he felt like everything would be ready with time to spare, and at others that he would never finish in time. Nausea hit every time one of the chefs came by to watch him. Fortunately, they didn't seem to want to talk to anyone, just watch, and Luke tried to blank out their presence.

It wasn't until he was stepping back from his plated food that he thought about the other applicants and wondered how they had done. The chefs worked their way around each candidate's finished food, examining it with forensic precision and making notes but speaking very little. Their faces also gave little away. All Luke could work out was that he hadn't done anything too awful.

There was little time to bask in the relief of completing a third of the challenges before the dread of the interview crept up on him. This was the part he feared the most—hearing himself stumble and struggle to explain what he wanted to say, and that was if he understood the question in the first place.

Waiting around for his turn, he listened in on the conversations developing around him. One of the applicants seemed very confident, describing cooking as a cinch and easy money. In Luke's experience, people who talked like that rarely knew what they were doing, but he could be an exception. Another candidate admitted he'd not cooked his chicken properly and had only applied because he hadn't been able to think what else he wanted to do. The woman was quiet most of the time, but she also seemed very focused and determined. The people who had already been interviewed sat slightly apart from those still waiting, and Luke couldn't decide if he wished they would talk about how their interviews had gone or not.

Luke's name was the fourth name called. At least it was Josh who took him through to the interview room. "They're not as bad as they like to seem," he whispered to Luke conspiratorially. "Don't let them faze you."

He took Luke into a room where Ralfe, Marianna, and another man sat behind a long table, with a chair stuck in the middle of the room for Luke. *All it needs is a spotlight and it would count for torture*, he thought as he tried to smile and sat down. The chair was plastic and uncomfortable. It seemed impossible to sit on it without slumping, and in the end Luke found he had to lean forward the whole time to avoid appearing too relaxed. The man he hadn't yet met was the owner of the restaurant, but as the interview moved on, Luke got the feeling that Ralfe would have the main say in the awarding of the apprenticeship.

There were some brief questions about Luke's visa and he confirmed that he had permission to work and study in the UK for the next eighteen months, and some clarification about when he'd left school that dwelled on his lack of academic qualifications. They were interested in his work experience as well, though—not just on what his job had been, but what he had learned from working at different places too. Luke's face felt hot. He had to focus to keep his breathing regular and he was aware of every gesture and fidget and how it could be interpreted. Was this ever going to end?

They saved the hardest question until the end. "Why do you think we should give you the apprenticeship?"

All three interviewers sat back and looked at him. Luke's mouth was dry, and his head was still full of all the questions that had come before this one. He did his best to form an answer, but it wasn't particularly eloquent. He told them that he loved cooking for people, loved creating and presenting recipes that people would enjoy, wanted to learn more, and wouldn't be put off by long hours or starting at the bottom. It was all said in a couple of sentences and somehow it didn't feel like it was enough, but equally there was nothing else to add.

Realizing he'd finished, they thanked him for coming and asked him to wait with the other candidates until they had completed all the interviews. When Luke sat down on the sofa in the waiting area, he felt as if he had run a marathon. Now he understood why the other applicants had been so quiet after their interviews. He briefly considered texting Paul while he was waiting for the others to go through the same process, but he didn't want to lose focus and there wasn't really much to say yet.

The last candidate came out of the interview room. "They want us to wait here for a few minutes and then they'll come out and say who they need for the afternoon," he told the expectant faces. No one said anything. Instead, they all seemed to find some point in the room to stare at or a thread to fiddle with. The knowledge that the decision was being made in the next room, and there was no more they could do to influence it, pressed down on everybody.

Although they were all waiting for it, all the candidates seemed to jump when the door finally opened. Ralfe thanked them all for attending before reading out the names of the three people they wanted to return in the afternoon. When Luke heard his name, he had to force himself to act composed instead of running around the room cheering. His heart was racing, and he was sure he was grinning like a fool.

They had a break before their task in the afternoon, and Luke was desperate to get outside and collect his thoughts. He walked until he found a small park and sat down on the bench, still smiling to himself. He had done it! Somehow he had gotten through the interview, and now, even if he didn't get the job, he knew he had done well. He hugged himself against the cold and savored the moment. Maybe this was something he really could do. Maybe he could get a better job than the one he had now, and a better one after that and... who knew where he could end up?

He didn't need to talk to Paul—he didn't feel the need to talk to anyone. This was just for him, because perhaps he had been the only one who hadn't seen it before. He knew that no matter what happened in the final task, he had achieved something for himself that morning and nothing was going to stop him from holding on to that.

Luke checked the time and walked slowly back to a shop he had passed earlier to pick up a drink and a sandwich. He ate his lunch as he wandered along, and by the time he was back at the restaurant he was ready to get going again.

It wasn't as if he didn't still get a cramp of nerves when he was faced with a pile of ingredients and two hours to make a main course and a dessert; he just knew that even if he got this wrong it wouldn't take away what had gone before. At first, he had too many ideas, but he remembered Paul's words again and focused—if he had this stuff in the cupboards, what would he make for Paul? He ended up making grilled lamb with a balsamic marinade, pea puree, and crushed new potatoes, followed by pistachio soufflé with dark chocolate sauce. Everything was a rush—he didn't have time to think too much about presentation and he had the feeling that his lamb was slightly overcooked, but his soufflé rose beautifully and he knew he'd done his best.

The chefs gave nothing away when they came around to judge each applicant's work. As before, they muttered to each other and wrote things down but seemed neither impressed nor disappointed. However, before they left, Ralfe did thank them all for working so hard and making his decision difficult, and he appeared to mean it.

Luke was supposed to call Paul to come and pick him up, but he wanted some more time with his thoughts so he caught a bus instead.

He liked the idea of surprising Paul and he had quite a bit of making up to do after the last few days. He knew he should be happy with what he had achieved, and he was, but he couldn't quite stop himself from thinking how it might feel to tell people he was a chef at La Perfection when they asked what he did.

CHAPTER NINETEEN

"NOT much longer," Luke said from the bed as Paul got up to throw away the condom.

"No," Paul replied, but there was something else behind it.

Luke felt a coldness in his stomach. "You having second thoughts?"

"No, I've just been thinking a bit. When I was twenty-two...."

"Back in the dark ages," Luke added helpfully.

Paul gave him a look, but got back into bed and continued, "When I was your age, I wanted to be out there, y'know, having a good time, and, yeah, sleeping with different guys. I wanted to try things and I enjoyed it."

Luke nodded in mock seriousness. "I understand what you're saying. You were a slut."

Paul punched him lightly on the arm while he laughed. "I don't want you to feel you've missed out on your youth or something. I don't want you to regret this later."

Luke shrugged and looked more serious. "I never really felt like that—like I wanted to try lots of guys. Every time I went with somebody, it always felt like a bit of a risk. I know some people like that, but.... When I first started going to clubs and stuff, I loved the music. I loved being with other people who were gay and out and having a good time, and, yeah, when I knew that another guy thought I was hot—I liked that too. But for a long time I thought that maybe for gay guys that's all there was, that was all you were supposed to want. I thought I was a freak because I wanted something else, and the thought that I would never be able to have it, y'know, the whole 'couple' thing… it made me feel really alone. And now, having you, it scares me because it's so much what I want." He sighed. "I have no idea what I'll regret later, but I'm pretty sure being faithful to you is not going to be at the top of my list."

Paul pulled Luke in for a long, slow kiss. "If I wasn't so old, I'd fuck you all over again."

"Oh, you will, but later. Don't want to be late for the party."

It had been Paul's brother's birthday during the week, and his parents were having what Luke had been promised was a small family get-together. That didn't mean he wasn't dreading the whole thing, but he had a secret curiosity about Paul's family that would only be satisfied by meeting them. As well as his brother, Simon, his wife, Hannah, and their two children, Luke would also be able to meet Paul's parents (Sarah and David, still married after thirty-nine years), his sister, Claire, and her husband, Brandon.

"We've got a little bit longer," Paul murmured, curling his arm around Luke.

"Nope. I'm hitting the shower. I don't want to meet your folks smelling of sex."

Paul enjoyed the view of a naked Luke walking out of the bedroom and sank back onto the bed. He was looking forward to being together with his family and he'd wanted them to meet Luke for a while. He'd talked to his brother about Luke several times since they had met, and he'd made sure to brief his mother on topics best avoided. He knew she would have a hundred questions for Luke and he didn't want him to feel like he was being interviewed all over again.

They were still waiting for the outcome from the apprenticeship interview. Nearly three weeks had passed, and the applicants had been told expect to hear whether they had the job three to four weeks from the date of the interviews. Luke seemed very calm about the whole thing; it was Paul who felt the most nervous. Luke appeared to have decided that he wouldn't get the position, but he had surprised himself with how well he had done and right now that was enough for him. Paul didn't think he should be so quick to believe he wouldn't get it— he knew that they were collecting references before finalizing the decision, and while his employer's reference might not carry a lot of weight, Henry could write a reference that could make Luke sound like a culinary wunderkind.

He heard the shower switch off and dragged himself out of bed and into the bathroom. Since Luke had started staying at Paul's most weekends, he now left some of his things there all the time, but he always seemed to need to use Paul's Elemis skincare products. Now he was shaving, and Paul recognized the familiar scent. *At least I know what to buy him for his birthday*, he thought as he opened the shower.

While he was drying off, Luke persuaded Paul to test him on family names and relationships, but he didn't seem as anxious as he had been when he had gone to Henry's barbecue. That felt like a long time ago now, when he thought back to how edgy and defensive Luke had been compared to his curious nervousness now; he seemed a bit more confident in himself and perhaps more confident in them as a couple.

Luke still fussed over what to wear and needed a final push to get him out the door, but once they were in the car he was happy to carry on chatting. He was particularly caught up in the fact that Paul's parents still lived in the house they had moved to when Paul was four years old, and he wanted Paul to point things out to him as they got closer—the first school he had attended, where he had ridden his bike, the pub where he had his first alcoholic drink. Luke wanted to see it all. He had moved around so much when he was growing up; he couldn't quite imagine what it would have been like to have stayed in one place.

The driveway they ended up pulling into sat next to a solid, detached two-story building with an attic conversion. They hadn't even had the chance to get out of the car before a young boy had the front door open and rushed out onto the path, where he proceeded to jump up and down and look back toward the door.

"That's Jack. He's allowed to open the door but he's not allowed off of the path unless his mum or dad are there," Paul explained. "You ready for this?"

"Yeah. Let's do it." Luke even managed a nervous smile.

Once they were out of the car, Jack couldn't hold on any longer and ran into Paul's arms to be lifted up above his head. Paul was still carrying him as Hannah arrived at the door carrying three-year-old Isabelle, or Issie, as she was nicknamed. Paul introduced Luke to his sister-in-law, niece, and nephew, and they were bundled inside, largely by Jack, who was eager to show Paul his new scooter. As Jack pulled them through the house to the utility area where his scooter had been quarantined, Paul greeted his sister Claire and Brandon, his father, and finally, his mother in the kitchen. Each time he managed to introduce Luke quickly before Jack realized he was losing momentum and gave Paul an extra tug.

Luke started to follow Paul in the direction Jack was pulling him, but Paul's mother wasn't going to let him get away so quickly.

"How are you, Luke?" she enquired, and Luke had to stop and answer while Paul moved on.

"Fine, thanks, Mrs. Blackwell."

"Sarah, please. Paul's told me lots about you, but nothing really useful, like if there's anything you don't eat. You're not a vegetarian, are you?"

Luke was glad he could confirm he wasn't.

"Thank goodness. We've got roast beef for dinner because that's Simon's favorite, and it was only this morning that I suddenly thought 'what if Luke's a vegetarian?'. It would be just like Paul to forget to mention something like that. Anyway, of course I could put something together for you if you were, it would be no trouble, but I did want everything to be right the first time you came to visit us."

Luke smiled and tried to work out the best way to respond. "Roast beef sounds great," he tried. Perhaps he was reading too much into things, but he liked the way she had said "the first time" as though it were obvious there would be many more times in the future.

Sarah rolled her eyes as if Luke had just given her the best news possible. "I'm so relieved. Now, if there's anything you don't eat, anything you don't like, just say so—there's nothing worse than thinking you have to eat something just to be polite...." And she carried on chatting away happily, delighted with Luke's nods and smiles and not noticing his occasional glances toward the door Paul had disappeared through.

Luke had never been in a "meet the parents" situation before and quickly realized he had no idea how much Paul's family knew about his life or how they really felt about it. Paul had said they were "fine with the whole thing" but that left quite a bit of room for uncertainty. He was relieved when Paul reappeared in the doorway. Paul remembered that the one person he hadn't spoken to yet was his brother and he got Luke away from his mother by pointing out he still needed to introduce him to Simon.

Back in the living room, Paul's siblings and their partners were spread out on armchairs and sofas while Issie played with her dolls on the carpet. Paul and Simon hugged warmly, and then Simon shook hands with Luke.

"It's great to meet you at last," Simon told him, and Luke had a nervous moment when he wondered what Paul had been saying about him. After the introductions, Luke found somewhere to sit and listened in on the catch-up conversation that took place between the siblings. Jack drifted back into the lounge—he had lost interest in his scooter now that he no longer had an audience. Looking around, he spotted that Luke wasn't actively engaged in a conversation (he knew he wasn't allowed to interrupt when they were talking).

"Do you like Legos? I've got lots of Legos. Do you want to see?" he fired at Luke.

"Sure," Luke replied, and it wasn't long before Jack had put him to work helping to build a "monster fort," which had a very specific design that only Jack seemed able to understand.

Paul got up and put his hand on Luke's shoulder. "Jack, I need to borrow Luke for a minute. C'mon—I want to show you my old room."

Luke hoped he wasn't blushing as he got up and followed Paul out of the living room. Paul reached back and took his hand before they got to the stairs and Luke shot him a nervous look. "It's okay," Paul said, laughing. "I told you, my family is fine. I mean, I wouldn't stick my tongue in your mouth in front of them, but then I don't think anyone would be too impressed if Simon and Hannah did that, either. Once I get you upstairs, though…." He laughed again and pulled Luke behind him.

"So which is your room?" Luke asked when they were at the top of the stairs.

"Well, when I was little I shared this room with Simon." Paul pushed open the door to a bedroom that now looked to be used as a guest room, with a view over the garden. "His bed was against that wall, and mine was here," Paul said, gesturing. "When we argued we used to have very detailed negotiations about dividing the room in half and exactly where the border would go. Eventually, my parents got sick of the arguing and converted the attic, which is where I'm taking you now."

Paul led him up a spiral staircase and pushed up a trapdoor to gain access to the attic. Inside, Luke saw the remains of Paul's old bedroom in amongst boxes labeled "Paul," "Simon," and "Claire." "Mum and Dad turned the bedrooms downstairs into a study and a spare room, but they just use this for storage." He sat down on a stripped single bed. "This is my actual original bed, right here."

Luke grinned at him and sat down next to him, testing the springs. "Did it see much action?"

"Absolutely none," Paul confessed. "But, God, the hours I spent lying here dreaming…." He smiled at Luke and leaned forward until they were kissing, soft and slow.

Before it got to be too much to resist, Luke leaned back and looked around the room again. He noticed the posters on the walls and couldn't help laughing. "Who the hell was C+C Music Factory?"

"Oh, I like the way you ignore the U2 poster, and the Red Hot Chili Peppers. I liked some cool music."

"Mmm-hmm," Luke replied, still laughing.

Paul looked around for something to hit him with, but was interrupted by his mother calling them down for lunch.

"I'll see to you later," he warned Luke.

"I hope so," Luke whispered back before dodging Paul's hand and climbing back down the stairs.

The meal went well, with even Luke feeling relaxed toward the end. Paul's family had a natural way of making him feel as if he was part of the conversation without actually asking him anything, so he never felt self-conscious. At times, he felt something that he had to acknowledge was jealousy as he found himself listening to childhood stories and comparing his own life with Paul's. They had been so different and it reminded him of the empty ache he had inside. He looked around and caught Paul's eye, saw the slight flash of concern, and found himself smiling again. Nothing was going to change the past, but that didn't mean he couldn't find a future for himself.

A FEW days later, Paul pulled up outside Luke's building and thought again about asking Luke to move in with him. The place reminded him of the kind of lodgings he'd had when he was at university, and anyway, he didn't want to visit Luke. He wanted to live with him. Now wasn't the time for that, though. He'd sent Luke a text asking if he could come round after work because he knew Luke should be getting notification about the apprenticeship that day. Luke had said that would be great, but hadn't mentioned if he'd heard anything. Of course, the mail could be slow and he might not have received anything yet. Paul also had a feeling that they would contact the person they wanted to offer the job to first, and if Luke hadn't gotten it, he might not hear for a few more days.

As always, Luke had the door to his apartment open before Paul got there. Paul quickly scanned his face for clues but couldn't spot any. Luke looked happy to see him, perhaps a little tired. Maybe he hadn't heard yet.

Paul caught a soft sigh from Luke as he pressed into him and he held him close for a minute, savoring the sense of "home" he felt when Luke was in his arms. Luke's body was familiar to him now and just felt so right against his. He found himself wondering if he could talk Luke into coming back to his place for the night; then he would be able to really enjoy everything he knew about that body.

Luke eased away and led Paul into the apartment. "I'm glad you said you wanted to come over. I got a letter from La Perfection today and I wanted to tell you about it."

Paul looked at Luke quickly. He was obviously trying to work out how to say what he needed to tell him. Paul started preparing to console him when instead he heard Luke say, "I got it. They've offered me the apprenticeship."

"That's fantastic!" Then Paul realized he was still the only one excited about the news. Luke's smile was tight, and he looked exactly as Paul had expected if he hadn't been offered the job.

"It's… it's great, but I'm gonna have to turn it down."

"I don't understand." And Paul really didn't.

"It's my choice, isn't it? And you always said it didn't make any difference to you what I did or whether I got it, so it doesn't matter, anyway."

Paul believed that he was a pretty patient guy, but right at that point he could imagine someone else wanting to strangle Luke. He took a deep breath and let it all out before he spoke.

"It's only natural to be anxious—everybody is when they start a new job. You're bound to find it really hard at first, but they wouldn't have given it to you if they didn't think you could do it. You have to give it a chance."

"It's not that. It's just…. Look, it's my decision. Why isn't that good enough?" Luke leaned against the kitchen counter. His face looked as if it couldn't decide if it was challenging or pleading.

"Because it isn't. We're supposed to be a team. I thought this was what you wanted. You can't just turn around and say it isn't without giving me a reason," Paul pointed out.

"I can't do it." Luke sighed heavily, as if Paul was forcing him to say things that he really didn't want to admit. His eyes were fixed on the floor. "I'd only be working four days a week because obviously the college days don't count, and the wage is lower, anyway. I should have thought about it before; I was stupid not to. I'd have to give up my flat and maybe find a room somewhere, but even then I don't think I can afford it."

"That's the only reason? Money?"

Luke looked up at him, and his eyes were cold and hard. "Says the guy who's always had it. I guess it must seem pretty stupid to you." His voice was low and controlled but there was a deep anger behind it.

Paul bit back his first response. Yes, there had been times when he was a student and he'd been budgeting and surviving on tinned spaghetti, but that wasn't what Luke was talking about. Paul had always known that a pleading phone call home would send a check his way (even if it was accompanied by a lecture on not wasting money). His parents weren't rich, but they had both worked in well-paid jobs their whole lives. Paul hadn't always gotten the Christmas presents he'd dreamed of, but he'd never opened a cupboard and found it empty, either. The bottom line was that he had always known financial security, and Luke's life had been the opposite.

"It doesn't seem stupid, but there is an obvious way around this. Look, I've been thinking about this for a while, and now, well, it seems perfect. I want you to move in with me. We could make a home together. You don't need to pay for somewhere else."

Luke sat down at the table and put his hand to his forehead.

"Don't get overexcited," Paul muttered. He knew the timing complicated things, but what he'd said was true—he really did want Luke to live with him, and it had taken him a while to get there. He'd expected Luke to respond a bit more positively.

Luke's head was whirling. He wanted to be with Paul and, yes, he wanted to live with Paul and to stop shuttling back and forth to his empty flat. However, that would mean giving up his independence. It was a square he'd never managed to smooth into a circle, even in his daydreams. It was so hard for him to give up his autonomy and depend on another person, but if he didn't, where did he see his relationship with Paul going? If he wanted his dream—a life shared with Paul—then he had to do it, but he just didn't feel sure.

"I wouldn't be able to afford to pay you the rent you should get for someone staying there," Luke said eventually.

Paul couldn't keep the anger out of his voice any longer. "I don't want any fucking rent! I'm asking you to come and live with me. Why are you making this so difficult? If you don't want to move in, just say so."

"I can't move in as any kind of equal. I'd be a freeloader. That's what all your friends expected me to be, and now it turns out they were right? I pay my own way. If I can't afford something, I do without. I don't get my boyfriend to pay for me."

"Fuck! You're so fucking inflexible!" Paul took some deep breaths. He gave Luke a look as sharp as steel, but Luke's face remained fixed, intractable. Someone had to give and neither thought they could be the one to back down. Paul had a horrible feeling that they could be moving toward something irreparable.

"You know what you're doing? You're trying to live by those nonexistent rules again. 'You shouldn't live with a guy without paying your way?' Well, I shouldn't be living in this big fucking house without paying a huge mortgage every month. But I am. That's how it turned out. There's no justice or reason to it. I could have hidden Craig's life assurance money in a box under the bed, telling myself I shouldn't benefit from his death, but what would be the fucking point? And you, you could waste your life doing a job you hate, or live in a stinking bedsit miles away from me and watch the damp creep up the walls, but what would be the fucking point? We don't have any choice about the shit stuff that comes into our lives. It seems pretty stupid to me to ignore a chance to grab some of the good stuff." He shrugged. "But you're going to do whatever you're going to do."

Paul flopped down onto the sofa that faced away from Luke. He didn't want to walk out or think about where things could lead if Luke wouldn't budge. He could imagine him sitting at the table behind him, a deep frown creasing his forehead. It wasn't like he didn't understand how Luke felt, and he wished he could make everything better by wrapping his arms around him and kissing him, but this wasn't that kind of thing. It wasn't just Luke who was taking a risk. He needed to know that Luke was prepared to give this relationship a real try.

He heard Luke get up from the table and move to the side of the sofa. When Paul looked at him, his face had softened a little and Luke's voice was quiet. "What if we break up?" Luke asked softly.

Paul managed to stop himself before telling Luke that it was never going to happen. Neither one of them was quite idealistic enough to believe it was an impossibility, however good things might be between them now. Luke needed something more hard-nosed than romantic proclamations.

"Well, if you're a total shit I'll chuck you out, and Henry will take you in until you get something else sorted. If he'll ever let you leave. The same goes if I'm a total shit. If we're feeling more reasonable, you could stay in one of the rooms upstairs until you have somewhere else to go." Paul sighed. "I'm not saying it couldn't happen, but even if it did—would you be any worse off than you are now?"

"I wouldn't have you." Luke's voice was so soft and broken that Paul had him in his arms in seconds.

"Hey, baby...." He started to cover Luke's face in kisses.

"What if I drive you crazy? What if you find you can't stand me anymore? What happens when you get bored? Maybe it would take longer if we didn't live together."

"You're not talking about me; you're talking about Kit."

"I'm talking about everybody." There were tears in Luke's eyes now. "It always happens in the end, and I don't know how I'm gonna stand it when it happens with you."

"Oh, babe...." Paul couldn't get Luke close enough, wanted to pull him inside where he could keep him safe.

"You're offering to do so much for me. I know I sound like the most ungrateful person on the planet."

"I'm not offering to do anything for you. That's just an accidental benefit. I want you to move in for *me*. I hate it when you're not there. I spend my whole time just thinking about when you're coming to stay next. I love knowing that you're just in the next room. I love seeing your stuff around the house. I love you. I want to share my life with you. I don't know what else to say."

Luke shook his head. "Getting the apprenticeship and moving in with you—it's all too perfect. Something's got to go wrong."

"I promise you now that living with me will not be perfect. Your job is not going to be perfect. But maybe we've already had our balance of things that go wrong." He held Luke's face in his hands. "Say you'll do it. Take a chance. Move in with me."

Luke saw everything he needed to know in Paul's face. His pulse was running at a thousand beats a minute when he heard the answer in his head. Reaching out to stroke Paul's face, he spoke with certainty in his voice, "I'd love to."

EPILOGUE

SUNDAY was the best day. Luke always woke thinking about what he needed to do that day and then he remembered—nothing. On Sunday there was no working at the restaurant and no college work—just him and Paul and a whole day.

The last four months hadn't exactly been a breeze—their working schedules clashed so that they barely spoke from Wednesday to Saturday, when Luke was working until midnight at the restaurant and Paul was leaving for school at seven thirty in the morning. Luke had offered to sleep in one of the spare rooms to avoid waking Paul when he came home, but so far Paul had refused. If he were forced to, he would have admitted that it was worth being woken just for that moment when Luke slid his body next to his and he knew that Luke was home, and safe, and close to him.

Luke felt Paul shift by his side and smiled, rolling over to face him. He still got that moment that squeezed his heart when he saw the guy who was sharing his bed, sharing his life. Since he'd moved in, his anxious side had been waiting for him to regret his decision, but so far it hadn't happened. They had argued, but the house was big enough for them both to be able to retreat to different corners when they needed to. Paul had told Luke to take one of the spare rooms for a study, although he didn't really need it. It made a good bolt-hole, though, and Paul had his office already set up, so they both had somewhere to go when they needed some space.

He stretched up to meet Paul's mouth with his. The first time they had fucked without a condom had been intense, fantastic, and quick. Since then they had adjusted a bit to the increased sensation and were getting back up to the longer fucks they had enjoyed previously. For Luke, it wasn't just the different feeling; it was also the thought of it that sent him over the edge—the knowledge of skin against skin inside him, and having Paul come in him with the come slipping out of him afterward—that he couldn't get enough of.

Paul rolled over so his upper body was on top of Luke as he took the kiss deeper. He looked down into Luke's sleepy blue eyes and saw nothing in his perfect face but a happy desire to follow where Paul would lead. He'd had his hair cut shorter recently because he complained it got in his eyes too much when he was working, and Paul missed the loose waves he had gripped before, but he was getting used to the new, sharper, more groomed Luke. He felt Luke's hand slide up his back and then down again to the dip in his spine and rest there, adding fuel to the fire that was starting in his belly. When Luke had agreed to move in with him, he had insisted that he collect some of his stuff then and there, and brought him back home before Luke could talk himself out of it. Since then, Luke had moved out of his flat completely and surrendered the lease. It had taken a while, but he now seemed relaxed in the house, and it made Paul glad when he heard him refer to it as his home because that's what it had now become—a home for both of them.

Paul let his own fingers play with Luke's nipples, squeezing and rolling the hard nubs between his thumb and forefinger and enjoying the increased hunger in Luke's kisses as a result. Kissing along his collarbone earned him a soft moan, and he felt Luke trying to reposition his hips so he could get the most contact from Paul's body against his cock. Luke reached out and grabbed the lube that was always kept near the bed and pushed it against Paul's hand—not exactly subtle, but certainly an effective way to communicate what he wanted.

When Paul slipped a wet finger inside him, Luke closed his eyes and focused on the sensation. Paul held his finger still until Luke's body had adjusted, and Luke let him know by pushing further against it, trying to get it against his prostate. Once he had bet Paul that he could recognize each of his fingers from the way they felt inside him, and Paul had been impressed at his success rate. Now Luke groaned as the finger found the right place to rock against.

Luke's hands found their cocks and pressed them together, adding the precome Paul was triggering from his prostate to Paul's own and slicking it down the shafts. He loved the rub of the underside of his cock against Paul's. His eyes found Paul's and saw the need there. "Fuck me," he whispered softly.

Paul never needed to be asked twice. Luke hitched his hands under his bent knees, pulling his legs up against the sides of his body and opening his ass to Paul. Then he felt the pressure of the glans against him, forcing his body to open just a little to let Paul in. When Paul eased the head through the opposing muscle, Luke caught his breath and bit his full lower lip, hearing the conflicting voices in his head. One telling him no, no, no, while the other groaned for everything—now. He was always tight and slow to stretch in the mornings, but there was something about the burning ache that he loved. It pushed him until he thought he'd have to stop and then melted into a slow, deep pleasure that spread through his whole body. Maybe it was knowing that if he ever did need Paul to stop, he would, that let him go to that place.

Paul stroked Luke's dick and leaned in to kiss his parted lips. As he finally pushed his whole length inside, Paul had total possession of his body—his ass, his cock, his mouth, and he pressed down over him, into him, reveling in that possession. Luke gave himself up freely. The doubts of the past were gone now, and slowly, without conscious thought, his trust in Paul had become complete.

Tremors of pleasure started to rock through them both with greater intensity, and they both fought to push against it, to keep this time where their bodies were locked into each other for as long as possible. But they both knew that when it did overwhelm them, when there was no more holding back, they would still find themselves left with each other and a life together ahead of them. Paul had promised Luke that it wouldn't be perfect, and it probably wasn't, but sometimes it was too damn close to call.

Reading and writing have always made life fun for H.J. HOLT, and the thought that one day her writing might reach other people has been a long-held dream. She writes about the things that interest her most: how people make sense of their lives and how they manage to connect with each other. She lives in southern England and spends her time teaching, baking, writing, and very quietly breaking rules.

www.ingramcontent.com/pod-product-compliance
Lightning Source LLC
Chambersburg PA
CBHW070009260626
47159CB00005B/1737